ALSO BY HEATHER TERRELL

The Chrysalis

The Map Thief

brigid of kildare

brigid of kildare

a novel

HEATHER TERRELL

BALLANTINE BOOKS / NEW YORK

Copyright © 2009 by Heather Terrell

Published in the United States by Ballantine Books, an imprint of The Random House Publishing Group, a division of Random House, Inc., New York.

BALLANTINE and colophon are registered trademarks of Random House, Inc.

LIBRARY OF CONGRESS CATALOGING-IN-PUBLICATION DATA
Terrell, Heather.
    Brigid of Kildare : a novel / Heather Terrell.—1st ed.
        p.   cm.
ISBN 978-0-345-50512-5 (pbk. : acid-free paper)
1. Lost books—Fiction.   2. Manuscripts—Fiction.   3. Brigid, of Ireland, Saint,
ca. 453–ca. 524—Fiction.   4. Mary, Blessed Virgin, Saint—Theology—Fiction.
5. Romans—Ireland—Fiction.   6. Ireland—Antiquities—Fiction.   7. Ireland—
Church history—To 1172—Fiction.   I. Title.
PS3620.E75B75 2009
813'.6—dc22   2009038973

Printed in the United States of America on acid-free paper

www.ballantinebooks.com

9 8 7 6 5 4 3 2 1

FIRST EDITION

Book design by Casey Hampton

For Jim, Jack, and Ben

A new order of life has been found out by Mary alone.

—The Gospel of Pseudo-Matthew

A NOTE ON THE TEXT

Throughout the centuries, Ireland has been called many names by many different peoples. For example, the Latin word Scotti (or Scoti) has been used to describe the Irish. Ireland itself has been called Hibernia in Latin. Among the many possibilities, I selected the words Gael and Gaels to reference fifth-century Ireland and its people, even though Gael is more commonly thought of as an ethno-linguistic term, in the hopes that the word would best connote ancient Ireland.

brigid of kildare

ROME

A.D. 470

Brother,

I write you in the utmost haste, trusting in God that I will find a safe way to deliver this letter unto your hands. For this very eve, I must leave Rome for an island so far outside the bounds of civilization it has never merited the attention of our dear Republic: the land of the Gaels.

That the Lord has summoned me to this mission, I have no doubt. Yet, as dawn broke and I finished my prayers this morning, I would have sworn on the cross that the day would progress like every other.

I settled at my desk in the chambers of the papal secretary just as the sun's rays began their full celebration of God's good day. Capturing the clarity of the earliest light is as critical to my work as a scrivener for the Lord as it is to your work overseeing the family land; thus I was alone in the study. I was preparing to record the edicts emanating from a recent council meeting when I heard my name.

I turned toward the sound and, to my surprise, saw a papal page in the doorway. He said, "Brother Decius, you are to follow me to an audience in the chambers of His Holiness Pope Simplicius, bishop of Rome."

The page started off down the long and winding corridors that lead to His Holiness's inner sanctum. I raced after him, wary of losing him in the labyrinthine route connecting the church's official buildings to the palace. I kept his pace, and he left me at the entryway to the pope's own chambers.

A crimson tapestry separated the sacred inner sanctum from the bustle of the rest of the palace. I approached it, and though I pulled the heavy fabric aside with reverence and care, my fingers caught on the pearls and rubies sewn into the silken embroidery. In that moment of disentanglement, I know not why, I hesitated before crossing the threshold.

My body began shaking, as it had never trembled before. Yet I knew I could show no fear. Courage is necessary—nay, mandated—for selection to one of Christ's missions. And somehow I knew that this was the purpose of my summoning.

To expel the devil's own trepidation from my heart and soul, I steeled myself with the image, oft described by you, of our father and mother stoic in the face of the barbarians. If our parents could suffer at their hands and never flinch before the final swing of the crude battle-axe, then, I told myself, I could take the simple step of entering the private chamber of Saint Peter's own representative on this earth.

Peace descended upon me, almost as though our mother and father spoke from heaven. I left the tapestry to swing in my wake and immediately knelt before His Holiness. Or so I believed.

"Rise, Brother Decius," the order sounded out.

I readied myself to confront the intimidating phalanx of aristocratic councillors that accompany His Holiness's every movement, which I had witnessed during my three prior papal audiences. Yet as I rose from my deep genuflection and lifted my eyes, a single figure greeted me. I knew the man only by sight and rumor, as he would never deign to enter the secretary's study: it was Gallienus, a priest and the most senior of the pope's councillors.

I bowed my head in respect, yet could not help but note the comfortable, nearly languorous, manner in which he leaned against the empty papal throne. "Your Eminence," I said.

"The twelfth eagle will soon fly," Gallienus said.

I did not answer at once, uncertain as to his meaning and even more unsure as to the safest response.

"Are you not familiar with the Prophecy of the Twelve Eagles, Brother Decius?" Gallienus asked.

"I am, Your Eminence." Indeed, I guess nearly every Roman citizen has heard the divination that the Republic's supremacy will last twelve centuries only, each one represented by an eagle. Even the masses must have heard it bandied about in the bars and streets of the bustling Aventine Quarter in recent times, as the Visigoths rule Rome in all but name and other hordes conquer more and more of the Roman provinces every day. Oh, but this is old, sad news to us true Romans.

"Then you know that twelve centuries of the Roman Empire's rule as foretold by the twelve eagles are nearly at an end?"

I paused before answering. I hate to speak ill of a fellow Christian, but the elite Gallienus is known for his wiles and I feared that the question was a trap. If I admitted to an awareness of the prophecy and the few years remaining on it, I could well be confessing to giving credence to pagan lore—a punishable confession, since Christianity was proclaimed the state religion almost one hundred years ago, as you know well.

I delivered a measured response. "I do, Your Eminence. Yet I also know that such prophecy is but heretical conjecture spoken by the masses."

Gallienus stared long at me, never blinking but keeping his eyes hooded in shadow such that I could not read his reaction. Then he nodded slowly and said, "That is true, Brother Decius. Still, we must be prepared."

"Of course, Your Eminence." Wary of this man, I was apprehensive of accusations that I had discounted the empire's military might with my answer. So I said, "Though the empire maintains a vast army."

"We cannot leave the fate of the Roman Christian Church to Emperor Anthemius's troops, can we, Brother Decius?"

Understanding that Gallienus's question brooked no response other than agreement, I said, "No, Your Eminence. We cannot leave the fate of the Roman Christian Church to the Roman army."

"I am glad we are of like mind, Brother Decius. Heartily glad."

I watched Gallienus saunter around the pope's chamber as if it belonged to him, pausing to touch the gilt arms of the papal throne and the intricate wall mosaic of birds in flight. As he gazed out between columns to the surging metropolis below, still crowded with marble temples and colonnaded forums dedicated to the pagan gods, despite the edict banning their worship, I waited for my mission.

"We must secure the land of the Gaels, Brother Decius," Gallienus pronounced without turning back toward me.

"The desolate isle beyond Britannia, Your Eminence?" My brother, I regretted the question the moment it slipped from my tongue. I knew, of course, where the Gaelic land lay, but I could not believe that the church would trouble itself with the unimportant, rocky outcropping on the precipice of the known world, an island so inconsequential that Rome did not bother to colonize it even in the Republic's prime. Not to mention that with Gael's lack of a central ruler, subduing its countless chieftains would have required more than fifty thousand troops, which Rome could ill afford due to mounting pressures on nearly all other frontiers. But I did not want the man to think I was a fool or, worse, an insubordinate in need of punishment.

"The very same," Gallenius answered, without rebuke or surprise at my response. He faced me. "Rumors are surfacing that its chieftains are uniting in power under the newly formed Christian monasteries. This news would be hailed—indeed, we always embrace new sheep in our flock—but for the reports that the Gaelic brand of Christianity is rife with heresy. We would not want Gael to unify under a Pelagian Christianity, now, would we? We must determine whether these reports bear truth."

Gallienus did not continue with any details, though, of course, I had long heard rumblings about Pelagius, the rebel monk from Britannia who had maintained that original sin does not exist and that man has free will, a belief condemned by the church's Council of Ephesus in 431.

"Would Bishop Patrick not be able to serve in this regard?" The Roman Christian Church had sent Patrick to Gael as a missionary some years before, in an unprecedented posting. The church had never before assigned a missionary to an uncolonized land, but Patrick had made constant, persuasive arguments about God calling him to convert the people who had once enslaved him.

"Inexplicably, Bishop Patrick is too enamored with the Gaelic people to report upon them objectively." Gallienus then made a broad gesture toward me.

I finished for him, as he clearly wished: "You would like me to make this appraisal, Your Eminence."

"Yes, Brother Decius. I wish you to study a particular abbey that grows in power, the Abbey of Kildare, which is run by a woman, Brigid, no less." He paused and then asked, "Do you understand the critical importance of this work?"

"I welcome Your Eminence's wisdom." I felt the need to remain guarded in my responses, though I had begun to intuit his designs.

"If, in fact, the Gaelic monasteries and churches preach heresy as charged, we must stamp out the leaders of this profanation and replace them with our own. Only then can we unite this disjointed, backward land under the true Christian faith and present it as a tribute to the emperor. To help him bolster the empire and . . ." He left the sentence unfinished.

"And, in turn, bolster the church, Your Eminence?" He seemed to want me to say this aloud.

"You do see, Brother Decius. I am well pleased."

And see I did, when he put it so plainly. The Roman Church stands on increasingly unsteady ground as the Roman government falters. It needs to shore itself against the barbarian onslaught by routing out all heresy. Efforts to keep the remote island fully Roman Catholic could prevent it from becoming barbarian—and create a fitting honorarium for the Roman emperor in the process.

Gallienus sidled up near me, drawing so close that, despite the early hours, I could smell his sour, wine-laden breath. "Do you wonder at your selection for this task?"

I lowered my head, away from his probing stare and his stench. "I trust in the sagacity of God, Pope Simplicius, and his learned councillors, Your Eminence."

Gallienus smiled. "Always cautious, Brother Decius. Almost as cautious as myself. It will serve you well." The smile vanished, leaving an unpleasant grimace on his lips. "We chose you not for your ardent faith or your private hatred of the barbarians, though you have both of these excellent qualities in abundance. We chose you because we need a scribe."

My dear brother, the light fades, and the horses assemble for the long journey. I have not the time to complete the description of my encounter with Gallienus or my mission to the Gaelic land, though I suspect you would reel at the notion of your pious, careful younger brother, whom you always protected as you dashed off on some adventure of your own design, heading off into the dark unknown. I pray with fervence to our Lord that He will deliver unto me the means to transport this letter to you. Until then, I will be in His hands. Pray for me, brother, as I pray for you.

Decius

GAEL

A.D. 456

BRIGID: A LIFE

Brigid readies her sword. She sizes up her competitor and fashions a fresh strategy. The call to battle sounds, and they rush at each other headlong.

The metallic shriek of their locked swords overtakes the battlefield. Brigid begins with a thrust and parry so they will seem even matched. But she knows her combatant well, and her standard swordplay serves as a trap. The rhythmic clash of their blades lulls him into thinking he commands the lead and wipes any strategy from his overconfident mind. She lures him to the edge of a ditch bordering the field and prepares her final strike.

An almost imperceptible tremor passes through the watching soldiers. Brigid averts her gaze momentarily and sees that her father has arrived. A faint smile curls on her lips as she thinks about the fortune of having her father watch her victory. She shifts her weight to muster all her force for the winning thrust.

But her competitor marks her fleeting distraction and subtly changes his position. When Brigid swings forward with all her might, she stumbles to the ground in pain and embarrassment. It is her opponent who delivers the ultimate blow—not Brigid.

She rises under her own strength, pushing aside her competitor's outstretched hand. If she must fall to another's sword, she will prove to her father that she can shrug off a blow as easily as his fiercest warriors. Brushing away a servant's attempt to dress her shoulder wound, Brigid passes her blade back into the scabbard hanging from a loop off her metal belt. She unrolls the hem of her long robe, which she had tucked into her belt, and strides off the field as if she had won.

Brigid glances in her father's direction. She hopes he has observed her stoicism, if not her victory. But he is gone, leaving her to wonder just what he witnessed.

She curses to herself as the crowd dissipates. Her overeagerness had caused her fatal misstep, one only a rank beginner would commit. She is furious with herself.

"Ach, don't beat yourself up about it, Brigid. Everyone knows you've got better sword skills than me."

She turns toward the voice. It is her opponent, her foster brother, Oengus, who has been sheltered by her family since the age of seven, according to Gaelic custom. He will return to his own family at seventeen, taking the newly made bond with him as a tie to his own family. "Easy for you to say. You just won to a warrior's crowd of a hundred, with my father at the center."

Oengus does not respond. Wisely, Brigid thinks. For she knows—and he knows—that she is right, that her father expects her to dominate in every respect. Even on the battlefield against a man. For her father is Dubtach, king of the Fothairt people of southern Gael, and he demands nothing less of his only natural child.

The long walk across the crop fields to the stone *cashel* ringing the royal homestead lessens her inner anger. As they pass the cattle and sheep fields, she forgets her troubles for a moment and unconsciously counts the animals' heads: they are the measure of her father's power, along with the slaves captured by raiding parties. By the time they cross the rampart over the ditch encircling the inner wall of the *cashel*,

Brigid has even mustered a laugh at Oengus's imitation of their instructor, an aging warrior of her father's. Oengus alone can make her laugh. At their approach to the two vast earthen mounds used by Dubtach for his ceremonies, she is able to pretend that she has forgotten about her humiliation. But she never really forgets.

Brigid and Oengus near the large heather-thatched building used for their studies. Though they are well ahead of their appointed time, they notice a number of unfamiliar people entering the structure. Brigid picks up her pace, pushes open the heavy oak door, and enters with Oengus hard at her heels.

"Fresh from the battlefield, I see?"

Brigid's eyes adjust slowly from the bright spring light to the dim interior. She does not need to see the face to recognize the speaker. It is her mother, Broicsech, queen of the Fothairt people, and from her tone, Brigid understands that she is fuming.

Brigid falls to her knees out of deference and custom, and Oengus quickly follows. Broicsech is every bit as formidable as Dubtach, and Brigid does not want to be the subject of her wrath. Her father is fond of saying that Broicsech wields a blade as well as any man, but her most fearsome weapon is her sharp tongue.

"You see that my daughter and foster son like their feats of martial skill and courage. They enjoy those skirmishes so much, they cannot bear to wash away the bloody badges, can they?"

Brigid wonders to whom her mother speaks, but she dares not raise her head until given permission. She chastises herself for not changing her dirty garb before entering the library, the place where her mother is most often found. She stays frozen in her position.

"Our Lord Jesus Christ implores us to turn the other cheek to our enemies, not brandish our swords before them," an accented voice says in response.

"He does indeed, and we try to heed His Words. But He did not know the Gaelic people, did He?"

Brigid is surprised to hear a deep laugh come from the serious-sounding stranger. "He might not have met the Gaels while still here on earth, but I feel certain He knows them well from his vantage point in heaven."

Broicsech chuckles at the retort, the kind she might have made herself. "Well spoken."

Brigid's knees begin to ache from kneeling and from her battlefield fall. She alters her stance the tiniest bit, and Broicsech says, "So impatient to meet our guest, Brigid? I suppose you and Oengus may rise."

With little of the grace her mother insists upon, Brigid struggles to her feet. Behind her lovely mother, immaculately dressed as always in a pristine robe and with a golden crown encircling her black hair, stands the stranger. A very strange stranger indeed, Brigid thinks to herself.

The man wears the dark robes of a monk or a Druid, though Brigid supposes that the reference to Jesus Christ marks him as a monk. He has dark hair tonsured in the Roman style and light eyes and seems of her mother's age, though much worse for the wear. Yet it is not these features that distinguish him as strange. His oddity comes from his eyes, so intense they seem as if fire lights them from within.

He meets her stare. "So this is your Brigid?"

"It is indeed." She gestures toward Oengus. "And this is my foster son, Oengus, of whom you have heard me speak. Brigid and Oengus, pay your respects to Bishop Patrick."

They lower themselves to the floor once again. Brigid is astonished that Bishop Patrick stands in their midst. That a senior Christian official visits their *cashel* does not startle her; her family is ostensibly Christian and certainly royal, and thus the visit is unusual but not unfathomable. That a stranger stops in their kingdom does not surprise her. No, her incredulity arises from the fact that Bishop Patrick pays *his* respects to the family of Dubtach, best known for the ferocity and frequency of his raiding parties for slaves in Britannia. For Patrick was born a wealthy Roman Briton, the son of a Christian deacon and the grandson of a Christian priest, but he was taken prisoner at sixteen by Gaelic raiders and served as a slave for six years, until he escaped. Astonishingly, Patrick then eschewed his own people to minister the Christian faith to the Gaelic people, who once enslaved him, and to preach against slavery.

"Shall we pray?"

Her mother nods her acquiescence, and the assemblage kneels. Bishop Patrick leads them in Jesus Christ's own prayer, then stands and addresses them while they continue to kneel before him.

"Broicsech, I know your family to be strong leaders of your *tuath* and ardent Christians. You serve as sublime examples to your people in the saving ways of our Jesus Christ."

As Broicsech gives her thanks, Brigid thinks on the cleverness of this Patrick. Patrick, though foreign, understands the Gaelic people well—from his years in Gaelic captivity, she supposes. By referencing the *tuath,* or kingdom, over which her father rules in all matters material and moral, he subtly reminds her mother that Dubtach is the sacred protector of the people's lives and their souls. Brigid wonders what Patrick wants that he raises the stakes so high.

"My monks and I will pass through your lands again in six months' time. I know your family to be good Christians, but as yet unbaptized. I ask in the name of our Lord that you will consider allowing me to baptize you and your family in a ceremony before your people. Where your family leads, your people will follow."

Broicsech is quiet for a time, then answers in an uncharacteristically muted voice: "Bishop Patrick, I vow to you that I will consider your request for myself, my daughter, and my foster son, but I cannot speak to my husband's willingness for a baptism or his appetite for a public ceremony of the rite."

Patrick is silent, but Brigid sees the fury simmering in his eyes. His voice rises in anger to match.

"Broicsech, I do not ask much of you as a Christian. Nor does God. Consider my ministry to convert the people of Gael. I am bound by the Holy Spirit to work here in Gael and never again see my own kin. I must extend God's mercy and kindness to the very people who once took me captive, and who made such havoc of my father's estate. God asks comparatively little of you."

Watching her mother offer apologies and promises, Brigid considers Patrick's statements. She finds him not only clever but convincing. For how could he bear his ministerial burden but for the grace of God? It is compelling evidence that his God must exist. She wonders how Patrick's words will resound with the Gaelic people, who would rather draw pools of blood from their enslavers than bestow mercy as did Patrick. And she wonders what this God would ask of her.

NEW YORK, NEW YORK

PRESENT DAY

The moment Alex feared before every flight finally happened.

The Transportation Security Administration agent grabbed her bag off the conveyor belt as soon as it passed through the X-ray machine. Inwardly, she flinched as he pawed through it, but outwardly, she smiled at the portly, overworked agent—as if the contents were perfectly normal to carry on board a transatlantic flight.

The agent signaled for her to walk through the metal detector and join him in the screening station on the other side. "Is there a problem, Officer?" she asked, careful to keep an innocent smile pasted on her lips and her voice even. A well-placed grin or a friendly remark had always warded off this dreaded level of scrutiny before.

"You realize that sharp objects and knives are prohibited in carry-on luggage, don't you?" He said it with a patronizing tone as he pointed to the sign making the logical prohibition abundantly clear.

"Of course, Officer—" She searched for his name tag, but had no luck.

"Then"—he reached into her black student's bag, a vestige from her Columbia University days, and pulled out the container of her instruments—"what exactly are these?"

Knowing how bad they looked, Alex tried to stay as calm as possible. "Appraiser's tools."

The agent fanned the items out on the inspection table. "They look like weapons to me."

Alex remained silent, realizing that any defense or explanation she might offer would only ignite the situation. The wrenches, the brushes, the magnification equipment, and the pliers were tiny—indeed, she'd made certain that they fell within the allotted seven-inch limit—but they did look unusual and ominous.

"You can check these items, but you cannot carry them on board."

"No—" Too late, she realized that her protest was too vehement.

"No?" He arched an eyebrow. Sweeping the tools into his meaty palms, he began walking toward the collection bin for banned items. "Okay, you've made your choice. I'll just confiscate them instead."

Alex knew that confiscation meant destruction. "Please don't take them. I need this equipment for a project appraising medieval relics for a church in Ireland, and I can't risk their getting lost in the baggage check. I swear they're just tools."

He looked her up and down, trying to squeeze her into some profile and realizing that a tall, blond, Caucasian woman in her early thirties simply did not fit the bill. "Do you have any proof?"

"Yes," Alex said. She dug out a business card identifying her as an appraiser of medieval religious artifacts, the letter of commission for her current project, and a completed appraisal for a related project that she thought might prove useful. The latter contained her full academic résumé as well as her photograph.

The agent stared at the papers, unsure of what to make of her credentials or the detailed description of a ninth-century Germanic chalice. He lumbered off to consult his boss. She watched as they studied her tools and measured each instrument against the seven-inch standard.

Please God, please God, please God, don't let them take my instruments, Alex chanted to herself. She knew it was risky—not to say foolhardy—to insist on bringing equipment on her trips. But she'd used these tools for all her appraisals since finishing her doctorate, and she'd experienced an unusual amount of success with them. She was too self-confident to attribute her success wholly to her instruments, but she was just superstitious enough to refuse to leave them behind.

The agent returned. Although he had broad authority to seize any object he deemed suspicious—and her instruments were certainly more suspect than the average nail scissors—he slapped a fluorescent pink label on her bag instead. "You can keep the tools in your possession until you get on board. Then you have to turn them over to the staff to keep in a locked closet until you land," he said, as he typed her particulars into a computer.

Alex didn't really exhale until she reached the gate for her Aer Lingus flight. She settled into an isolated seat near the windows, and, still clutching her worn bag like a life preserver, she closed her eyes and breathed deeply.

She opened them to a jam-packed tarmac. A veritable United Nations of airplanes—emblazoned with the white-on-red cross of Swissair, El Al's Star of David, and the bright green shamrock of Aer Lingus, among them—jockeyed for positions. By now, Alex had seen similar sights hundreds of times as she jetted off for her work, but it never failed to infuse her with anticipation over the possibility of fresh discoveries.

After a moment of indulging in the view, Alex reimmersed herself in her work. Always work. She unzipped her bag and slid out photographs from a hand-labeled manila envelope. She'd reviewed them in the office, of course, but she wanted one last look in the natural light.

The amateur pictures, with grainy color and poor lighting, showed three liturgical vessels of obvious antiquity: a chalice; a paten, or communion plate; and a rectangular reliquary box. Even the amateur photography couldn't mask the beauty and rare craftsmanship, not to mention the intrinsic value of the gold, silver, and inlaid gems. The owner of the items—a small convent in the countryside near Dublin—believed the relics to be very old, from the sixth century perhaps, but solving the riddle of the pieces' exact age and value was her task. Her privilege, she always told her clients.

The boarding announcement sounded, and Alex gathered up her

things. As she shuffled the photos back into a pile, a close-up of the reliquary box caught her attention. She brought it near the window to better capture the dimming daylight and drew her magnifying glass close. The reliquary box, designed to hold the physical relics of a saint, had a sumptuous gold overlay of a cross bearing the symbols of the authors of the Gospels—Matthew, Mark, Luke, and John—in the corners and the Virgin Mary at the center. Alex sensed some discordant element in its design, though she couldn't quite place a finger on it.

The second call for boarding crackled over the speaker. Reluctantly, Alex slipped the pictures back into the envelope, zipped up her bag, and slung it over her shoulder. Leaving New York behind her, she boarded the plane.

DUBLIN AND KILDARE, IRELAND

PRESENT DAY

The plane took a sudden dip in altitude, jolting Alex awake from a surprisingly deep sleep. She slid open the window shade and gazed out. The plane hovered at the cloud line, a nether place between sky and earth. Until it took another dive.

They plunged through the cloud layer and entered a world of blackened skies. Alex stared down at the dark chop of the Irish Sea and waited for the first sight of the coast. One more cloud strata, and she saw it. Huge jetties darted out from the craggy shore, braving the rough force of the sea. An incongruous blend of tidy white housing developments and rugby pitches and the crumbling remains of stone structures—both lavish and humble—decorated the shoreline. She loved coming here, and not just because it served up such a rich array of ancient artifacts.

Finally, finally the airplane touched down, and the landing bell rang with a soft ping. The tired passengers launched themselves into the aisles and reached for the overhead compartments. After working her way through immigration and customs, Alex got into the car waiting to take her to Kildare.

The car wove through Dublin's packed morning rush hour, a far cry from the few workaday cars that had trickled into the city center when

Alex had first started coming to Ireland years earlier, before the days of
the Celtic Tiger. Once clear of the city and its sprawling suburbs, they
entered the verdant terrain of most Irish-American fantasies. Sheep
and horses dotted the lush countryside, especially when they approached the famous Curragh Racecourse, and the villages provided
charming pubs aplenty. But Alex knew that the fantasy—if it had ever
really existed—began to disappear when the Irish economic boom
changed the traditional landscape.

The car pulled in at an orderly, picturesque town square, which announced itself as the center of Kildare. The driver, who'd been chatting amiably throughout the ride, pointed to a weather-beaten
limestone church sitting on a rise above the square, calling it Saint
Brigid's. From her window, Alex studied the church's massive central
tower, which rose above an impressive nave with double defensive
arches, and its attractive green, containing one of Ireland's famous
round towers of disputed sixth-century origins. She remembered reading about the on-site remains of Saint Brigid's Fire House, thought to
be a pagan sacred fire structure Christianized by Brigid herself.

She'd started to gather up her things when the driver said, "Wait a
second, luv. Do you want Saint Brigid's Cathedral or Saint Brigid's
Church?"

Alex was perplexed. "I don't know."

"Ah, it's a common enough source of confusion." He pointed to the
imposing structure she'd been examining through the window. "That's
Saint Brigid's Cathedral. It actually sits on the land Brigid developed,
but it's run by the Anglicans. The Church of Saint Brigid is around the
corner, and it's run by the Catholics."

Her client was a convent, so Alex guessed: "I believe I need the
church."

"Then that's where we'll go, luv."

He drove around the square and down a small hill. Alex thought
how the distance between the Anglican church and its Catholic counterpart was short in length but long in grandeur. The Catholic Saint
Brigid's bore the familiar hallmarks of post–Vatican II architectural
overlay—with none of the majesty and historical punch of the cathedral.

Alex gave the driver instructions to drop her bags at the Silken Thomas Inn and got out of the car. Immediately, she drew her coat around her like a protective blanket against the cool drizzle and wind. The harsh weather made her glad that she'd worn wool slacks, a sweater, and boots.

Before she even reached the church's front doors, an older woman wearing the unmistakable black garb of a nun raced out onto the street to greet her. Sticking out her hand, she shook Alex's hand with a firm grip. "Sister Mary Kelly."

"It's a pleasure to meet you, Sister Mary. I'm Alexandra Patterson."

"Good to meet you, Miss Patterson. I've been waiting for you. Let's talk while we walk, all right?" she asked, but she didn't wait for Alex's response before marching off. "Do you know much about our Brigid, dear?"

Alex's work mandated that she have at least a decent grasp of most saints' biographies. She had found, however, that if she allowed her clients to share their stories first, she learned more about the speaker and the pieces she'd come to assess than if she admitted her knowledge from the start. "Just a bit."

"Good. Where to start, where to start. The Brigidine legends just abound, liberally, and often incorrectly, mixed in with historical facts, of course. We believe she was born in the middle of the fifth century. Her father was pagan, and her mother Christian, but Brigid embraced Christianity from the start. Some say Saint Patrick himself baptized her." Sister Mary paused in her words but not her walking, clearly awaiting a reaction.

"Really?" Alex obliged.

"Really. Well, her father wanted her to marry, but Brigid would have none of it. She was determined to become a nun, and after taking her vows, she traveled the countryside, converting people as she went. Eventually, she settled in Kildare and built an abbey right here in town. Although our church is not built on the site of her abbey—the Protestants absconded with her actual lands some time ago, so the abbey remains are found at the Anglican Saint Brigid's Cathedral." Sister Mary sighed. "Brigid's one of the great Catholic saints, and she helped Christianity take hold in Ireland."

"So I understand," Alex said. Sister Mary seemed to want validation.

"Bet you wonder why we'd even consider selling her precious artifacts?"

"There's no need to explain, Sister Mary. Our clients have their reasons, and that's not our business or our concern."

"Ah, but I should tell you. I *need* to tell you." She broke from her brisk pace and looked at Alex. "People are always demeaning Saint Brigid and her very real miracles and contributions by trotting out the fantastical legends about her—that she turned water into beer for her visitors, or hung her cloak on a sunbeam, or made animals do her bidding. Whether you believe the old tales about Brigid's miracles or not, we want the people to know that early Irish Christianity had at least one very impressive woman: Brigid. So we're selling the relics as a necessary measure to combat patronizing talk about a formidable Catholic saint. To ensure that the message is properly delivered and widely disseminated, we need to do it ourselves."

"And you need money for that undertaking. Hence the sale of the relics."

"Exactly. Money that Rome isn't exactly clamoring to hand over to our Order of Saint Brigid. Even though Rome's got money aplenty for other projects." Sister Mary nodded with satisfaction. "I can see I won't have to explain things twice to you."

Sister Mary led them into a small, nondescript building adjacent to the church. The quiet weekday morning found the church community center empty and peaceful, though postings on the bulletin boards showed it to be a bustling neighborhood hub for the older set, at least. Reaching for the jam-packed key ring at her waist, she unlocked one of the front doors and motioned for Alex to follow her inside.

The center had that musty, institutional smell that immediately conjured up Alex's childhood trips to the Sisters of Mercy convent, where her aunt lived. As a child, she'd been scared by the convent's dark wooden images of Jesus on the Cross, the saints, and the Virgin, but as a young adult, she'd grown intrigued. She'd begun to see sacred images as imbued with a sort of power. Not religious power, nor miraculous properties: the secular nature of her childhood home—Protestant father and Catholic mother turned Christmas Christians—made her too skeptical for such belief. No, she began to believe that the images held historical mysteries that she could draw out. And since grad school, she'd built up a track record proving just that point.

The nun continued talking as she unlocked her office door. Alex liked the tenacity and bullishness of Sister Mary; no passive, "will of God" religiosity for her. "The relics have been kept by our order for well over a thousand years. We don't know for certain the exact year Brigid entrusted them to us, but our oral tradition tells us that we have protected the pieces since at least the ninth century, when a Viking fleet of thirty vessels sailed up the river Liffey to raid the Abbey of Kildare. We buried them deep in the root system of the famous oak tree at the center of the abbey."

Alex waited while the nun genuflected before a small Madonna shrine in the office's back corner; then she sat in the indicated chair on the visitors' side of the desk. As soon as it was seemly, she whipped out her notebook and began scribbling down the artifacts' provenance. "How long did your order hide them under that tree?"

"The abbey was attacked by the Vikings at least sixteen times before the year 1000. They took anything that looked valuable—covered in precious metals or stones, that is—and destroyed the rest. Since the Vikings were largely illiterate, that meant burning the countless manuscripts stored at the abbey after they ripped off the ornamental covers, among other things. So, for safekeeping, Brigid's artifacts remained under the abbey's oak tree until the final defeat of the Vikings, around 1014. At that time, our order determined that the relics could be safely used in the Mass and displayed as an emblem of the Celtic independence and triumph over the loathed Vikings. And we did, for over a century, at least."

"Until what year?"

"Until Ireland was defeated once again in 1172. That time, the English conquered us." Sister Mary didn't bother to conceal her typical Irish dislike of the English. "We had tried to reassert our autonomy against Rome when we refused to pay its tax, 'St. Peter's penny.' As punishment, Rome offered us up to King Henry II, making him Ireland's tax collector and setting the stage for later English control." Sis-

ter Mary seemed to hold a grudge against Rome as well, not a view
Alex typically heard spoken aloud by a nun.

"Even under the English," she continued, "our order stayed in control of the abbey's female community, but the men came under the direction of the English bishops of Kildare. With so many English at the
abbey, you can understand if we didn't trust the relics to be out and
about. So we hid them again."

"When did your order bring them to light?"

"Not for a good long time. As I'm sure you know, in 1532, Henry
VIII, who was also king of Ireland, broke with the Catholic Church.
Ireland became a battleground between native Irish Catholics and the
English forces—again. Kildare's own ruler Silken Thomas renounced
Henry VIII's rule, and he was hanged in 1537. By 1539, Henry had
dissolved all monasteries and confiscated their goods. Even if he
hadn't, the English stole our lands and goods whenever possible and
destroyed relics and sacred images."

"So you kept the relics in hiding?"

"Yes. In fact, by 1540, our order itself was forced to go into hiding.
The abbey and the convent were in shambles, and the Catholic persecution under way. We unearthed our relics and left the abbey, setting
up a quiet, almost invisible community for ourselves in the remote
countryside outside of Kildare. We stayed there until the Roman
Catholic Church of Saint Brigid—an early version of what you see before you—was built, in 1833, and we were invited to participate in its
community in the mid-1800s. We renamed ourselves the Order of
Saint Brigid at that time."

"Did you finally exhibit the relics then?"

"No, we'd waited nearly seven hundred years at that point; we
could wait until it was completely secure. In 1921, when Ireland became free from Protestant England, we celebrated by using the relics
again for sacred occasions. Over time, they had really become emblems—not just of Catholic Christianity but of Irish independence. In
some centuries, they represented freedom from outside political
forces and in other centuries, freedom from the church."

Alex was impressed, and not just because the order had managed
to keep premedieval sacred artifacts in the same hands for over a thou-

sand years. Assuming that the provenance research bore out that claim, of course. "Your pieces are true witnesses to the history of Catholicism in Ireland, Sister Mary."

Sister Mary turned a steely gaze on Alex. "Indeed, they are—and witnesses to the Irish struggle for independence as well. You can see that our order has risked much to protect these relics, for over a millennium. The decision to sell them is not one we take lightly."

Alex's clients often felt the need to justify parting with such valuable items, but she could understand Sister Mary's compulsion to do so. Even though she had tried to assure the sister that such explanation was unnecessary. "Of course not; I'm sure it was a difficult, even painful, determination. But our firm can assist you in placing them with an individual or institution that will respect and honor the integrity and importance of your pieces—a place that will tell their stories fully and truthfully."

"That is what my Vatican friends tell me. That's why I picked you and your firm."

"You will not be disappointed to have placed your confidence in us."

"I certainly hope not, Miss Patterson. I don't want to be answering to God for my choice."

Alex wanted to steer away from the religious course the conversation was taking. Talk of belief and faith always made her uneasy, a fact her boss found amusing, given her chosen line of work. "Do you have any written documentation of the relics' history?"

"No. The history has always been passed down verbally from keeper to keeper."

" 'Keeper'?" Alex had heard the phrase used in connection with Irish museums—they termed their curators "keepers"—but never outside that context.

"Yes, the keeper. Our order selects one of our members to head up the care of the relics. Our most recent keeper, Sister Augustine, became dangerously sick four weeks ago after serving as keeper for nearly five decades. The order chose me to succeed her, and Sister Augustine passed on the history to me while she was still able, although she was grievously ill at the time. And so she remains."

The date struck Alex. She thought back to the first letter her firm had received from the order, almost certain that it dated to exactly four weeks ago. Instead, she said, "I'm certain the order trusts your judgment implicitly."

Sister Mary bowed her head in humble prayer, but Alex thought she saw a flinty gleam in her eyes before she lowered her gaze. "As long as God has faith in my decision, I'll be pleased."

KILDARE, IRELAND

PRESENT DAY

Alex watched as Sister Mary struggled with the lock to the church entrance, which bore a modern design incorporating the distinctive cross of Saint Brigid. Declining offers of help, Sister Mary finally made just the right deft turns, and the lock yielded. She insisted on pushing open the heavy bronze doors herself.

The church interior was even darker than the stormy spring morning outside. Without turning on a single light, Sister Mary crossed the church with her quick, officious step. Hurrying to keep up with the nun, Alex followed her into the Madonna Chapel, at the far end of the church. She paused while Sister Mary genuflected, stepped behind the shrine's little altar, and knelt down on the floor. Alex assumed that she was squeezing in one last prayer before they began.

Instead, Alex heard the rattle of keys and the scrape of metal. Sister Mary emerged from behind the altar with a chalice. Even the faint light could not diminish its radiance. About twelve inches high, the hammered silver crucible bore golden bands of filigreed ornaments around its rim and base, each of which gleamed with colored gems and amber also set with delicately worked gold filigree. It was a masterpiece.

One by one, Sister Mary carried the equally beautiful paten and reliquary from the storage space; each piece rivaled the chalice in artistic handiwork, lavishness of material, and aesthetic impact. She laid them next to the chalice on the white linen cloth spread out on the altar. Alex itched to hold them in her hands, but didn't dare touch them until given permission from their guardian. Instead, she stayed back and drank them in with her eyes.

Sister Mary joined her. "What do you think of our sacred charge?"

Alex looked directly at her; she wanted to make sure the nun understood the import of her words. "Sister Mary, I've been privileged to study a few early-medieval liturgical vessels that I consider world-class, truly incomparable. Even without in-depth analysis, I'd say these pieces fall within that category."

Sister Mary graced Alex with a broad, beatific smile. "Well, then, let me introduce you to them."

They approached the altar slowly, as if performing a sacred rite. At least it felt that way to Alex, whose only religion was her work. Sister Mary held up the chalice, paten, and reliquary for Alex's visual examination, but not for her tactile inspection just yet. She had more to say. "Our order's history tells us that Saint Brigid herself commissioned the two communion vessels—the chalice and the paten. As I mentioned, the early Abbey of Kildare housed a famous scriptorium and a highly advanced metalworking studio. Brigid was determined that God's glory should be manifest in man's world—just one of the many reasons we'd like to properly honor her."

"What about the reliquary?"

"Brigid ordered its creation as well."

"Brigid commissioned her own reliquary?" The construction of reliquaries, shrines to house the physical remains of martyrs and saints, dated back to very early Christianity, and Alex had studied many of them. But she'd never heard of a saint or martyr directing the formation of his or her own reliquary before he or she died. It seemed presumptuous, like declaring oneself a saint in one's own lifetime.

Sister Mary did not hear—or chose not to hear—the skepticism in

Alex's voice. "Yes, she did. They are all early-sixth-century pieces cre-ated at Brigid's behest."

Alex realized that she would gain nothing by arguing with the au-thoritative nun. If her assessment produced a formation date different from Sister Mary's, she'd allow the scientific results to speak for her. Instead, she asked, "Do you know if the reliquary still contains the original relic?"

"No, it doesn't. Our history tells us that the relic was removed in the ninth century and taken, along with Brigid's full remains, which rested in the abbey church, to Downpatrick to protect them from the Vikings. The relic and Brigid's body were destroyed in the 'Reforma-tion' "—the nun spat out the word—"of the sixteenth century, except for her head, which was saved and presented to the Jesuit church in Lisbon."

Alex was relieved. The Catholic Church had all sorts of rules about handling reliquaries that still contained the vestiges of a saint, and the regulations invariably delayed the appraisal and sale process. And Alex didn't think she could withstand the delay; her mouth watered at the thought of moving forward with haste. "Do you know what the relic was?"

"I believe it was corporeal, possibly a bone."

For all Sister Mary's detailed historical knowledge, Alex found it surprising that the nun did not know the precise nature of the relic of Saint Brigid the order had once held. She took another look at the reli-quary. It was rectangular and quite large—approximately eighteen inches long, twelve inches across, and ten inches high—making it an unusual design and size for a bone relic. The shape and size seemed more suitable for a book shrine, which traditionally contained sacred texts that had been handled or owned by a saint or martyr. Again, Alex thought she'd hold off on challenging Sister Mary. "Where would you like me to conduct my appraisal?"

"Here."

"Here? In the church?"

Sister Mary nodded. "Sadly, this chapel to the Virgin Mary gets lit-tle use these days. If it is satisfactory to you, you may work in here during the daylight hours. I have a table set up for you to the side of the altar."

"Of course, whatever you wish."

"I will lock you inside the chapel," she said, pointing to an iron grill-work, "to ensure your safety and the security of the relics. I will return periodically throughout the day to check on you and then at day's end to return the items to the protection of the Virgin."

GAUL AND THE IRISH SEA

A.D. 470

Brother,

Forgive my long absence, as I pray the Lord will absolve me as well. The road affords scant few chances to pray, let alone write.

I call this dusty treacherous rut on which we travel a road, but I give it undue praise. This crude axe slash in the rough terrain of northern Italy and Gaul bears no resemblance to the ordered pavement of our Roman roads. Yet I should expect nothing more since it is barbarian-wrought.

We ride through lands that Rome once held and cultivated, but that now succumb to the barbarian destruction and ensuing decay. The Ostrogoths, Burgundians, and Franks charged through these hills and plains in a wild, tattooed stampede of bloodshed and triumph, leaving any evidence of Roman civilization to molder in the wake of their battle lust. These barbarians hunger only for the fight and the victory, not for caretaking of their conquered lands. They leave not societies but scars.

But, brother, I launch headlong into my journeys. You must wonder who constitutes this "we" I mention. The only salve in my crossing through barbarian mayhem has been my traveling companion and fellow Roman, Lucius. Gallienus assigned the monk to accompany me as far as the seaside cliffs of northern Gaul to prepare me for my mission. When the road permits, Lucius instructs me in the language, manner, religion, and nature of the strange Gaelic peoples. He knows their ways well; when he was a young monk, the Gaels stole him into slavery from his posting in Britannia, much like the notorious Bishop Patrick. After some unmentionable years, Lucius was traded back into freedom, and returned to Rome. All this I learned from Gallienus. But for one instance, Lucius has not mentioned his own time in Gael.

We travel not as priest and monk but as middling merchants with no particular loyalties except to gold. The lands through which we pass do not suffer representatives of the true Christian church, but they welcome any other manner of society's scum to enter and trade. These barbarians hold fast to their pagan beliefs or, in smaller but growing numbers, their heretical Arian Christianity, with its offensive denial of Christ's very divinity. Though it bristles, we must hide all badges of our Lord if we are to accomplish His mission.

The road offers me much time to study this Lucius. I marvel as he transforms from a quiet monk who rides with steadfast solemnity at my side to a jocund merchant in a swaggering search for the local whorehouse or wager game, when the circumstances demand such proclamations. And he accomplishes all this with the smallest alterations in facial expression, posture, and tone. He astonishes further when he changes back again the very moment the situation permits, only to prostrate himself in a mad rush for our Lord's forgiveness for even mentioning such sins. I believe that the pious monk is his truest self, yet his easy way with transformation amazes and I learn much from it. For soon—too soon—I must don my own mask.

Still, with all of my watching of Lucius, a question has surfaced. I have tried to disregard its sinful whispers, but it has returned again and again as a tormenting reminder that I carry some doubts about my mission. Prayer helped stave off this plaguing query for a time, yet I find I have not the resolve to ignore it entirely. I imagine that this confession will surprise you, brother, for you oft maintain, with a chuckle, that my cautious and resolute nature is nigh inhuman and so must be God-given—an indication that not only our parents but our Lord

marked me for His service. Though even you must own that I ill suppress a certain rashness of spirit when it comes to the barbarian hel-
lions or a perceived injustice to family or God.

Despite my efforts at divine intercession, the question refused to
be silenced one evening after Lucius gave his lessons. I said to him,
"You speak the language with ease, and have an excellent feel for the
Gaelic tribes and their lands, Lucius."

"My thanks, Brother Decius. It is God's doing," Lucius answered as
he stirred the fire. He never fails to use the formal "Brother" when ad-
dressing me, though I have often suggested that the informality of the
road makes it incongruous.

"And you have the undeniable gift of transformation."

Lucius paused. "That too is God's doing, though it is hard for me to
give thanks for it." He looked up from the embers and stared at me.
"Surely you see that assuming the merchant role pains me."

"I do, Lucius. Still, I wonder. Why does the church not send you to
this mission, Lucius? You are eminently suitable, far more fitting than
me."

He broke my gaze. "I would not go."

"Even if ordered?" There is nothing so precious to a monk than his
vows, and obedience ranks high among the oaths.

"Even if ordered."

Embedded in Lucius's answer was a plea to halt my inquiry. I tried
to still my tongue and heed him, but my usual reserve deserted me.
"Why?"

"Brother Decius, do not ask such questions of me. Just know that I
could not serve the Gaelic people in the fullness of the Holy Spirit."

I had overstepped and was heartily sorry to this man who had
served me well. "Forgive me for pressing you, Brother Lucius. They
must have harmed you deeply."

"No, Brother Decius, worse. They tempted me."

Lucius will leave me here, on this desolate Gallic coast, and return to
Rome. I am to await a band of holy men, exiled from their own lands
by the barbarian hordes, that we hear will soon arrive. I am to meld
into their ranks for the arduous sea journey across to Britannia and

then beyond, to the land of the Gaels. I am to reassume my monkish robes and become an outcast among outcasts, looking for the shelter that the Gaelic monasteries afford. But, brother, I head to a land where even the most stoic of our Lord's followers faced temptation. I wonder what will befall me.

These letters burn in my bag. We have passed no messenger, no worthy Roman citizen, to whom I can entrust them. I ask the Lord nightly to send a means, to help lift the worry about my well-being that surely must have settled on your shoulders. He does not answer my prayers.

I know our Savior is here even among these soulless barbarian peoples and the dregs churned up from their wars, but I strain to see Him as I never have before. I see only the wings of the twelfth eagle in flight.

I will write you again when I know next where He will direct me.

Brother,

The voyage to Gael lasted but four days, yet seemed an eternity on a stormy sea churned up by Satan himself. I sailed on a small pirated merchant ship with five other outcast monks, and the northern chop maddened and sickened us all. We clung to the ship's rails in futile attempts to steady ourselves and our stomachs, experiencing relief only when the ship becalmed for brief instances.

During those rare tranquil moments, we huddled together over hurried meals of stale bread and flat ale in the ship's sole belowdecks cabin. Over this meager sustenance we shared our stories, as refugees do, though mine was fiction and uncomfortably revealed. Brother, how often I wished during the journey for even a small measure of your natural gregariousness and fluid way with truth. Instead, I struggled through the communing of histories and blurted out the new identity Gallienus had forged for me, that of a Christian monk and scrivener seeking refuge from a former Roman region beset by a warring mix of pagans.

Somehow my clumsy rendition of Gallienus's fabrication passed muster, for I learned much of the other exiled monks on board. The bone-thin ascetics Rabbula and Shenoute, from Syria and Egypt, took flight from unsympathetic political regimes. Francoveus and Gaudiosos hailed from former Roman regions beset by Visigoths and Burgundians intolerant of Catholic Christians. Only Alanus remained silent. Initially, I attributed this to a reticent nature not unlike my own, until I heard him recite a somewhat unusual Lord's Prayer. I began to wonder if he kept close counsel because he sought refuge not from barbarians but from Rome. I longed to ask questions and tease out his story, but knew that uncovering the biography of one lone monk—no matter how unorthodox and no matter which monastery welcomed him—was not Gallienus's intention for me.

Occasionally awkward silences reigned, and stories of Bishop Patrick's life leaped to fill the void. Adoration for this Briton enslaved by Gaels who—by the grace of God—upon his escape embraced and converted his captors shone through in each word. Though Patrick died years ago, the men spoke of him as though his mission and zeal were alive. I learned details lost to Rome in the vast landscape of Patrick's success in converting great numbers of Gaels to Christianity: his fearlessness in confronting chieftains, his determined eradication of slavery in a society bent on slave raids, his use of a local plant—the shamrock—to explain the Trinity. I heard their lamentations that no Christian leader has arisen from the landscape, or has been sent by Rome, to replace him. Of course, I did not share with them the gentle derision with which he is discussed in Rome, for his poor Latin and interrupted education. It would only offend.

When tales of Patrick waned, the monks enthusiastically discussed the speed with which Patrick's conversions had yielded Gaelic monasteries and abbeys—with the exception of Alanus, who kept his tongue still. Though all extolled the surging growth of these Christian communities, they debated their diverse approaches, as each monk embraced a different path and, thus a different community. Rabbula and Shenoute held fast to the hermetic lifestyle of the nearly inaccessible island settlements, where the monks worshipped in the most extreme conditions of isolation and hardship imaginable; Francoveus and Gaudiosos praised the newly emerging monastic city-states, like Patrick's own Armagh, where a few bishops and abbesses ruled over religious and layfolk alike in small unified village-like communities. When they learned that I traveled to Kildare, however, they set aside their disputes to agree that Brigid's abbey—known for its assiduous tolerance and generosity—indeed held a special place. For Brigid was sanctioned by Patrick himself.

At dawn on the fifth day, the ship lurched forward and then halted its relentless rocking. The impatient crew yelled for us to appear on deck, and we were unceremoniously dumped close to—but not on—the rocky Gaelic shore. On unsteady sea legs, we waded through shallow yet surprisingly violent surf, holding our precious packs high over our heads. I had no doubt that manuscripts crammed the monks' packs, though no one had mentioned texts on board. We stumbled onto the rough beach and knelt in prayers of thanksgiving.

We dried and reassembled our belongings, foraged for a shared meal, and then gained our bearings by exchanging maps and directions. Then we took our leave of one another. In truth, brother, I was sad to part with them, even though it relieved me from playing a role for a short while. For I know not what I face as I begin the long trek inland toward Kildare.

Rome seems ever more distant with each passing day, and I cannot imagine encountering a Roman soul traveling homeward to whom I can entrust these letters. Particularly since Lucius gave me to understand that so few Romans other than us refugee monks, who cannot return home, walk on these shores. Still, I will continue to write you, brother, to keep our connection in spirit, if not in person.

Pray for me, brother, as I head into the heart of my mission, as I pray for you.

Decius

GAEL

BRIGID: A LIFE

The Words encircle Brigid. Beautifully bound leather manuscripts, tightly wound elongated scrolls, and heavy folios ring around her in a divine dance for her attention. Brigid longs to select from them, but she does not have the liberty to single one out. Her mother directs the order of her review.

Broicsech undertakes this final stage in Brigid and her foster brother Oengus's religious education. Available Christian tutors have been interviewed and summarily rejected as not erudite enough to guide her daughter and foster son through the sacred texts. Therefore Broicsech takes on their initiation into the Words herself, a first for the busy queen. But the sacrifice is necessary. She wants them perfectly trained for Patrick, for the pure waters of their baptism.

With careful deliberation, Broicsech reveals the blessed books to them. She has quietly amassed these singular texts over the years, procuring them from wandering Britons, outcast Romans, and the odd Copt. A deft exchange of a golden armlet here or a silver cloak pin there, and the manuscripts join her collection, one so private that none have seen it before.

In her lyrical voice, she reads the Words aloud to Brigid and Oengus, lulling them with the accounts of Matthew and Luke and the letters of Paul. Brigid is just as seduced by Mark's realistic reports of Jesus's daily life as she is by the dreamlike meditations on His suffering depicted in the poetic Round Dance of the Cross. Yet with every breath and every word, Brigid hears the reluctance in her mother's voice at divulging the texts' secrets, so long closely held.

The Jesus enfleshed by these manuscripts entrances Brigid. He is no longer a deity known only from afar. He becomes real and vulnerable, utterly different from the elemental spirits whirling around the Gaels' rituals. She would never utter such thoughts aloud, even to Oengus, for she knows Jesus to be divine no matter how human He seems. The texts of His friends and followers assure her of this again and again. More than any other aspect of His teachings, Brigid becomes convinced by the solid logic of His virtues; they appeal to her practical and rational nature.

As Broicsech guides them through her library, scroll by scroll, folio by folio, Brigid grows unsettled. For days, she cannot put a name to her unease. She wonders whether it stems from the slight variations in the accounts of His followers or the unusual nature of His world. She considers whether His monotheism troubles her or His assertions that He is the Son of this only God.

Then, with a sudden rush, the source of her discomfort exposes itself. Brigid cannot believe she did not recognize it before. It is that the texts barely reference women.

She knows how Broicsech will react if she interrupts—and she fears her mother's sharp tongue and sharper belt—but she cannot wait another moment to question this. "Pardon me, Mother, but where are the women in this Jesus's world?"

"What do you mean?" Broicsech does not look up from her folio.

"We have heard tale after tale of His ministry, yet His followers seem to be exclusively men. Even stories of the towns through which He passes and the people they encounter mention few women. In the atypical instance when a woman is discussed, she is a passive female family member or a serving girl or a whore. I can understand that women do not figure in His deity as goddesses do in ours—but I cannot fathom the lack of prominent women in His earthly world."

Broicsech marks her place in the dense text with her finger and answers: "You overstate your argument, Brigid. Certainly women other than serving girls or whores figure in His world. Still, His world is different than ours. His women cannot play the same roles they do in ours."

Brigid shakes her head at the incomprehensibility. "How can I believe in a God who disregards the intelligence and strength of women? Who only knows women to be passive vessels for the doings of men?"

"Do not mistake the lack of reference to women as a sign of His disregard for them. His world was—is—unlike our own. Women were not permitted to serve as lawyers or priestesses or bards, as they do here in Gael. But do not let this diminish the truth or potency of His message, just the parity of the world from whence He comes."

Brigid watches Oengus sink back into the arms of his chair, as if it could rescue him from the rising exchange. Or render him invisible, at the very least.

"Mother, I want to embrace this Jesus, truly I do. But how can I have faith in a god who comes from a world without women leaders?"

"Brigid, you must accept my pledge that Jesus bears women no ill will and, in fact, respects them wholly. Do not forget that He included women in His ministry against the protest of many."

"Mother, you have hired too many Druids and lawyers for my education for me to take such a blind leap of faith."

To Brigid's surprise, Broicsech does not raise her voice in response, but sighs. "Your misgivings wear on me, Brigid. You should listen to your mother and queen when she offers you assurances."

Broicsech rises from her chair and begins searching through the piles of precious manuscripts. She slides out a surprisingly small text concealed within a mass of much larger folios and walks toward Brigid.

Broicsech hands her the text. "Here is the woman you seek. Here is a Jesus you will abide."

Brigid looks at the palm-sized manuscript her mother has placed in her hand. She asks, "May I read from it?"

"Yes, but with great care. This text—"

A call sounds from behind the closed library doors, staying their conversation. The noise grows louder until the doors slam open with a jolt. Suddenly Dubtach stands at the entry. "Broicsech, time to ready yourself for the royal progress. The Druids say the weather will hold for the journey."

Brigid slips the manuscript into her bag, and they enter the bustle of the *cashel* in Dubtach's wake. All of its members—free and slave—scurry in a mad rush to prepare the royal entourage for the regular tour of their lands. The Fothairt people beholden to Dubtach depend on the king's annual visit as an affirmation of their mutual obligation to one another: kingly protection against attack from other chieftains in exchange for livestock and tillage of land.

The *cashel* teems with charioteers, warriors, slaves, Druids, and bards, all packing for the imminent departure. Brigid and Oengus have never accompanied the kingly procession, so they are free to pursue their whims. They race to secure their swords and head toward the neglected practice fields.

Just as they reach the gate, Brigid hears Broicsech summon her. "Brigid, you have no time for warrior training. You must prepare for our departure."

"I am to accompany you?" Brigid is surprised. Never before has she joined the royal progress.

Broicsech sighs. "Brigid, you are of an age to join me and Dubtach in the representation of our family. Besides, it will give you ample opportunity to display the Christian charity of which we have been reading."

"As you wish, Mother," Brigid answers with a curtsy. She smiles at Oengus, whom she assumes will come as well. But Oengus's expression offers no confirmation, only confusion.

She dares to ask the question she sees unspoken on her foster brother's face: "What of Oengus, Mother?"

Broicsech's queenly arched brow lowers, and her tightly clenched jaw slackens. With unmistakable regret and an atypical softness, she says, "Oengus nears seventeen. By Samhain, he will be returning to his birth family, after nearly ten years fosterage with us. It would not be appropriate for him to join the royal progress, Brigid."

Broicsech pivots back toward her quarters to undertake her arrangements. Brigid and Oengus both know that Broicsech's hasty departure is born from too much emotion rather than too little, but Brigid feels that Oengus deserves actual consolation. She turns toward him to offer her apologies. Though her ever affable foster brother's eyes brim with tears, he smiles and says, "Ah, Brigid, we all knew the time would come. It's just that I've been with your family for so long, I hardly remember my birth family. You have become my true sister, you know?"

Brigid grabs Oengus and holds him close. "And you have become my true brother. We do not need blood to bind us."

GAEL

A.D. 456

BRIGID: A LIFE

Oengus's absence taints Brigid's excitement over her first royal progress. She knows that were Oengus at her side, she would revel in every aspect of the lengthy rides through the verdant countryside and the elaborate banquets of their hosts. Her foster brother has long filled the unoccupied hours that make up the only child's days, and she feels oddly empty without him to share this new experience.

Her spirits are dampened for another reason as well. Her attendance on the annual tour sends a message to the Fothairt people of southern Gael: Brigid has come of age. Her long walks with the Druids memorizing verse and history will end. Her afternoons in the library challenging her mother's latest tutor will cease. Her time with the silversmith and scribes learning their craft will stop. Her beloved warrior's training will finish. For soon, Brigid must choose a life path.

Her mind and heart weigh heavy on their final evening at the estate of one of Dubtach's favored chiefs, Eaghan. As Brigid has become accustomed, she stands to Broicsech's right as the gifting ceremony begins. She ensures that the baskets of cheese, bread, and ale stand at the ready, and nods to her mother that she may start the distribution of goods to Eaghan's people.

The horn sounds, and Brigid backs away to let her mother, the queen, commence. Instead she feels Broicsech's hand at her elbow, pushing her forward. She resists and whispers to her mother, "What are you doing?"

"Guiding you toward your duty."

Brigid stumbles to the front of the assemblage, trying to remember the exact steps of the ritual. She kneels before the band of children at the front of the large group of commoners. After signaling to the servants to bring the food baskets to her side, one by one, she hands the children loaves of bread and immense blocks of cheese. The children giggle with delight at her modest gifts, and for long moments she forgets that she is the daughter of Dubtach undertaking her duty. She recalls only that she is a child of God, helping those in need. It is a uniquely satisfying experience.

She reaches into the last basket only to find it bare. Standing, Brigid apologizes to the few empty-handed children and then concludes the gifting ceremony with the traditional utterances of thanksgiving for the bounty of the harvest. Turning back toward her father's retinue, she notices that a royal, one of Eaghan's sons, stands at the edge of the commoners' crowd. He is staring at her. His gaze does not waver when she looks into his eyes; in fact, he nods in pleasure that she has noted his interest.

They take their leave of the people and retire to the immense thatch-roofed hall at the center of Eaghan's *rath,* the earthen enclosure around his royal structures. Brigid hears the strumming of fine harpists as they approach, and eloquent *filid* recite poems to them as they settle into their seats. Servants present gifts of finely embroidered cloth to Dubtach and his family, and parade delectable cheeses and honey cakes before them.

Brigid notes that her father seems oddly merry, a contentment that continues throughout the evening. He applauds with gusto at the performances, and shouts compliments about the meats and ales. He even asks Broicsech to dance with him, and Brigid admits to herself

that her parents make a fine, lithe pair. Watching them, she understands why her mother selected him from all her many suitors.

Dubtach's satisfaction is contagious, and Brigid finds herself enjoy-
ing the festivities—until her mother asks her to perform a piece of poetry for the gathering. She mentally reviews her memorized poems and,
nervously, selects a poem by the famous bard Amhairghin. The piece
demonstrates the intellectual curiosity and strength of the Gaelic people. And herself, she hopes. It is a deviation from the courtly love
poems that most young women would perform.

Brigid closes her eyes and recites the words:

I am the wind which blows over the sea,
I am wave of the sea,
I am lowing of the sea,
I am the bull of seven battles,
I am the bird of prey on the cliff-face,
I am sunbeam,
I am skillful sailor,
I am a cruel boar,
I am lake in the valley,
I am word of knowledge,
I am a sharp sword threatening an army,
I am the god who gives fire to the head,
I am he who casts the light between mountains,
I am he who foretells the ages of the moon,
I am he who teaches where the sun sets.

She opens her eyes. The seated crowd is quiet, almost motionless.
Brigid wonders whether she has performed poorly. Or perhaps she has
offended with her choice, and they would have preferred a more traditional love poem. But she does not want to be perceived in such a
manner, as some lovesick girl seeking a mate.

Brigid hesitates, uncertain whether to remain standing or take her
seat. A loud clapping emanates from the crowd. She sees that two men
stand to applaud her recitation: her father and Eaghan's son. Heaving

a sigh of relief, Brigid returns to her seat. She grasps her cup of ale and drains it to calm her nerves. Half-hidden by her goblet, she hears her father whisper to her mother, "Odd choice, that. But she showed herself well nonetheless. She may assist us in the unification against Rome and the barbarians yet."

Brigid sneaks a glance at Broicsech to gauge her reaction. But her mother's face bears its usual impenetrable regality. Brigid is left to speculate about in what way her father hopes to utilize her in his efforts to designate a single king for Gael, one capable of mustering all resources to fend off the Romans or the barbarians in the coming days. Himself, preferably. The Gaels' notorious lack of leadership unity has served them well so far—making it hard for the Romans to defeat them without the strength of many troops—but rumors abound that Gael will need a single powerful force to maintain their ongoing independence. And most chiefs bristle at the thought of uniting under the growing power of the Christian church. Brigid arrives at a singular conclusion about her usefulness.

Broicsech and Brigid return to their quarters as the men continue with their drink and games. They are both quiet as the servants help them undo their heavy ceremonial dresses and jewelry. In the stillness, Brigid carefully fashions her questions and waits for the servants to leave.

"Why did you ask me to perform this evening, Mother?"

"Isn't the answer self-evident, Brigid? I have made certain you were trained in all the arts so that you can properly represent your family. And you have done well."

"I think the answer is not quite so simple, Mother."

The blade of her mother's voice begins to sharpen. "If you knew the answer, Brigid, then why did you ask the question? Pray do inform me of this answer."

"I think you and Father were displaying my qualities to Eaghan's clan like cattle available for purchase."

Broicsech's lovely brow knits in frustration and anger. "Brigid, do you think so little of me? Do you think for one moment that I wish to thrust my only daughter—my only natural child—into the marriage ring? I have no alternative but to do so."

"Why do you believe you have no free will in the matter of my future?" Brigid answers her. It is the first time she has dared to truly challenge her formidable mother.

"Politics and the survival of our people leave me with little choice. If you make an advantageous marriage, you may assist our future greatly. Had we other children, perhaps I could have sheltered you better."

"Why did you bother to raise me with the belief that I would be able to choose my own path? Why did you expose me to so many callings? I would have been better off knowing little but the domestic realm if this was to be my fate." Brigid wants—has always desired—to please her family, her oft-absent father in particular. Yet she has always hoped to achieve that goal not through marriage but through her own accomplishments in her studies, or on the battlefield.

"Do you remember the story of your birth? Born neither within nor without the house?" Broicsech references the tale Brigid knows well. Broicsech's labor was fast and early, forcing her to bear Brigid alone on the house's hard stone threshold.

"Yes."

"I had to prepare you for all worlds, Brigid. For I do not know—I have never known—upon which you will settle."

GAEL

A.D. 456

BRIGID: A LIFE

The return to the *cashel* does not bring the usual excitement of returning rulers, at least not for Brigid. For their homecoming also brings
the parting ceremony for Oengus, months before originally planned.
His parents, adherents of the old gods, want him back early, long before Patrick revisits Dubtach and his family. Though Brigid paints a
smile upon her face during the banquets and entertainments and offers good wishes to her foster brother and his family, she feels empty
and sad. Without Oengus, Brigid is alone, now more than ever.

She retreats into her studies, though this means time with Broicsech. Her mother acts as ever, yet Brigid senses the distance between
them. Logically, she understands the reasons for her parents' plan and
even concedes that measures toward Gaelic unity may be necessary.
Still, she cannot help but feel betrayed that her own mother would
sacrifice her to that end, no matter how noble, without heed to her desires.

Never discussing their rift, they continue with the examination of
the sacred manuscripts in Broicsech's collection. Periodically, Broicsech interrupts her textual instruction with more practical training in

the divergent forms of Christianity and the battles brewing—or already brewed—between the Roman Church and its outliers. She explains to Brigid that the heresy most associated with Gael is that espoused by the late Briton Pelagius, who argued that individuals have moral responsibility over their own actions because God gave them free will. Though mother and daughter agree that Pelagius's tenet bears a certain logic, akin to the Druidic beliefs, they agree to keep such accord private so as not to risk alienation.

Queenly duties periodically force Broicsech to break from their studies. Whenever they do stop, Brigid flees the library with a text in hand. She longs for the openness of the plains and the coolness of the early spring air to free her from her anger and sorrow, and finds solace in reading His Words outdoors in His creation.

She rediscovers the manuscript handed to her by Broicsech on the day of their departure. Sitting in a knoll by the Liffey riverbank, she opens the small book titled the Gospel of Mary the Mother. She hears the leather-bound spine crack a bit as she turns to the first page. Her eyes strain as she attempts to decipher the cramped Latin script, the ink and vellum faded with age. Yet from the first moment she makes sense of its prose, she is entranced.

As Broicsech had promised, the manuscript contains the story of a woman, a most impressive female from the world of Jesus Christ. The text contains a full account of Jesus's mother, Mary, a narrative utterly different from any other Brigid had read with Broicsech in the Gospels of Matthew, Mark, Luke, and John.

Brigid learns that Mary, at the young age of three, enters the famed Temple in Jerusalem to study with the priests. It is an honor normally reserved for boys alone and, even then, for a very select few. From the start, Mary's maturity, learning, and piety distinguish her and engender adulation among the people of Jerusalem. She bears the gift of sight and the ability to converse with the Lord's messengers. While at the Temple, the text says, "no one was more learned in the wisdom of the law of God, more lowly in humility, more elegant in singing, more perfect in virtue. She was indeed steadfast, immovable, unchangeable, and daily advancing to perfection."

Suitors seek her hand when she comes of age. In contravention of the wishes of the priests and her family, Mary forbids them, saying, "It cannot be that I should know a man, or that a man should know me. . . . I, from my infancy in the Temple of God, have learned that virginity can be sufficiently dear to God. And so, because I can offer what is dear to God, I have resolved in my heart that I should not know a man at all."

But then an angel appears before Mary, saying, "You have found grace before the Lord of all. You will conceive from His Word." Mary resists at first, adhering to her vow of chastity. She acquiesces when the angel explains the virginal nature of the conception and the fact that Mary will bear "the Son of the Most High . . . who will save His people from their sins." The angel guides Mary to accept Joseph, assuring her that he will not be a true husband and saying that since "she had found favor with God, she would conceive in her womb and bring forth a King who fills not only earth but Heaven."

When the Temple priests hear of Mary's pregnancy, they assume defilement by Joseph. But Mary says—"steadfastly and without trembling"—"if there be any pollution in me, or any sin, or any evil desires, or unchastity, expose me in the sight of all the people, and make me an example of punishment to all." Before the priests, she approaches the Lord's altar boldly, circles the altar seven times, and no sign of impurity appears upon her. Thus she convinces the people of Jerusalem of her innocence.

Brigid is moved by Mary's endurance and strength on the long journey to Bethlehem and in the bearing of her precious child without complaint or bloodshed. Yet the account of the bond between mother and Christ child sways her most. For she learns how Jesus drives fear from Mary's heart in moments of terror, and listens to His Mother's guidance in times of crisis and youthful misbehavior when He will heed no one else. In one tale, His Mother comes to the youthful Jesus after He has killed a childhood rival in anger and says, "My Lord, what was it that he did to bring about his death?" When Jesus explains what happened, Mary says, "Do not so, my Lord, because all men rise up against us." And He, "not wishing to grieve His Mother," causes the child to rise. Again and again, he returns to her side, and she encourages Him to strive to His Father's calling when all others cower in fear before Him: "Jesus returns to His Mother."

The Gospel of Mary the Mother lures her. For here is a strong woman of Jesus's band worthy of emulation—resilient, bold at times, and learned. She is not afraid to instruct her Son—even chastise Him—when His behavior demands it, and He heeds her, recognizing her as a woman worthy of respect. Brigid returns to the text's Words again and again, whenever her circumstances permit. And this text, this Gospel of Mary the Mother, plants a seed.

One particularly fine summer afternoon, a cry interrupts Brigid's solitary reading by the riverbank. As the sound grows closer, she recognizes the voice as that of her mother's personal maid, Muireen. "The queen summons you immediately," Muireen announces. "Bishop Patrick is due to arrive."

Brigid rises from her knoll. As she hurriedly walks back to the *rath,* she is careful to brush off the dust and grass from her cloak and smooth her hair into neat plaits. She does not want her second meeting with Bishop Patrick to commence as her first did. Too much may depend upon it.

She pushes through the gate and, from the state of the *cashel,* sees that Patrick has yet to appear. Relieved, she walks to her quarters to further refine her appearance. As she thinks on which gown to wear and with which pin to fasten it, she walks by her parents' rooms. She is surprised to hear her father's voice from behind the closed door; he is rarely found within the *cashel* during the busy daylight hours.

Slowing nearly to a stop, Brigid hears her father say, "Broicsech, I have made myself abundantly clear on this point. I will not play host to a mass baptismal rite for a personal aim of Patrick's." He pauses and then spits out, "Or whatever master he serves, the bastard Britons with their Saxon mercenaries or the Roman government with its unquenching desire to conquer our lands."

"Dubtach, do not speak such heresy. You know that Patrick has allegiance to neither Britannia nor the Roman government. In fact, he has made enemies of both Britannia and the Roman government in even coming to minister to us in Gael. He had to convince the Romans that we were worthy of conversion, and he made himself suspect in Britannia by desiring to minister to the Gaels at all. Patrick's fealty is to the Roman Church—and to God in the purest sense."

"Are you so certain that the Roman Church and the Roman government are not one and the same? Or that the Roman Church is so separate from the church and government of our enemies in Britannia? I do not trust him, and I will not be used for his schemes."

"Please, Dubtach, I beseech you. Bishop Patrick has asked to baptize us before our people, and I believe it is our Christian duty to honor that request."

"I am a king, first and foremost. I must protect my cattle, my land, and my people and heed their needs. Not Patrick."

Her mother's voice sounds horrified. "What do you mean, Dubtach? As king, the leader of your *tuath*, you are charged with the care of your people's souls. As a Christian king, you should guide them toward the true faith."

Brigid smiles. Her mother is using the same tactic with Dubtach that Patrick had used on her.

"My role is practical leadership, not religious conversion. The people must choose their own spiritual guides, and if they do not feel compelled by our God, I will not drive them from theirs."

Brigid's smile fades. It seems that Broicsech will experience less success with the *tuath* strategy than Patrick had with her. Brigid strains but can hear no more from the chambers. After a long moment, she hears Broicsech ask in a small voice, "What of Brigid?"

"What do you mean?"

"Will you allow her to be baptized by Patrick?"

Her father is quiet for a time. In the stillness, Brigid saddens at the thought of her otherwise intimidating mother having to beg her father for permission. She wonders whether women's subservience to men will grow more common with the infiltration of Roman and barbarian notions of women. Then Dubtach responds: "You may have her baptized—in private. I do not want Brigid's religious status to become known and jeopardize any plans we might form for her. She must be preserved for the role in which she can serve us best—as a wife."

X

GAEL
A.D. 457

BRIGID: A LIFE

Brigid is slow and deliberate in her preparations. She selects a gown of unblemished white linen and closes it at her shoulder with her simplest silver pin, shunning all other ornamentation. Drawing her red-gold hair back from her face, she braids it into three layers of plaits. She washes her face and hands, scrubbing them until they are raw. Then she steals a glance at herself in the highly polished silver pitcher on her table, and nods in approval at the austere visage staring back at her.

Alone, she solemnly walks the short distance to the smaller of the *cashel*'s two reception halls, as if marching along one of Dubtach's ceremonial routes. The *cashel* no longer bustles with the arrangements for Patrick's welcome. The bishop has already arrived, and, in any event, Dubtach's decision has halted the need for any intricate plans. Thus Brigid passes, almost unobserved, into the hall.

Broicsech sits with the bishop at the large dining table at the hall's center. They talk quietly, while the bishop's monks and Broicsech's maids stand idly behind them. No one notices Brigid, leaving her to wonder what words pass between the bishop and the queen that so engross them. Do they discuss the finer points of Christian doctrine? Or is Broicsech trying to appease Patrick for Dubtach's rejection?

With a start, Patrick stands. Her mother rises in quick succession. "Come," Patrick says, "we have been waiting for you."

Brigid approaches the bishop and kneels in respect. At his behest, she settles into the chair to which he points, across from him and Broicsech. She keeps her eyes lowered and her hands clasped as if in prayer.

"Your mother tells me you are ready for the rite of baptism."

"I hope you find me so, Bishop Patrick," she says, without raising her gaze.

"I am certain that I will. I understand that, with your mother's guidance, you have been undertaking good works and reading the Words of our Lord, as is required for the sacrament."

"Indeed, Bishop Patrick, I have prayed that the study of His Words will prepare me well for my *first* initiation into His Kingdom." Brigid chooses her phrases, and her emphasis, carefully.

He seems not to have perceived her implication. "I have no doubt that He has answered those prayers, Brigid. And that His Words have brought you closer to Him. I know that the Words returned me to Him when I had wandered far from Him during my years in Britannia before I was taken to Gael."

"To be sure, I have found the stories of Mary—and her decision to take the veil—to be of particular comfort." Brigid wants to ensure that her meaning is understood and that her groundwork is laid.

"You speak of the stories of Mary, Mother of Jesus Christ?" Patrick's voice grows cold.

Brigid does not understand the change in his tone. "Yes, Bishop Patrick."

He turns to her mother. "Broicsech, has Brigid been reading the Gospel of Mary the Mother?"

Her mother is quick to answer: "Bishop Patrick, we live in a land far from Rome's civilizing influence, as you well know. We must study the limited sacred literature available to us."

"Surely, other, more appropriate texts are available to you? You do know that the Gospel of Mary the Mother was forbidden by Irenaeus, bishop of Lyons and a leader of our church, nearly three hundred years ago—along with other self-proclaimed Gospels—as apocryphal and unorthodox? And that His Holiness the pope has adopted Irenaeus's views?"

"I have heard of that edict, Bishop Patrick, and the pope's agreement. But Brigid understands that the true Gospels are only those of Matthew, Mark, Luke, and John. She does not read any of the other texts for the veracity of their words, only for the texture of their tales. I will let her assure you of this herself."

Brigid hears the command underlying Broicsech's gentle assurances. She knows how to placate her mother, and she is in accord. Though she sought to invoke Mary the Mother, she nonetheless wants nothing to impede her baptism. "My mother is correct, Bishop Patrick. I only meant to say that I find Mary's devotion to be moving and inspirational."

"Ah, if that was your sole meaning—"

"It was indeed, Bishop Patrick."

"Then I do not think that you have damaged your faith or imperiled your soul by reading her self-proclaimed Gospel. And, among the three of us, I have read a copy of the manuscript as well. I find myself charmed by the anecdotes of Mary's life, though, of course, they are not to be treated as Gospel. "

A palpable relief descends upon the table. "May we proceed with the rite of baptism for Brigid and myself?" Broicsech ventures to ask.

"We may," Patrick says with a signal to his monks.

Brigid watches as the robed ascetics fill a vast basin with water from jugs marked with the sign of the cross. "We will not be baptized in the river Liffey?" she asks.

Patrick shakes his head. "It is true that our Lord was born anew in a river. However, I understand that your father would prefer that you and your mother experience a more intimate rite. As would our pope."

Broisech and Brigid kneel before the basin. Bishop Patrick articulates the sacred words of exorcism to ensure the purity of the women's souls before the sacrament. He then anoints them with blessed oil from a tiny jar hidden within the folds of his black robe.

Patrick asks, "Do you believe that you cast off the sin of your father and mother through baptism?"

In unison, Broisech and Brigid say, "We believe."

"Do you believe in penance after sin?"

"We believe."

"Do you believe in life after death? In the resurrection?"

"We believe."

"Do you believe in the unity of the church?"

"We believe."

Patrick then turns his back to them, genuflecting and praying before the basin.

Broicsech motions for Brigid to rise. They retire to an antechamber off the hall, with their servants in tow. The maids undress them and wrap them in white cloth to protect their modesty during the immersion ritual. They hang Broicsech's and Brigid's pristine robes with particular care, as the later wearing of these garments will signify their new life in Christ.

Taking advantage of the servants' preoccupation, Broicsech whispers, "What game are you at, Brigid?"

"Pardon me, Mother?"

"Your references to Mary and the veil—what are you about?"

"I do not understand your meaning, Mother."

"And I do not comprehend yours, Brigid. But I will, mark my words."

KILDARE, IRELAND

PRESENT DAY

Alex's second day in Kildare quickly fell into an excited rhythm. She woke at dawn and hastened to Saint Brigid's Church, where Sister Mary had already beaten her to the bronze doors, despite Alex's early arrival. She stood there on the marble floor of the Madonna Chapel while Sister Mary unlocked the relics from their storage space and spread them out on the altar. She waited until she heard Sister Mary lock her back into the chapel and leave the church altogether before she launched into her work. It was the most satisfying appraisal of her career to date, for the pieces lived up to every one of Alex's initial expectations.

The chalice and paten bore the hallmarks of a true artisan. Alex's magnification equipment revealed a remarkable minuscule design embedded in the gold filigree of the communion vessels, a pattern of interlaced knots, birds, and animals alternating with kneeling men and women. On the chalice bowl, she discovered a nearly invisible inscription, the names of the apostles and the Virgin Mary. And when she turned the chalice upside down, she uncovered the most elaborate handiwork of all: a gold filigree circle inlaid with an enormous rock crystal. The craftsman had reserved his finest work for God, as the crystal could be seen only when the chalice was tipped up toward heaven as the celebrant drank of the communion wine.

Yet for all their beauty, Alex did not think the two objects were of sixth-century origin. Their unique Gaelic design and iconography—called Hiberno-Saxon, a fusion of the earlier abstract La Tène Celtic style and the animal art then common elsewhere in Europe—were well developed, really too well developed for the sixth century, when the style had just begun to evolve. And the materials, many of which were not native to Ireland, spoke of an established trade relationship with the Continent, a tenuous tie at best in the sixth century. To be sure, she believed they were ancient, but they seemed born of the early ninth century, in the days before the Vikings began their invasion of Kildare. Not that the later date diminished the value tremendously, Alex would assure Sister Mary. The chalice and paten were of a quality and age similar to those of the Ardagh and Derrynaflan chalices—both considered to be priceless treasures of the National Museum of Ireland.

Dating and placing the sumptuous gold and silver reliquary box proved a greater challenge, one Alex puzzled over that night at the Silken Thomas Inn. Huddled in a corner booth at the inn's pub, she scarfed down her fish and chips while studying the array of photographs before her. The reliquary simply did not make sense. The shape was unusual for a small corporeal artifact, and its iconography—the symbols of the Gospel authors Matthew, Mark, Luke, and John in the four corners of the cross—made it a natural design for a sacred-text reliquary. The piece looked much closer to the book shrines in the National Museum—the Shrine of the Stowe Missal, the Miosach, the Domhnach Airgid, and the Shrine of the Cathach—and those reliquaries contained books that claimed saints' ownership and were of much later origin than the sixth century.

Other incongruous design elements made Alex's head spin. The base of the reliquary was exceptionally deep and bore a much simpler pattern, one Alex might have expected to see in sixth-century La Tène art prior to the period when the Hiberno-Saxon style took hold. To further complicate matters, a beautifully crafted golden representation of the enthroned Virgin Mary with the Christ child on her lap overlay the cross frontispiece, but the image of the Virgin Mary arguably was not seen in Western art until the famous ninth-century illuminated manuscript the Book of Kells. So was the reliquary from the sixth century, as Sister Mary insisted, or had it been fashioned sometime in the ninth century, after the Book of Kells?

Perhaps the justification for the disparity was simple, Alex tried to reassure herself. Maybe craftsmen had reworked the reliquary over time; Alex had seen eighth-century book shrines that had been retooled as late as the sixteenth century. Yet somehow that explanation didn't fit. The overall effect of the reliquary was too cohesive, and its materials had aged uniformly.

"Care for another, miss?"

Alex looked down at her glass and then up at the waitress as if waking from a dream. She'd drained her beer without even realizing it. "Sure, thanks."

Rubbing her bleary eyes, Alex glanced around the room. The other tables were crowded with couples and families eating dinner, and the bar was packed with a bunch of sweaty football players fresh from a match. A roaring fire enhanced the lively, cozy feel, and Alex enjoyed the atmosphere and companionship vicariously. Then she noticed a young woman at a nearby table staring at her with a curious, pitying look.

The compassionate expression took Alex aback, almost like a slap. She'd grown used to working alone, dining alone, and living alone. During her many years at Columbia, she'd always had a few close friends, but she'd shied away from groups, seeing their games as a drain from her pursuits. Even when she selected her career, she stayed away from the predictable museums, auction houses, and academic institutions for the same reasons; all the traditional avenues seemed riddled with time-sapping office politics. There'd been boyfriends, though she was always attracted to men whose artistic endeavors demanded freedom from convention. She'd always told herself that she'd chosen the margins; but now her painful reaction to the stranger's expression made her wonder.

The next morning Alex actually made it to the bronze church doors before Sister Mary. A highlighted reproduction of a seventh-century *Life*

of Saint Brigid practically burned in her black bag, propelling her there
early. She had turned to one of the several extant histories of Saint
Brigid the night before as a way to take her mind off both the puzzle of
the reliquary and that of her own life. Though she'd reviewed the narrative by the seventh-century cleric Cogitosus before her flight, a
reread passage suddenly struck her and took on new meaning. Cogitosus mentioned that in the seventh century, the Kildare abbey church
contained a reliquary holding Brigid's body, "decorated with a variega-
tion of gold, silver, gems, and precious stones, with gold and silver
crowns hanging above them."

Obviously, Sister Mary's reliquary was not that described by Cogitosus—her smallish box could not possibly hold Brigid's body—but if
a lavish shrine had existed as early as the seventh century, was it also
possible that Sister Mary's reliquary had been created in the sixth century, as she claimed? If Alex could pin the reliquary to the sixth century, she'd pull off quite a coup; the oldest known book shrine dated
from the eighth century. And if the reliquary dated from the sixth century, perhaps the chalice and paten did as well.

Alex said nothing of her hopes to Sister Mary. She didn't want to ex-
cite her unduly if the theory proved incorrect—and she didn't want the
prickly nun to know she'd questioned her assertions about the relics'
dates in the first place. She waited patiently as Sister Mary undertook
the slow process of removing the relics from the altar safe. Or so she
thought.

"Antsy today, aren't we, Miss Patterson?"

"Just anxious to start working. It's a real honor to study your pieces."

Sister Mary nodded in agreement, but she scanned Alex warily as
she did. "Well, I'll let you get down to brass tacks." She pulled out two
keys from her crammed key chain and said, "I'll be back a few times
before nightfall. Are you all set?"

"Absolutely." Alex couldn't wait for Sister Mary to leave the shrine
so she could get to work.

"All right then. I'm off."

Alex paused until she heard the sound of Sister Mary locking the
church doors behind her. Then she set upon the reliquary, intent upon
examining it with fresh eyes rather than her usual skeptical vision.

Scrutinizing every design, every material, and every nuance of the exterior with her equipment, Alex determined that her theory was indeed *possible*. She would face criticism—doubters would say that the materials were too exotic, the style too inconsistent, and the Virgin Mary all wrong—but her hypothesis that they indeed hailed from the sixth century was *possible*.

Alex finished her inspection by gingerly lifting up the reliquary's lid to examine the inside once again. The simple interior left her no reason to rethink her theory, so she closed it. She thought about the many legendary false bottoms in her line of work. Such devices were rare, though not unheard-of, with reliquaries. After all, the designer—and the owner—wanted to protect, even hide, the precious saint's remains above all else, especially if they bore magical properties, as so often claimed. But Alex had never come across one herself. An impulse overcame her to run her sterilized fingers along the border between the ornate lid and the simpler, wide base. Deep inside a decorative filigree knot in line with the Virgin Mary, she felt a groove. Reaching for her pliers, Alex gently pressed the little furrow with her instrument. The bottom of the reliquary flung itself open.

Almost afraid of what she might uncover, she looked inside. Instead of a decaying finger bone or a rotting scrap of a burial shroud, a leather-bound manuscript lay within. Just as she reached for it, she heard the fast clip of footsteps across the church's marble floor. Acting on instinct, Alex slipped the manuscript into her black bag.

KILDARE, IRELAND

PRESENT DAY

Her hands trembled violently as she unlocked the door to her room at the Silken Thomas. Alex couldn't believe what she'd done. She tried to tell herself that she'd only borrowed the manuscript for further study. But she knew better; hubris—her belief that she alone could uncover the relics' full story—had pushed her to jump from the periphery into the abyss.

How she'd managed to make it through the day, she didn't know. She'd gone through the motions of photographing and examining the three pieces as she'd planned, all the while obsessing about the manuscript secreted in her bag. Sister Mary's watchful gaze had had to be navigated, as she'd unexpectedly returned—and stayed—more frequently than normal throughout the day. What did she sense, Alex wondered? Or suspect?

Locking the hotel room door behind herself, Alex grabbed the desk chair and lodged it firmly beneath the handle. Intellectually, she knew that no one was going to come barreling through her door, but emotionally, she couldn't help herself. She knelt next to her bedside and placed her black bag on the chintz coverlet. Slowly, Alex unzipped the bag. She'd carefully wrapped the book in a protective sleeve during a rare moment alone. She slid the book out of her bag and then out of the sleeve, onto some plastic sheeting she'd spread out on the bed. It was larger than she'd remembered, nearly twelve by ten inches.

Alex was as afraid to look at it now as she had been when the base sprang open, though for a very different reason. What if the find didn't meet her wild dreams of a late-sixth- to ninth-century illuminated manuscript? The text was probably just some seventeenth-century printing-press Bible inserted by some superstitious nun long after the reliquary's completion.

She stared for a long moment at the manuscript's red binding and its thick, tooled leather cover. Spirals and knots and swirls—typical for La Tène art—so densely blanketed the entire front that not a single empty area remained. Mustering up her courage, she opened it the tiniest bit and heard a crack. Alex winced; she knew it to be the sound of a book spine, untouched for centuries, expanding dangerously.

Slowly, she opened the book a little farther. A breathtaking female face stared out at her from the very first page. Four delicately wrought angels and an intricate border of emerald green, cobalt blue, bright yellow, deep gold, mauve, maroon, and ocher surrounded the image. The backdrop was so distracting that it took a minute for Alex to realize that she recognized the central figure. It was the enthroned Virgin Mary, with the Christ child on her lap, the same image as the reliquary lid.

Mesmerized, she kept turning the vellum folio pages. Ethereal angels, symbolic evangelists, Eucharistic emblems, and images of Christ leaped out at Alex, all wrapped and woven and interlaced with the distinctive and colorful La Tène and Hiberno-Saxon patterns. Even the text pages, covered with biblical words rendered in plain brownish iron-gall ink, contained bold decorative letters and icons. Each folio was more arresting than the last—except for the first. In Alex's estimation, the Virgin Mary image surpassed all that followed.

Alex could translate only a few words of the insular majuscule Old Latin script. Her work required only that she decipher the names and places critical to appraising early liturgical vessels, and she knew her gifts were visual, not linguistic. Yet she also knew that a proper translation would give her the quickest sense of the text's age and import.

Regardless of the gaps in her knowledge, her professional instinct told her that the reliquary had been created to house the manuscript. And that this manuscript was the priceless relic.

KILDARE, IRELAND

PRESENT DAY

Alex rose at five A.M. She went through the motions of greeting and chatting with Sister Mary the next morning. Uncertain as to her next steps, she allowed the nun to lead her to the place she'd requested access to the day before—the basement storage housing the convent's archives.

Sister Mary had assured Alex that this would prove fruitless to her appraisal, that the convent had preserved no documentation earlier than the mid-1800s. Still, Alex felt honor-bound to complete the typical next stage in her provenance search, to ascertain whether the records contained any reference to the artifacts. She was grateful for the silence and the solitude of the subterranean space. She needed the mental and physical room to decide what to do with the manuscript.

Pawing her way through countless musty cardboard boxes, she began to believe that Sister Mary was right. The Order of Saint Brigid had saved only a scant few documents from earlier than the late 1800s. Perhaps the secretive nature of the order in the midst of all the Catholic persecution had mandated sparse evidence of the convent's early existence. The nuns had relied on oral tradition to keep their long history, after all.

Regardless, Alex felt compelled to look through each box with methodical care. She paged through decades of detritus reflecting the convent's mundane daily activities: the convent's financial accounts, inventories of supplies necessary to feed and clothe the nuns, lists of donations received over the years, and records of the order's ever-diminishing numbers. Prayer pamphlets and religious literature she found aplenty, and these too she thumbed through with her usual attention to detail.

The dim basement light and the jet lag began to hit Alex, and she yawned and rubbed her eyes as she knelt down to examine yet another cardboard box. She was sifting through the unorganized piles of old financial records when her hand brushed up against a leather object buried within the papers. Reaching in with both hands, she pulled out not one but two small leather-bound books tied with cords.

Her exhaustion evaporated as she held the books up to the flickering fluorescent light: the leather looked and felt old. Certainly nowhere near as ancient as the cover and binding of the manuscript she'd found in the reliquary, but far older than the nineteenth-century documents contained in the boxes. Possibly even centuries older.

Normally, Alex would have held off on opening the books until she was in a more protected environment, but her heart beat fast at the thought that the books might contain some provenance evidence for the relics. And her experience of finding the manuscript made waiting impossible.

Drawing closer to the faint available light, Alex untwined one of the books and opened it up. Ancient Latin script on vellum pages much older even than the antique leather cover stared up at her, scribed in a hand familiar to her from the reliquary's hidden manuscript. And the second book bore the exact same qualities. With sudden clarity, Alex knew what she must do.

Sitting on the church steps, she rehearsed her excuse for Sister Mary over and over again. Even though she didn't think of herself as religious, she hated lying to a nun. But she wanted to piece together the hidden tale of the reliquary, the manuscript, and the trunk's books more than anything, and she could not be certain that Sister Mary would grant her that honor.

The loud jangle of Sister Mary's keys made its way up the steps before she did. The forewarning gave Alex a moment to compose herself and stand up before the imposing nun arrived.

Before Alex could offer her greetings, Sister Mary said, "Done so early today?"

Alex eked out a smile at the nun's attempt at banter. "Actually, I waited out here to tell you that I need to go to Dublin for a few days to do some research."

"So urgently? You didn't mention a peep about a trip when I left you this morning."

"I was hoping to deliver you some good news today. But as I reviewed my notes at midday, I realized that I need to tie up some loose ends first."

"Good news?"

"I'd really feel more comfortable sharing my assessment when it's finalized."

"Ah, you're not going to make an old nun like myself wait, are you? Who knows how long the good Lord might grant me?"

Alex almost guffawed. For a daunting figure like Sister Mary to play the part of an ailing woman of God was laughable. The smile disappeared from Alex's face, however, when she remembered that she was about to tell a lie of omission. "If you insist, Sister Mary. I have come to believe that your chalice, paten, and reliquary box may come from the sixth century. This would make them the very oldest Irish communion vessels."

Sister Mary looked confused. "But I already told you that they were made in the sixth century."

"You did indeed, Sister Mary, and I wish I could take all my clients' representations at face value. But my job as an appraiser is to reach my own conclusions. My assessments would be meritless if I didn't approach my work with some modicum of objectivity."

"I understand," the nun said, though her face revealed her disagreement.

"I tend to agree with your order's history that the pieces were made in the sixth century. If my final bits of research pan out as I hope, my appraisal will describe your relics as literally priceless."

"Priceless, you say?"

"Priceless. Not to worry, though. I'm sure we'll be able to put a price tag on their pricelessness, and I'm certain we'll find a very willing—but respectful—buyer."

The nun paused and then gifted Alex with that saintly grin. "Well, then, let's get you on that train to Dublin. And may God be with you."

GAEL

A.D. 470

Brother,

My bag grows heavy with the weight of my unsent letters to you, letters that might ease your undoubted concern over your long-missing brother. I have accepted that my words cannot reach you, that no Roman messenger will ever appear on these hills, but I keep writing. The words save me. On my sea voyage, our imagined conversations were my only authentic exchanges during long days of playing the fellow outcast, and since I took my leave of that kindly band on the Gaelic shores, our invented talks are my only companion.

Other than God, of course. Strangely, our Lord has begun to seem more visible to me here in this simple country than He did on the long trek through the marginally more civilized Italian and Gaulish countryside or in the chop of the seas of Britannia. I marvel that Lucius felt tempted in this land where He feels so near.

Perhaps His presence can be explained by the natural lushness of this island so untouched by the hand of man. As soon as I left the crashing surf of the rocky beaches and stepped onto firm soil, landing alone on a rare sunny morn, I experienced the most curious sensation. I entered a landscape so awash in shimmering green that I felt as though I were diving deep into God's emerald waters rather than emerging from them.

This peculiar impression did not leave me, even though nature and man conspired to shake it free. I found that the stormy days of stinging rain and ever-blackening skies only enhanced the feel of deep waters. Even when I passed a rare long-abandoned gray stone ring fort or an enigmatic circle of boulders scrolled with concentric circles, my sense of submersion only increased. I swam through a landscape of green grass, moss, and leaves.

I suspected that the reputedly rough Gaelic people might release me from this strange sensation, but of them I saw little on my way to Kildare. I had only Lucius's account of them as a warrior people with quick wits and quicker tempers, deep stores of pride, and a love of tales and music; as a folk whose women were allowed to be queens, warriors, judges, even priests. I stopped my guessing at them, as I knew I must make my own assessment soon enough.

After weeks of this unsettling travel, I stood at the gateway to the plains of Kildare. I surveyed the open expanse at dawn, taking measure of the final steps I must make toward my destination. Yet the terrain looked so different from Lucius's description and so unlike the rough map I had drawn from his and the other monks' accounts, I despaired of having lost my way.

As I stared into the plains, I spotted a patch of heather at the base of a small hill. I crept toward the nook quietly, thinking it might conceal a hare or pheasant suitable for my meal. I'd crouched down slowly and readied my bow when the heather moved. It shifted not with the gentle rustle of a bird's wings or the leap of a rabbit but with the bold movement of a human being standing upright.

I froze. After so many days without human contact, I could not conceive it so. I reasoned it to be a trick of this land's changeable light, so unfixed at dawn particularly. Yet the being walked toward me.

The shape drew closer, and I realized that the swath of heather was actually a hooded tartan cloak, a sort of camouflage for its wearer. I quickly stood, dropped my bow, and reached for my blade; then I realized that the shape was not man but woman.

The woman pulled back her hood and revealed a striking face. Long tresses of a color unlike any I had seen before spilled out. Despite the meager sunlight, her hair shone neither red nor gold, but both. The style was distinct, designed in three sections, two wound upward and a third hanging down her back in waves nearly to her knees. It served to enhance the unusual hue. I found her age difficult to discern; her face bore the color and freshness of its first bloom, yet I noticed fine lines around the outer corners of her eyes.

Having been long estranged from any company, I struggled to speak. Cobbling together nearly forgotten words from Lucius's instructions, I offered greetings. I then asked, "Do you know the way to the Abbey of Kildare?"

She stepped back, placed her hands on her hips in a most impertinent manner, and took the measure of me. This forthrightness, from a woman no less, startled the words right out of me. I collected myself and repeated in my stammering Gaelic, "Do—do you know the way to the Abbey of Kildare?"

She smiled and answered in speech much more melodious than the rough intonation of Lucius: "Cill Dara?"

My pronunciation, borrowed from Lucius, must have been the source of confusion; thus I corrected myself. "Yes, Cill Dara."

"I do know the route to Cill Dara." Her eyes squinted in deeper discernment of me.

"Will you show me the way?"

"We are always hospitable to strangers traveling in our land," she answered with a nod. Pulling her hood back over her startling hair, she headed back up the slope from which she had emerged.

I scrambled after her, for she was lithe and quick on her feet, affecting no delicacy of movement as Roman women are wont to do. Once at her side, I calmed my breath and asked a few innocuous questions about the plain and its topography. She answered me cordially enough, but with brevity rarely displayed in polite Roman conversation. During one of the many silences, it occurred to me that, with effort, I might learn something of the leader of the Kildare abbey and monastery from this woman—who might be a peasant or novice, for all I could detect.

"Know you the abbess of Cill Dara?"

"Indeed."

"Is she your mistress?" Though her cloak and manner seemed ill-suited to a nun, I thought anything possible in this strange land.

She slowed her pace and turned toward me. One corner of her mouth turned up, and if she had been other than a Gaelic woman, I would have taken it for a coy smile. "She is, and she isn't," she said.

Her mildly mocking tone confused me. I had not intended to amuse or insult by my question, and yet somehow I had. I determined quietude to be the safest course, and we passed the following hour in an increasingly comfortable silence.

We reached the pinnacle of a steep hill and looked down upon a most agreeable plain, through which a sleepy river meandered. At the plain's center stood a giant oak tree around which a vast settlement grew.

The woman pointed and said, "Cill Dara."

I understood her words for the first time: "Cill Dara" means "Church of the Oak." I will be certain to call it Cill Dara now. I stared down in amazement at the sizable community and the massive oak tree that held court in the center. An enormous wall, twelve feet high, penetrated by various gated openings, encircled the development. At the wall's inner perimeter stood dozens of stone structures in beehive shapes, with dozens more just outside the wall. Closer to the center, where the oak dominated, three immense wooden buildings prevailed. One of these edifices connected to a round stone tower rising to nearly one hundred feet, topped off with a roof like a conical cap; another displayed a sculptured high cross of curious design.

"It looks near to a Roman village," I said to myself. In Latin.

"So they say," she answered in Latin. Latin, brother.

If my face had borne amazement before, at spying a considerable town in this barren land, it now revealed shock. Lucius had given me to understand that very few Gaels had exposure to Roman citizens, let alone a Roman education, so I'd expected the language from abbey inhabitants only. And even then, only the religious men. I asked the obvious, if only to hear our mother tongue again: "You speak Latin?"

"I do," she continued in Latin with a wry smile. "Some of us Gaels are not as ignorant as rumored."

I am certain my face grew red; she spoke aloud what I had thought. It seemed that I had done nothing but entertain or offend the first Gael I had met. This did not bode well for my reception and integration into the abbey.

She hastened down the hill. I ran after her, uncertain as to the introductions she would make on my behalf to the abbey's gatekeepers, but reliant on her presentation. I caught up to her just as we approached the largest aperture in the wall.

The guards rushed out to greet her. I stayed a few steps behind, listening as they conversed in quick, unintelligible Gaelic and observing broad gestures in my direction. I waited until they gave me leave to enter.

Once we were inside, one of the guards barked out orders, and a rotund monk emerged from one of the large wooden structures, hurrying to my side. I turned to give my thanks to the woman for her guidance, but a swarm of nuns had flocked around her. I watched as they slid off the heathery cloak to reveal an ankle-length white robe fastened at the shoulder with a gold pin, a circle pierced by a lance. The nuns' fussing motions hid her face, so I could see only the hint of an ornate golden necklace around her neck and a matching armlet around her upper arm.

The monk ushered me off toward the building from whence he'd come, preventing me from staring further at the stately woman who'd appeared from beneath the mantle of a common girl. Before I entered the interior, I looked back one more time to call out my gratitude. But she was gone.

And I realized that I did not know her name.

I wait here in the abbey's refectory for an offered repast and for my fate. I know not our Savior's plans for me, brother. Whatever they may be and however strange this land, I feel His purpose beginning to unfold. The wily Gallienus may have set me on the Lord's path, though for his own ends.

Brother,

Only hours have passed since I last wrote you, but how much has transpired. I wonder how you would view the conclusion of my first day in

Cill Dara. I have been chastising myself, but your nature is more agreeable and optimistic than my own, so perhaps the events would provide you a good dose of laughter. I know naught for certain, other than my own discomfiture, which I will relay in due course.

I write to you in dim candlelight from the hut assigned to me by Ciaran, the monk who welcomed and fed me on my arrival, after a thorough questioning. My hut is one of the many beehives I spied from the hill. These unusual round structures, outwardly cramped, with some made of stone and others of wood, wicker, and thatch, provide a warm, surprisingly spacious living space within. Each religious person—monk, priest, or nun—has their own hut, in which they may sleep, meditate, and pray.

Dining and working takes place elsewhere. The religious folk—men and women alike, mind you—dine communally in the refectory building. Work occurs in a myriad of locations, depending on the task, a function of "our God-given gifts," as Ciaran explained to me. But forgive me; I skip ahead.

Over a simple meal of cured fish and dense bread, Ciaran quizzed me in his paltry Latin, and I responded in my sad Gaelic. We conducted this halting exchange for some time, during which I divulged my "identity" as a Christian monk and scrivener seeking refuge from a former Roman region beset by warring pagans. He seemed less interested in my status as a religious exile—for these Gael has aplenty—than in my skills as a scribe. Ciaran asked me question after question about my trade—what materials I used, whether I could read and write languages other than Latin, how I fared in my image making—but nothing intrigued him quite so much as my mention that I'd brought with me some manuscripts the barbarians otherwise would have burned. He requested that I turn over these minor texts, in accordance with Cill Dara's policies. I had procured them for this exact purpose from Gallienus's own library, and, as I handed them to him, I mistakenly passed him a small Gospel book I had created for myself, for my own worship. From his look, I knew I could not reclaim this item.

Brother, you would have been proud at my ability to don another identity, a talent you would deem necessary for any man calling himself Roman in these mercurial times. For somehow, this stumbling conversation satisfied, and Ciaran assigned me to the scriptorium, a place I will visit tomorrow when the light permits. When the monk made this decision, after plodding consideration, I could almost hear Gallienus applaud; this assignment was his particular goal. For he believes that in the Gaels' texts we will uncover the firmest evidence of their heresy.

Once my belly was full and my work determined, Ciaran led me on a tour of the abbey. We began at the impressive elliptical stone wall, or *cashel,* as he called it, and moved inward to more substantial buildings. From the desolation of the countryside, the plainness of the refectory, and Roman rumor, I expected little. I was wrong to so judge.

True enough, the design of the wall, the huts, the outer structures, and the refectory were basic, nothing to the grandeur of our Roman buildings. And the materials were rudimentary, only the rough stone, wood, and minerals that the land yielded. Yet as we moved toward the interior, inching ever closer to the seemingly sacrosanct oak, I saw evidence of craftsmanship and inspired creation. Every available surface, whether a building exterior or a freestanding sculpture, sprang alive with curvilinear shapes, swirls, and figures. On first glance, I took the decorations to be primitive, yet on closer examination they revealed a delicacy and subtlety, different from our Roman sensibilities but still beautiful.

Nowhere was this artistry more impressive than in the church, to which Ciaran and I retired for evening Mass. As daylight faded, we made our way toward this large rectangular structure, through a crowd of other religious men and women offering greetings to me. The people amazed me with their warm salutations, so unlike the guarded warriors' reception I had anticipated.

We entered through the main doors, flung open wide like an embrace, to a soaring oak church of spare beauty. The benches were nearly full, and from their dress, I could see that regular folk occupied many of them. I was shocked to notice the departure from the strict delineation and hierarchy of seating of our Roman services, where every man knows his place and where woman has none. Scattered among the male and female commoners were the monks, nuns, and priests; the religious held no special accommodations.

Ciaran took my elbow and led me toward one of the few open benches in the back. I struggled to see the altar over others' heads. I noted that the worshippers included monks bearing the curious style of shaving the front of the head from ear to ear so reviled by my superiors as a sign of disobedience. Rome had long mandated the shaved crown alone for its followers; the Gaelic tonsure resembled the old Druid style.

A sudden shift by an unusually tall woman in front of me revealed an altar splendid in its simplicity. A single enormous stone, polished until it glistened, sat atop a pedestal. Along its edge, I saw a chorus of intricately wrought sculptures in the shape of men. Ciaran witnessed my staring, nodded with pride, and said, "The apostles."

The carvings indeed depicted Jesus Christ's twelve apostles. On their sturdy backs stood a silver and gold chalice and paten, the sacrosanct articles of the Mass. Though I found the details hard to discern from a distance, the items seemed of excellent workmanship, equal to what I'd witnessed during my walk with Ciaran.

Bells pealed. Knowing well this signal of the service's commencement, I rose along with the others. The procession started down the center aisle, and the incense drifted toward the high arched ceiling as the celebrants passed. I breathed deeply of its heady scent, and it drew me into the pleasing ritual of the Mass, with its attendant proximity to God.

A white-robed priest stood before the altar and uttered a few words. They were strange in their pronunciation but familiar in their cadence. I closed my eyes and folded my hands in prayer, feeling closer to our Lord than I had for some time. Then a woman began speaking from the altar.

A woman, brother.

My eyes opened. I strained to see the altar over the sea of tonsured heads and hoods. Try as I might, I could not discern the source of the forceful voice. Yet I could not help but notice that it did not alarm the other worshippers.

Knowing the importance of securing the trust of my new peers, I maintained my composure. This will not surprise you, brother, who knows my reserve so well. I confess, though, I writhed within at the thought of a woman performing the Mass, in clear violation of all Roman precepts and all church tenets. In the apostle Paul's letters to the Corinthians, does he not instruct, "Women should remain silent in the churches. They are not allowed to speak, but must be in submission, as the Law says"?

Without warning, the worshippers knelt in prayer, affording me a fleeting view of the altar. I lifted my eyes while keeping my head locked in a respectful nod. The woman stood, arms outstretched, each one bearing a sacred vessel, uttering the secret words of transubstantiation. Garbed in white, her brow encircled by a gold headdress, she was undoubtedly Brigid, the abbess of Cill Dara I had come to learn about. But to my surprise, I recognized her face.

She was the girl from the plains. And she recognized me, for she stared directly at me with the ghost of a smile upon her lips.

Brother, I hope you understand the import of this account. It is heresy enough that a woman performed the sacrament of the High Mass, turning wine to blood and bread to flesh. This profanation I will report to Gallienus when I am able, and the news will surely assist him in his directives. But there is more. Brigid's challenging gaze unnerved me, setting me to wonder whether she guesses at the reasons for my presence in Cill Dara.

So I leave you to your undoubted laughter at my missteps, my amiable brother. For myself, I am left to my prayers that my gaffes today with this girl from the plains—this Brigid—do not cost me the work God calls me to undertake.

Pray for me brother, as I will for you.

Decius

GAEL

A.D. 457

BRIGID: A LIFE

A shake wakes Brigid from a deep slumber. She sits bolt upright but cannot will her eyes to focus. She rubs the sleep from them with her fists; when her pupils finally adjust, she stares into the face of her mother's maid, Muireen.

"The queen wishes your presence in her quarters."

"At this hour? What cannot wait until morning?"

"I know not the nature of the summons, Mistress Brigid, only its urgency."

Brigid throws a cloak over her bedclothes. She walks to her parents' quarters as her mother's maid holds a candle aloft to light the way. Muireen steps aside so Brigid may push open the door to her mother's bedchamber. She finds Broicsech fully dressed in her queenly finest, necklaces, armlets, crown, and all.

"Mother, what is going on?"

Broicsech gestures to the chair before her. "Please sit, Brigid."

She lowers herself with trepidation. She guesses at the worst: the death of her father or the overthrow of his kingdom. Dubtach has been undertaking the dangerous business of assessing his cattle for many long days, so either end is possible.

"Your father has returned to the *cashel* with wonderful news," Broicsech announces, though Brigid hears little delight in her voice. "Eaghan's son Cullen has made a most generous offer for your hand in marriage. A union with a son of your father's favorite chieftain would be blessing enough, but it carries even more gifts. Cullen was foster son to Cormac, king of the Connaught province. Cormac just passed on, leaving Cullen as his heir. Cullen has agreed that his marriage to you will allow your father to join our lands and cattle with that of the late king Cormac—making your father high king of two of the five provinces of Gael and you and Cullen queen and king beholden to him. Dubtach will have unprecedented strength to fend off any invaders. We must act with haste, to ensure no revocation of the offer."

Brigid is unable to speak. She has feared news of a marital union for some days and, in fact, has fashioned a plan to stave off its seeming inevitability. Yet this announcement carries such deep implications for her father's rule—indeed, Gael's rule—that she finds herself oddly immobilized, as if in a terrible dream.

"Brigid, did you hear me?"

"Yes, Mother." The two words are all Brigid can manage, though her heart speaks silent volumes.

"I have already sent my serving girls to assist your maids in the packing of your goods. All you need do is to allow Muireen to dress your hair and help you into this gown." Her mother points to an ornately embroidered robe, one of Broicsech's finest, rarely worn except for high ceremonies.

"Ah, my beloved Brigitta," her father bellows as he bursts into the room. Dubtach has not called Brigid by her childhood nickname for some years, and it further unsettles her. He lifts her from the chair and swings her about the room, making her feel like a cloth doll stuffed with hay.

"You have brought your father unbridled happiness on this day. Cullen desires your hand so fervently, he is willing to cede high rule of his new province to me. Gael will be well suited for the fight, should it come."

Dubtach lowers Brigid to the ground with a gentleness not seen since her milk-tooth days. She still finds herself unable to speak, so he talks for both of them. "I am well pleased with you, Brigid. But not a mention of your recent baptism, do you understand? Eaghan's people hold to the old gods, and I do not want your faith to put Cullen off the marriage."

He leaves the women to their ministrations, calling over his shoulder, "We will leave at first light."

The odd malaise that settled upon Brigid during Broicsech's announcement does not lift during the long ride to Eaghan's lands. Her mind whirls with the conundrum in which this union has placed her, but her body does not reel in accordance. She knows not what course to take; even constant prayer yields no solution to her puzzle.

The regal procession of king and queen, followed by Brigid and a trail of warriors with banners flying and horns sounding, arrives in the borderlands between Dubtach's original lands and Eaghan's. Two large tents, one crimson and one amethyst, stand in a flat field adjoining a grove. The warriors dismount at Dubtach's signal and escort Brigid and Broicsech toward the tent woven of rich purple cloth.

Before she passes over the threshold, Brigid turns around. She watches as her father nears the other tent. Eaghan himself pushes back the tent's opening and stretches out his hands in welcome to Dubtach, his imminent kinsman.

Brigid steps into the darkness of the tent's interior, so black it matches her despair. Her mother has taken a place on the rich carpet covering the forest floor and motions for Brigid to join her. Brigid declines the invitation, preferring to remain closer to the fresher air outside.

"You are unnaturally quiet, Brigid."

"I thought that is what you wished, Mother."

Her mother stands. "I did not raise you to docility and meekness, Brigid. I raised you to strength. Strength, however, does not mean that we always get to pursue our will. Strength means that we must follow our destined path with fortitude and grace."

"And strength sometimes means that we must act as our conscience and our God dictate—even if that course does not accord with
the designs of our family or our land," Brigid says in a near whisper.
With her words comes the insight she seeks.

The warriors' horns call for them. Broicsech leaves the tent with
Brigid and a bevy of maids in her wake. The women make a colorful
stream as they weave across the field to the ceremonial mound where
the men await.

Dubtach and Eaghan stand at the flattened top of the mound.
Their crowns and jewel-encrusted swords gleam in the dying light of
day. A place awaits Broicsech next to Eaghan's queen in the semicir-
cular terrace just below Dubtach and Eaghan on the mound. With a
warrior at each elbow, Broicsech climbs to her position.

And at the mound's base stands Cullen, waiting for Brigid. He is
handsome, with his black hair, green eyes, and crooked nose. As she
stares at him, Cullen smiles at her with gentleness and curiosity. She
thinks that he looks a kindly man, and in another life he might have
made her a good husband. Yet she knows with certainty that this union
is not the path to which she is called.

Custom requires the exchange of commitments between Dubtach
and Eaghan before Brigid takes her position at Cullen's side. Disre-
garding the ritualistic order, she approaches Cullen directly. She hears
her mother gasp and her father call out to her, but she continues her
advance.

Standing before Cullen, Brigid says, "I am so sorry, Cullen. You
seem a good man, and I wish I could honor my father's vows. But I
cannot."

"What—what do you mean?" he stammers in shock, making Brigid
like him all the more. No false warrior's bravado for him. "If you act out
of doubts as to my feelings toward you, I promise you that they are
true." His pledge of affection makes her task more difficult, for only a
gentle man would reassure her rather than lash out at the insult to his
honor.

Ignoring the protests of her parents, she reaches for his hands. She
squeezes them and says, "I do not doubt your feelings, Cullen. And
your words make me wish even more that I could enter into this mar-

riage. I am fortunate that a man such as yourself wants me for his wife." She smiles at him, and a tiny, hopeful grin appears at the corners of his lips.

"Then be my wife," he says.

Tears form in Brigid's eyes at his sincere plea. They course down her cheeks as she says, "Cullen, I would like nothing more than to be called to a traditional life. But the decision is not in my hands. I am newly baptized in the Christian faith, Cullen. And my God summons me to a different existence, an existence that requires my total commitment. It will be a life where I will pledge to follow the original calling of Mary, the Mother of God, and take no husband."

"No husband?" He seems shocked and relieved at once.

"No husband." Brigid touches his cheek with her finger. "Goodbye, Cullen."

Before her parents or her emotions can overtake her, Brigid runs from the ceremonial mound, across the field. She spies her horse, hitched along with the others. Without even bothering to secure her belongings other than the small bag still strapped to the horse, she mounts her steed and rides away. To where, she does not know.

GAEL

A.D. 457

BRIGID: A LIFE

Brigid rides aimlessly for days through forests and plains. She eats what little she can forage and stops only when exhaustion demands. Prayer alone sustains her through the hunger and fatigue, and the distress over her family's certain displeasure, but it does not provide her with a path.

She never wavers in her decision to reject Cullen's hand, but as the days pass, she begins to despair. She longs for a clear way to her new existence as a servant of God. The dream of following in Mary's initial footsteps—taking the veil and serving only the Lord—begins to seem rash and foolhardy. And she does not feel that she can turn to Patrick, the only Christian leader she knows, to shine a light on her path: he is too strongly allied with Broicsech. She falls to her knees beneath a bright half-moon and entreats God to show her the way to serve Him.

Hours later, Brigid awakens in a landscape somehow familiar. She recognizes the distinctive shape of an oak tree overhead and the unique roll of the hill at her feet. She does not remember coming to rest in this place.

After all these days of riding, she has unwittingly returned home.

Her fatigue and anguish had blinded her to the recognizable features of her familial terrain.

It is not yet dawn. Gauging the time remaining before day's light breaks and her father's vassals rise, she dashes down to the riverside. She stoops and drinks of the cold water, slaking her thirst. Dipping her hands in one last time, she rubs her wet fingers over her weary eyes.

Her eyes open to see Broicsech staring into them. Brigid starts to run, but her mother is quicker than her regal manner would suggest. Broicsech catches the wide fold of Brigid's sleeve and pulls her to the ground. Mother and daughter tumble down the knoll and land in a heap.

Panting from her exertions, Broicsech says, "Brigid, you have no need to fear me. I am not like one of your father's raiding parties, ready to cart you off to a life of enslavement."

"Mother, I did not intend to pass so close to the *cashel*. I beg you to let me leave before Father finds me on his lands."

"He knows you are here."

"And he permits me to stay? Without being taken into his custody?" Brigid is astonished. She would have guessed that if he discovered her trespass, her father would have ordered his warriors to return her to the *cashel* for punishment or another try at marriage to Cullen.

"For the moment—"

"I would have thought him furious beyond measure."

"He is indeed. The injury done to his honor exceeds any from the battlefield, I can assure you. But he remains your father."

"I am surprised he would still call himself such."

"Brigid, he loves you, though he would not confess it aloud right now to anyone but me. Once you were spotted last evening, he and I discussed the situation. He knows that I have come to speak with you."

"He does?"

"Yes. He is in full accord with the message I bear."

"Pray do share it, Mother."

"We understand that you have chosen a Christian path, one that contemplates singular devotion and dedication to our Lord, without familial distractions. We will not force you into an unwanted marriage, though it would serve the Gaels' greater goals of continued independence." Broicsech raises her eyebrows. "We are not Romans, after all."

"Thank you, Mother." Brigid grasps her mother's hands and kisses them in appreciation.

"Do not be so hasty in your gratitude. We ask something of you in return. Something that may assist us in reaching the same end your marriage might have."

Brigid winces at the mention of her failed union to Cullen. "Anything you wish."

"We request that, as you serve our Lord, you also serve your people. We believe that Christianity will be the foremost power and religion in the coming days—whether the land remains under Gaelic rule or is overcome by Roman or barbarian. Thus, we want you to prove that Gael—through its Christian piety and prowess—is a land entitled to preservation and self-rule."

Before Brigid can curb her tongue, she blurts out, "Is not Bishop Patrick God's chosen vehicle for the Christian conversion of our people?"

"Patrick is Roman Briton, not a Gael. He may convert our people, but he will never convince Rome or the coming tide that Christian Gael deserves its autonomy. And he will never convert the sheer number of people that a Christian Gael can. The people will always harbor suspicions of a Roman and a Briton; we need a Gael to prove our mettle and bring our people round."

Brigid does not respond at first, judging Broicsech's request to be nigh impossible. After some deliberation, she says, "Mother, you and Father deserve nothing less. You have bestowed upon me the greatest gift, the gift of choosing my own path. Yet how can I—a woman alone—achieve a goal that an army would be better suited to seek?"

"Do not trouble yourself with that; Dubtach will tend to the warriors, as he always does. In any event, an army, by itself, could never meet our objective."

"I cannot fathom how I can succeed where an army would fail."

As if privy to a secret, Broicsech smiles curiously and says, "You must begin by making our people believe in Jesus Christ. And then you must inspire them to manifest that belief in magnificent accomplishments that will make Christian Rome and Arian Christian barbarians take heed of the Gaels."

"How shall I begin?"

"Let us choose your cloak well, for it is a mantle you will wear for all eternity in the minds of our people. If you are to inspire our people to embrace God and render magnificent testimony to Him, your Christian persona must build on what the people already know and love."

"What do you mean?"

Broicsech has an answer so fully formed that Brigid becomes certain that her mother has long considered this alternative to her marriage. "You are called Brigid. Our people worship the goddess Brigid, the source of all healing, the creator of all decorative arts and poetry, and the protector of women. So become the goddess Brigid, but a Christian one. Honor the rituals of the Gaels' Brigid and deliver our Lord's message to them through her voice and her customs. If you do so, the people will listen to you as you bear the saving Word of the new God—and then honor Him in ways our conquerors may heed."

GAEL

A.D. 457–61

BRIGID: A LIFE

Her robes fly behind her like a flag as she gallops through the forest. Astride a white mare and garbed entirely in pure linen, Brigid seems more a spirit than a human. This otherworldliness is her intention, for it eases her way into each village she enters.

She finds that the people accept a ghostly, yet oddly familiar goddess creature into their perimeters more readily than they would a lone woman—though she quickly shows them that her earthly ministry is anything but ethereal. As soon as she enters their enclaves, Brigid rolls up the sleeves of her white robes and offers her healing services to the sick. The people typically ignore her at first. Inevitably, a maimed, desperate villager finally accepts her assistance and the wary people see their crippled friend walk without a cane. Then they descend on her in droves. She sets injuries gotten in the fields; stitches gaping strife wounds; applies poultices to festering sores; and helps women birth their children. And always she refuses the people's efforts at payment.

Instead, she waits. Never preaching, never sermonizing, she quietly prays and observes the basic rituals of the goddess Brigid, the perpetual fire keeping and the holidays. She anticipates the questions that inevitably come. The people muster their courage to gather at her feet and ask about the source of her healing power or her unusual appearance or the nature of her gods.

"Who are your gods?" a bold villager, pushed forward by neighbors, predictably asks.

"I have but one God."

"One God? One God to rule over the rivers and seas and mountains and plains? One God to govern all the tribes and the cattle over which they war?" The person invariably taunts her with a voice full of disbelief. For a society that cannot agree upon one king, the concept of one God seems inconceivable.

"Yes. My God is the God of all people, the God of heaven and earth, of the sea and the rivers, the God of the sun, moon, and stars, the God of the high mountains and deep valleys. His life is in all things. He sparks the light of the sun, and sets the stars in place. He makes wells in arid lands and dry islands in the seas. He has a Son who is eternal with Him and of His nature. The Son is not younger than the Father nor the Father than the Son, and the Holy Spirit breathes in them. The Father, the Son, and the Holy Spirit are not separate. I pray that you will come to believe in my one God."

Brigid quiets and lets the words settle in their ears and minds and hearts. She knows that by describing Him in this way, she makes Him seem not so different from their familiar gods. He sounds like the Dagda, the head chief of the Gaels' pantheon of gods.

Village by village, chieftancy by chieftancy, and province by province, Brigid converts them. But she does not merely gather their pledges like plunder; she instructs them in His ways of living. She tutors them in basic writing and reading so they can share His Word with others. She teaches them how to build structures in which to worship Him and to carve stones to proclaim His majesty to all who pass. And then she chooses one of their women to join her in her ministry.

This selection, at first resisted, becomes highly desired. The female villagers vie for the chance to join Brigid's growing band. Taking the veil—with its heady mixture of freedom from tradition and devotion to God—becomes an emblem of Gaelic womanhood.

Though her followers grow large in number, Brigid keeps her approach simple and uniform. She takes the lead with her group as it nears the villages, although she always remains humble with the people and in her prayers. Her followers assist her with the initial offers for healing, and together they undertake their grueling work. When the people are ready, the women help her instruct the villagers in ways of His artistry and in His Words. Their numbers, however, allow Brigid to reach increasingly large populations. From the start, Brigid is careful never to tread on Patrick's northern territory. She has no reason to believe that he would condemn her efforts, but she is cautious nonetheless.

Yet from his seat in Armagh, Bishop Patrick takes notice as her company of women enlarges and the rumors of Brigid's accomplishments reach him.

Finally, Bishop Patrick summons her. Recollecting his quick temper, Brigid fears his displeasure at her self-appointed ministry. She certainly has no wish to alienate the Roman Church in these early days of her work, so she contemplates the best way to placate him. She determines to leave her women to their work and ride to Patrick's headquarters in Armagh alone.

The journey is arduous and long, but she has grown accustomed to the little hardships. She perceives the time away from her work as a blessing, a rare solitude in which to consider her calling and her approach with Patrick. Although she had remained at a distance from Patrick, she has learned much about him in the days since her baptism and has warmed to the man from afar. She and Patrick are both royal-born, but drawn to the Christian path. Each has been willing to sacrifice much to convert the Gaelic people, even if that conversion requires unseemly acts, such as bribery for safe conduct. Most of all, Brigid believes that Patrick advocates for a new kind of church—one that breaks from the rigid Roman model and theology yet retains its core truths. She feels a kinship with him, both personal and religious.

When she dismounts at the gates to Patrick's Armagh *rath,* she feels ready to defend her work and even sway Patrick to her vocation, if he should resist. Though a guard welcomes her and takes her horse to the stalls, Brigid finds Patrick's *rath* curiously empty. She had expected the bustle of a bishopric—a place of worship and work—even though she knows that Bishop Patrick spends as much time among the people as does she. Instead, an eerie stillness greets her. Seeking to announce her presence, Brigid encounters a monk she recognizes from her baptismal day.

"Brother, I do not know if you remember me, but I am Brigid from the house of Dubtach. You assisted Bishop Patrick some years ago, during my rite of baptism."

"I recall you well indeed—from that blessed day and from news of your Christian works ever since. The bishop has been waiting for your arrival for some days now."

"My apologies. The vagaries of the road are unpredictable."

"I am pleased to see that our Lord watched over you during your journey. I am called Brother Lergus. Please let me take you to Bishop Patrick."

Brigid nods in gratitude, but she finds the monk's haste curious. The Lord charges those who run His houses to offer food and hospitality first to their visitors. The rush to Patrick is unusual.

Still, she says nothing and matches his brisk pace. They approach a building larger than most of the others, and pass into the dark interior. The reek of sickness assaults her. Not the smell of wounds and birthing to which she has grown accustomed, but the rancid odor of decay. Brigid does not need to be told that Patrick is gravely ill.

She gathers her bearings and kneels before a hay-stuffed bed lodged in a shadowy corner. Although Brigid nods her head in silent prayer, her mind whirs with her prepared words of persuasion. The blankets covering the motionless mound at the bed's center begin to stir.

Brother Lergus rushes to the bedside and assists Patrick in sitting upright. With obvious effort, Patrick rasps, "My child, you have been busy since your baptism."

"Indeed, Bishop Patrick. Our Lord spoke to me on that fateful—"

He interrupts her rehearsed speech. "I have received reports of your numerous conversions in the south. I am well pleased with your inspired works, my child. You have followed well the Lord's exhortation to 'go now, teach all nations, baptizing them in the name of the Father and of the Son and of the Holy Spirit, teaching them to observe all that I have commanded you.' "

Patrick's acceptance of her mission shocks her into uncharacteristic silence. She had anticipated, at the least, a scolding for her unsanctioned efforts, or, at the worst, banishment from the church and her vocation. His approval moves her.

The bishop fills the quietude. "Brigid, the state of my health is undoubtedly apparent. Our Lord demands I leave this mortal body behind and join my soul to His in heaven, though Gael still requires much work. His timing is not ours, however."

"I am so sorry, my bishop. You will be heartily missed, and I do not know how Gael will become fully Christian without your guidance."

A sound like a chuckle escapes from Patrick's dry throat. "Our Lord does not need me to work His wonders. Still, I would like to pass my worldly mantle to one who has proven dedication to His goals."

"Of course, Bishop Patrick," Brigid says, though she cannot imagine a worthy—or successful—candidate among his small, soft-spoken band of monks and priests. His Roman religious do not know how to speak to the Gaels, literally or figuratively.

"I choose you, Brigid."

"Me?" In the periphery of her vision, she sees that Brother Lergus is as astonished as she.

"Yes, I choose you to fulfill my calling to minister to and convert the Gaels. Based on your triumph in bringing countless souls to our Lord in a few short years, I believe your achievements in converting Gaels will have no parallel. You, a Gael, will succeed where Roman priests and monks would perhaps fail."

"I am deeply honored, Bishop Patrick. Thank you."

"This selection is the Lord's doing, Brigid. Reserve your prayers of gratitude for Him." Patrick reaches a skeletal hand from beneath the heavy covers. "Come a bit closer to a dying man, my child. I wish to bless your mission."

Brigid draws as close to Patrick's bed as decorum permits. She resists the urge to gag as she nears his sickly smell. She kneels, and he places his wasted hand upon her head.

"In the name of the Father, the Son, and the Holy Spirit, I consecrate you Brigid, daughter of Dubtach and Broicsech, as bishop—"

"Please stop, Bishop Patrick," Brother Lergus cries out. "Your illness robs you of your senses. You are uttering the rite of consecration of a bishop, not the blessing for a nun."

With great unsteadiness, Patrick rises to his feet. For the first time since Brigid's arrival, the anger and fire for which he is known blaze to the surface.

"Brother Lergus, do not dare to challenge my words and actions. For in so doing, you contest the very Words and actions of our Lord. He means to make Brigid a bishop through my hands."

GAEL

A.D. 462

BRIGID: A LIFE

She stands on the plains of Cill Dara. One hand on her hip and one hand to her brow, to shield her eyes from the unseasonable brightness, Brigid surveys the vast, uninhabited expanse of lush grass and foliage. Her gaze settles on a craggy, ancient oak tree near a bluff.

Its branches stretch like arms reaching for the sky. The oak seems to yearn, and reminds Brigid of the oak presiding over the cherished knoll near her family *cashel*. She smiles. Of all the lands she has appraised in recent days, this feels most like home. And the oak tree, forever sacred to the Gaels and the Druids, bodes well for the people's adoption of the spot as hallowed.

She calls for Cathan, her first follower and her most loyal. "Rejoice, Cathan. Our Lord has directed us to the lands that the late Bishop Patrick ordered us to settle."

"Truly, Brigid?" Cathan asks. Brigid insists that all her adherents address her informally and certainly not with her formal title of "Bishop." She wants none of the hierarchy and differentiation of treatment rife in Roman institutions—including the Church—for her establishment.

"Truly." The women beam at each other in relief. They have spent many long months searching for the most suitable land on which to build the abbey commanded by Patrick. Converts of many southern and central provinces have offered Brigid pieces of their territories, but none called to her until now.

"Race you to the others?" Brigid challenges Cathan, with a mischievous grin. She feels light and youthful again for the first time in many years. She longs to sprint across the fields—her fields.

"It will be my great pleasure to beat the new abbess of Cill Dara on her own land," Cathan retorts, her playful mood matching Brigid's. The women hitch up the hems of their long robes, tucking them into their belts, and dash across the plains.

Brigid delights in the design and construction of her abbey. During the years tramping across the Gaelic countryside, seeking souls to save, she had often dreamed of building a sanctuary where strangers would receive a Christian welcome, monks and priests and nuns could pray in solicitude, and scholars and artisans might celebrate the Words and beauty of His Kingdom. Her abbey will be that haven.

Brigid garners stores of timber and stone from wealthy new Christians eager to pay their way to their new God's heaven. She sets about assembling teams of laborers and craftsmen to assist her and her followers, who plan on working alongside them at every stage. She accumulates provisions to feed her crews through the easy months of spring and summer as well as the barren months of fall and winter. All this she accomplishes with surprising ease, as if the Lord Himself provides.

Though she believes in the protective power of Jesus Christ, she is practical and understands the warlike nature of her countrymen and their thirst for plunder, and so she oversees the creation of a stone *cashel* around her planned abbey. Once her teams complete the fortifications to her satisfaction, she guides them through the building of her ideal structures. Around the *cashel*'s inner perimeter she places huts for the religious folk, so they may pray and rest in solitude. She arranges the communal buildings—the refectory, the storehouse, the abbess's quarters, the guesthouses—closer to the busy center. And at the abbey's heart, she positions her church—a soaring, light-infused edifice with room enough for religious and commoner—and her most treasured space, her scriptorium, where His Words will be studied, copied, and celebrated.

Yet she forgets not her mother's cautionary words to honor the people's gods as she worships the Lord. She selects one of the people's traditional means of venerating the goddess Brigid: the eternal fire. Constructing a stone firehouse near her church and scriptorium, but not close enough to endanger them, she vows that a fire will blaze in Brigid's honor in perpetuity.

Brigid allows herself and her women one week of rest and prayer upon the abbey's completion. She spends this week alone in the scriptorium. Brigid crafted this space with the utmost care, drawing upon memories of pictures of the great ancient libraries she had studied from her mother's tomes. Working closely with her master builder, she designed numerous, unusually sloped apertures to allow for maximum daylight while still safeguarding the interior from the elements. She ordered the construction of ingenious wooden cabinets and hanging leather shelves, in which she will store and protect the many sacred texts she hopes to collect. And, of course, she provided ample working tables, chairs, and bookstands for the scholars and scribes, along with braziers to warm their hands during the cold winter months. Sitting alone in the scriptorium's waiting splendor, Brigid believes that, of all the work she has undertaken for His glory, this handiwork may be her finest. She thanks the Lord and prays that the scholars and scribes come.

At the close of Sunday's services, her time of reflection ends, and her real labors commence in earnest. Brigid begins by forging alliances with the neighboring chieftains. The strength of her father's name and reputation carries her only so far—into their *raths* unharmed—and she knows she must convince the warriors of her merits and her peaceful motives. She enters their *raths* in her ethereal guise, much as she had throughout Gael's countryside. Once within the guarded walls, she does not preach but speaks to the leaders of their shared heritage and training, of her disdain for Roman and barbarian rule, of her plan to leave the Gaelic gods alone if the people reject her Jesus Christ, and, above all, of their like desires to fashion a Gael that no outsider would dare try to conquer. Her plain speech expels from their minds any suspicions that she is Gael without but Roman within.

Once Brigid secures the abbey's safety—insofar as safety is possible in Gael's shifting warrior culture—she turns her attentions to practical matters. She ensures adequate farmlands to supply the abbey's daily needs. She trains small groups of nuns to take over her work of combing the countryside for poor to feed, bodies to heal, and souls to save, though always cautioning them to rein in any behavior that might anger the chieftains. She starts holding High Masses every day in her newly wrought church, and encourages all to attend, often with generous feasts at holiday time. And on every wall, every gate, indeed, every surface, she guides her artisans to sculpt swirling shapes, exotic creatures, intricate foliage, and the Words of the Lord; she wants her abbey to shimmer and dazzle in its dedication to Him.

By day, Brigid is the essence of the fire and the cross, a living embodiment of the Gaelic goddess and the Christian God. She knows that she cannot waver in her conviction of these dual roles. Yet in the darkest hour of the night, she is only human, the Brigid of her birth. Alone, she kneels before her private altar, abject and afraid, praying that her work satisfies Him and her promise to her parents.

DUBLIN, IRELAND

PRESENT DAY

Alex waited for her expert to arrive at the Shelbourne hotel. Like most appraisers, she had a go-to list of consultants when a piece strayed outside her area of expertise. Keepers from the National Museum of Ireland and professors from Trinity College Dublin appeared on that list, but she could never confer with them on her "borrowed" manuscript. Her situation required that she seek out an expert with his own shop who wouldn't ask too many questions.

Tourists and locals alike packed the deservedly famous Lord Mayor's Lounge at midday. The sumptuous, confectioner's-sugar setting—with its crystal chandeliers and rococo wall moldings mounted on damask—lured them as much as the lavish afternoon tea. Alex listened to the relaxed chatter of older ladies mixed with the clipped discourse of businesspeople, a mélange that spoke of attempts to maintain the economic luster of the fading Celtic Tiger more than anything, as she stared out the window at the daffodil-carpeted Saint Stephen's Green for signs of her appointment.

Her expert was notoriously late, so Alex had armed herself with reading materials to pass the time productively. She'd stopped at the nearby Trinity College Library Shop just before her meeting and picked up the key texts on seventh- and eighth-century illustrated manuscripts. Part of her had been tempted to peek at the famous Book of Kells or its lesser-known counterparts, the Book of Armagh and the Book of Durrow, for a quick comparison with her manuscript. But she couldn't risk running into one of the researchers or conservators she knew who worked in the Old Library, where the books were housed. She'd used them for expert advice in the past, and they'd want to know all about her latest assignment.

She'd given up her watch and delved into the first scholarly text in the pile when she heard her name: "Alexandra Patterson, you've become a tourist at long last."

Alex stared up into the eyes of Declan Lamb, who was staring down at her tower of Trinity College books. "Good to see you too, Dec."

"Is this seat taken?"

"By you. Although it's been empty for"—she looked down at her watch in mock irritation, though, in truth, she'd expected a longer wait—"half an hour."

"Ah, Alex, you'll never become accustomed to Irish time, will you?" he said with a winning smile that bore no hint of apology. Not that Alex expected one from the devil-may-care Declan, who proudly wore this distinctive Irish characteristic like a flag.

"I do try," she said with an equally wide smile.

Declan settled into the deep upholstered chair next to hers. He sized her up without any pretense or subtlety. She'd purposely chosen an outfit that was professional rather than appealing, but it didn't deter him. "You're looking well, as always, Alex."

She returned the stare. "As are you, Dec." Although she mirrored the slightly taunting tone that Declan nearly always used, she meant it. His black hair and blue eyes might have overpowered his natural fairness, but for the fact that his cheeks were eternally ruddy from countless afternoons on the rugby pitch. He wore a battered brown tweed blazer, decrepit jeans, and a rumpled blue-checked shirt, yet somehow he managed to do it as though with the help of Ralph Lauren stylists. He frustrated and charmed simultaneously—only his brilliance saved him.

The waitress appeared. "Your food will be ready in another fifteen minutes. May I refresh your Earl Grey?" she asked Alex.

"Please."

The waitress had begun pouring the steaming water into Alex's freshly filled tea strainer when Declan interrupted: "Give us a pint, luv?"

"A pint?" Alex blurted out, then wanted to take it back. Although she'd specifically chosen teatime to avoid Declan's notorious Saturday afternoons in the pub—she needed him present and sharp—she hated to sound like a prim schoolmarm.

"You're right—what am I thinking, Alex? We'll have the champagne."

Alex groaned in protest, but in truth, she enjoyed the champagne. Three years had passed since they'd worked together on a cache of inscribed liturgical vessels found in the ruins of a Derry church basement, and the drinks softened the edge between them. She was more at ease asking about his "decision" to leave a coveted posting as assistant keeper of the treasury at the National Museum of Ireland after his hasty departure from a professorship at Trinity College. And he felt more comfortable answering with a bullish proclamation that he wanted to start his own business—though she suspected that the real explanation lurked in too much time on the rugby pitch and in the pubs mixed with his own dislike of playing academic games. The latter Alex could relate to.

Alex skirted the reason for their meeting as long as she could. She needed his renowned translating skills desperately, but she didn't trust him entirely. He always played the rogue, and she wasn't sure if it was an act or the truth. Still, she had no one else.

"Dec, I need you to be serious for a minute."

"Don't tease me, Alex. You know I'd love to get serious with you." He was only half-kidding; she knew he'd happily pass through any door she opened. He'd made that clear enough in the past.

"I mean it." She allowed her voice to become raw and solemn.

"Okay." The haze evaporated from his eyes, and she saw the serious scholar behind them emerge.

"I need you to translate an insular majuscule Old Latin manuscript for me."

"That's my stock-in-trade. If that's all you need, there's no cause for concern."

"You can tell no one about the manuscript, Declan. No one."

"All right then. It'll be our little secret." The somber moment over, he took a swig of champagne and allowed his natural joviality to escape. He teased, "What'd you do, Alex? Steal it?"

She'd gone this far—what was a little farther? "Something like that."

DUBLIN, IRELAND

PRESENT DAY

They left the Shelbourne and walked through Saint Stephen's Green on one of its manicured serpentine pathways. Declan told her that they were headed to his office, but it seemed a meandering route until he took a quick left out of the park. The exit deposited them in front of a row of Georgian town houses, and Declan strode directly to an attractive four-story brick building covered with ivy on the verge of turning green after a long brown winter.

He pulled his keys from the pocket of his tweed jacket and unlocked the front door. Alex was astonished that Declan could afford an office of this caliber. Saint Stephen's Green sat in the heart of Dublin, and its real estate had become exorbitant in recent years; even basic flats and office suites had cost in the millions of euros. Perhaps there was a grain of truth in the long-circulated rumors that he came from money, or maybe he dabbled in the black market side of their business. As long as he did his work and kept his mouth shut, she didn't much care.

She followed his lead up two steep flights of stairs that seemed increasingly residential in feel. Then he unlocked a nondescript oak door and ushered her into a handsomely decorated foyer. After she refused his offers to take her coat and bag or get her a cup of tea, he guided her

into a large rectangular room with park views that obviously had once
been the parlor but now served as a combination office, sterile labora-
tory, and reference library. She barely recognized this professional Declan.

He sat down at a long white worktable, completely devoid of any
objects other than the necessary tools of his trade, and put on sterile
gloves, handing her a pair as well. Gesturing for her to sit in one of the
two ergonomic chairs pulled up to the table, he stretched out his hand.
"Shall we have a look?"

Her heart quickened as she reached into her black bag for the manuscript. Intentionally, she had held back mentioning the other two
books she'd found in the convent archives. She didn't want to reveal
too much too soon, particularly if Declan's initial assessment of the
manuscript did not match her expectations.

The manuscript slipped out easily due to the protective sheeting
she'd wrapped around it that morning. She hesitated before handing
over her precious discovery, but Declan's surprising seriousness
calmed her nerves. "Here it is."

Laying the manuscript on the table, he slowly turned through the
folio pages. Alex could feel her palms sweating and her stomach
churning as she awaited his initial reaction. But the minutes stretched
on, and soon she lost herself in the beauty of the manuscript. So much
so that she jumped when he spoke.

"Where on earth did you get this?"

"I'd rather not say just yet. Is that important?"

"Not for my translation. But it will become important. Very, very
important."

"What do you mean?"

"Alex, you've just handed me the most artistically proficient, ancient illuminated manuscript I've ever seen outside the Book of
Kells—maybe even including the Book of Kells. I wouldn't swear to an
origin date until I've translated it and done some tests on the vellum
and ink, but I'm a gambling man. I'd place good odds on a date near
the ninth-century creation of the Book of Kells."

"You're putting me on, Declan."

"Do I look like I'm taking the piss, Alex?"

She stared at him. He looked as somber—and sober—as she'd ever seen him. "No."

"Alex, you've just rocked the world of illuminated manuscripts." He grinned. "My world too."

A few drinks later, Alex set the ground rules. She must be present when he worked on the manuscript: She would take it with her whenever she left his apartment. Declan must share with her each translated page immediately upon completion. If he began to draw firm conclusions about the date or nature of the manuscript, he must tell her straightaway. And, most importantly, no one else must be consulted.

Alex didn't need to tell him why they needed secrecy. But to his credit, Declan didn't probe, and he readily agreed to all her conditions.

The next day, she sat in one of the upholstered chairs near the bay windows while Declan worked. After she read through the books she'd bought at Trinity College the day before, she decided it might prove helpful to digest Declan's collection of scholarly texts on the great seventh- to ninth-century illuminated manuscripts containing the four Gospels. Supplementing her rudimentary grad school understanding, she learned that the Irish had led the way in creating the golden age of illuminated texts, utilizing the same intricate Hiberno-Saxon style and iconography she'd come across in Sister Mary's liturgical vessels. Although the early-ninth-century Book of Kells was the most famous and, arguably, the quintessential manuscript, earlier books—the Cathach, the Book of Dimma, the Lindisfarne Gospels, and the Book of Durrow among them—contained exquisite imagery as well. Some scholars argued that the Irish proliferation of those manuscripts—and their copies—helped re-Christianize the European continent in the Dark Ages after the fall of Rome.

Intermittently, Declan interrupted her reading with a handwritten sheet. The page invariably contained the words of a New Testament Gospel decoded from insular majuscule Old Latin into modern English. Alex had begun to wonder how the translation would help them date the manuscript when Declan suddenly asked, "Alex, did you find this book in Kildare?"

She panicked inwardly but tried to stay cool on the surface. "Why do you ask?" she said casually, without looking up.

Pushing back from his worktable, Declan stood and walked to his bookshelves. He reached to the highest shelf, which, Alex had noted, contained the oldest-looking reference books, and pulled out a slim volume. The book fell open to a dog-eared page, and he said, "I'm going to read you an excerpt from *The Topography of Ireland,* a late-twelfth-century historical treatise and travel narrative. The author was Giraldus Cambrensis, a Welsh clergyman and historian accompanying Prince John, the heir to English King Henry II, on his subjugating tour of Ireland in the 1180s.

"In describing the Abbey of Kildare, Giraldus says:

'Among all the miracles in Kildare, none appears to me more wonderful than that marvelous book which they say was written in the time of the Virgin Saint Brigid at the dictation of an angel. It contains the Four Gospels according to Saint Jerome, and almost every page is illustrated by drawing illuminated with a variety of brilliant colors. In one page you see the countenance of the Divine Majesty supernaturally pictured; in another, the mystic forms of the evangelists, with either six, four, or two wings; here are depicted the eagle, there the calf; here the face of a man, there of a lion; with other figures in almost endless variety. If you observe them superficially, and in the usual careless manner, you would imagine them to be daubs, rather than careful compositions; expecting to find nothing exquisite, where in truth, there is nothing that is not exquisite. But if you apply yourself to a more close examination, and are able to penetrate the secrets of the art displayed in these pictures, you will find them so delicate and exquisite, so finely drawn, and the work of interlacing so elaborate, while the colors with which they are illuminated are so blended, and still so fresh, that you will be ready to assert that all this is the work of angelic, and not human skill.'

"This description," Declan noted, "has been applied repeatedly to the Book of Kells."

"I thought it sounded familiar."

"You can see why people think Giraldus saw the Book of Kells. The excerpt certainly describes an illuminated manuscript with a decorative scheme very similar to that of the Book of Kells. But there is a major problem with that leap of logic."

"What?"

"Giraldus wrote these words in 1185, while visiting Kildare. An entry in the Annals of Ulster for A.D. 1006 shows that the Book of Kells arrived in Kells as early as the beginning of the eleventh century. If for some reason you doubted that evidence, there's proof that Kells had possession of the book in the early twelfth century, when land charters pertaining to the Abbey of Kells were copied into some of the book's blank pages. Either way, by 1185, when Giraldus visited Kildare, the Book of Kells was elsewhere, if it had ever been in Kildare at all. Giraldus saw a different manuscript."

Before Alex could interject, Declan continued. "Listen to another of Giraldus's entries for Kildare, it purports to describe the way in which this book was created:

"Early in the night before the morning on which the scribe was to begin the book, an angel stood before him in a dream, and showing him a picture drawn on a tablet which he had in his hand, said to him, 'Do you think that you can draw this picture on the first page of the volume which you propose to copy?' The scribe, who doubted his skill in such exquisite art, in which he was uninstructed and had no practice, replied that he could not. Upon this the angel said 'On the morrow, intreat your Lady to offer prayers for you to the Lord, that He would vouchsafe to open your bodily eyes, and give you spiritual vision, which may enable you to see more clearly, and understand with more intelligence, and employ your hands in drawing with accuracy.' The scribe having done as he commanded, the night following the angel came to him again, and presented to him the same picture, with a number of others. All these, aided by divine grace, the scribe made himself the master of, and faithfully committing them to his memory, exactly copied in his book in their proper places. In this manner, the book was composed, an angel furnishing the designs, Saint Brigid praying, and the scribe copying.' "

"What book was Giraldus describing?" Alex asked.

"Some believe that Giraldus is describing the lost Book of Kildare, which—who knows—you may have just found."

GAEL

A.D. 470

Brother,

Long days have passed since I last wrote you. I find myself busy, swept as I am into the monk's life here in Cill Dara. My hands so ache at day's end from the scribe's duties I find it hard to rouse them to write—especially words that I know will lie buried in the secret hole I dug out beneath a loose stone on the floor of my hut, words that may never reach you.

You have not left my thoughts, however. I imagine you assessing the olive groves' health after the harsh winter. I envision your young boys tearing through our family fields as we once did in the early spring, freed from the confines of the dark, frigid months. And I pray to God that someone, somehow has provided you with some measure of comfort as to the whereabouts of your younger brother. Who would defy Gallienus's strict command of silence about my mission in order to perform such kindness, I cannot imagine.

Though I can picture your days in vivid detail, I doubt you can visualize mine. Shall I walk you about this unfamiliar world I now inhabit? I can almost see you nod as we set off. Although this time we will not be embarking on one of your many mad larks, as we did so often in childhood, with you leading and me protesting in tow. Instead, we will embark on my own adventure.

Let us begin with my first day in the scriptorium. As promised, Ciaran arrived at my hut just after dawn that first morning at Cill Dara. I had finished my early prayers and was waiting for him. We broke our fast together in the refectory. The room buzzed with tantalizing phrases in not only Gaelic and Latin but Greek and countless local dialects. I noted this to Ciaran, whereupon he introduced me to scholarly monks and priests and nuns outcast from so many countries that it made my head spin. I tell you, brother, though this place lies on the very edge of, if not beyond, civilization, a number of its inhabitants are the very essence of it.

We took our leave and walked the brief distance to the scriptorium. Ciaran held open the door, and I entered a vast, bright room much larger than the church itself. I could almost hear you tease that perhaps the size of the buildings was telling—that the residents of Cill Dara stressed words over God. But no matter.

Most people had not yet begun to arrive after the morning meal, so Ciaran and I had the building nearly to ourselves. An astonishing amount of daylight flooded the work space, as the walls were cut with cunning openings designed to admit light yet shield one from the weather. Long desks, stands, and chairs stood in strategic locations around the room to best capture any hint of brightness. Each table offered ample writing materials—wax tablets, parchments, vellum, ink, brushes, rulers, and quills—so sophisticated I might have procured them from my study in Rome. Yet this cache of scribes' instruments was not the room's biggest surprise.

I reserve that honor for the manuscripts. They populated the scriptorium by the hundreds, perhaps even thousands. They lay on tabletops and were stacked on the floor. They were splayed on stands and suspended from the ceiling in leather satchels. They reclined with their spines outward in cupboards with hinged doors. In all my days, I have never witnessed so many manuscripts in one location, not even in the papal library.

As we walked about the room, I stole a glance at a page from an opened manuscript on one of the stands. I could not discern the script, but its exquisite style struck me. Elaborate scrollwork, abstract animal and human figures, and vivid patterns, all in brilliant pigments, embellished the letters and borders. The work was masterful.

In our imagined dialogue, you interrupt me with an impatient question: But what of the decor? Does the scriptorium not have gilded moldings, fine mosaics, and marble columns, as in the papal buildings? Surely it has silken tapestries and a vast fireplace stoked by servants to keep out the bitter cold?

No, I answer with a laugh. The Cill Dara scriptorium bears none of the luxuries seen in the Roman papal offices, save the manuscripts. For a scribe like myself, however, it contains all that I require and more: light, instruments, and inspiration. I know this would not satisfy you, my worldly brother.

The Abbey of Cill Dara is a working institution, however, and my day did not consist of a languorous walk about the scriptorium. Once more people arrived in the scriptorium, Ciaran began scanning the room. He took me by the arm, explaining that he needed to introduce me to the monk who would be my tutor.

Ciaran hurried over to an enormous man with a barrel chest and a wizened face; this was Aidan, my teacher. Ciaran gestured for me to sit at the chair waiting by Aidan's side, and left.

I settled into the chair as instructed. I offered my greetings to Aidan in Gaelic, and he answered in tenable but brusque Latin. Then, without the pretense of polite exchange, we got to work.

Aidan invited me to watch him add emerald-colored details to the wings of an angel. I observed as this great hulk of a man, gray-haired and with meaty fingers, painted nearly invisible brushstrokes, rendering the celestial figure even more ethereal. His skill mesmerized me for hours. I had never seen its like.

Then I reminded myself that Gallienus had sent me to Cill Dara to learn about heresy, not to hone my techniques as a scribe. I steeled my nerves, cleared my throat, and asked Aidan, "Where did you learn your craft?"

For a long while, he did not answer. He kept at his work. With his eyes fixed to the page, he finally said, "You are Roman?"

"Yes."

"And you learned your trade at a formal school, did you not?" he asked as he added the lightest touch of the green to the angel's harp.

"Yes."

"Well, I was taught in a field—under a large oak tree."

"You learned your skills as an illuminator in a field under an oak tree?" I should not have so sputtered, but, brother, you can imagine my confusion. For how could one learn such mastery in such conditions?

"In that field, under that tree, over a twenty-year period, I learned almost everything I know. Almost."

I was utterly perplexed.

He continued regardless: "That is where I became a Druid."

The confession of his heretical background shocked me out of my silence. "You are a Druid?"

He stopped working and stared at me. "I was a Druid priest before I became a Christian monk."

Although this conversation yielded a damning piece of information, I learned a critical lesson that day, brother, one that deepens the longer I am in Gael. I cannot ask direct questions of these people and expect direct answers, for they answer in riddles. By way of example, Aidan said he learned his illuminator's trade during his Druidic training, yet I now know that Druids consider it improper to commit anything to parchment. To find what Gallienus demands, I must seek knowledge by observation and investigation, not inquiry.

But, what of Brigid? I imagine you asking, Why does this letter contain no mention of her? After all, at my last writing, I worried about her reaction to my presence here in Cill Dara, and she is my primary objective.

Ah, Brigid. Oh yes, I call her Brigid, at least to the other monks, who refer to the abbess as such without a title or deferential address. I see her daily: in the refectory, where she dines alongside the other monks, priests, and nuns; on the abbey's grounds, where she tends to the Cill Dara residents' troubles as if she were a community priest; and, of course, in the church, presiding over Mass. And my fellow scribes discuss her often (some would say overmuch), always with respect, care, even fear, but not transcendent reverence.

Yet I have had no direct contact with Brigid. No formal introductions, no shared mealtime tables, no hallway passings that would require us to acknowledge our original encounter on the plains of Cill Dara. Or her bold stare during that initial Mass.

So I play at the deferential monk, a refugee from the barbarians, like so many here, grateful for the sanctuary. And she remains only my abbess. For now.

Brother,

Pray, fast, study, work. Pray, fast, study, work. Brother, you would bristle at the daily routine of Cill Dara, at its relentless monotony, religious practice, and retirement from the secular world. But for me, after years of Roman papal bureaucracy that served as a distraction from our Lord's labors, it satisfies.

Particularly since the work is God-sent.

The prayer and fasting, I need not describe, especially to you, who would shudder at the very description, despite your ostensible adherence to the Christianity of our parents. Know only that my fellow religious are a solid lot, even the Gaels: approachable, ardent in their faith, and some of them learned. But I cannot risk closeness with any, since I have not your talent—the Roman talent, you would call it—at deception. I believe I exhausted my small reserve of trickery during my initial interrogation with Ciaran. Thus, I stay quiet and respectful—not a difficult role for me, as you might guess.

Yet of the studying and the work, I must share with you. I explained to you the abundance of manuscripts at the scriptorium. This account might not have intrigued, as you have never been a reader at heart. But, brother, even you would be amazed at the beauty and types of the manuscripts I study every morn. Psalms, letters from Jesus's apostles and church fathers, lives of our Christian martyrs, Virgil, Horace, and lavishly decorated Gospels are my daily fare.

Aidan prescribes these readings like a medicinal, as the necessary poultice for our work. We study them not only for their textual encouragement but also to understand their artistic mastery. These manuscripts illuminate the Word in ways I have never encountered. The circles, the spirals, the trumpets, and the figures all interlace in a never-ending golden and multicolored celebration of our Lord's own infinity and the majesty of His Word. The artistry takes the breath away.

I am ordered to scrutinize these texts with more diligence than the other scribes, as Aidan says I must gain familiarity with their scripts, so different from the Roman, with its even, gracefully curved capital letters. This unusual Gaelic lettering style flows from one character to the next like a great tidal wave, with each fluid letter growing successively smaller from the first in the line.

The proper execution of both this script and the inspired decoration of the text requires more than just technical skills, or so Aidan tells me. The scribe must believe that the illumination helps direct the priest through the Gospels' many pages to the desired text, honors the mystery of the Word of God, and, with its sublime paintings, inspires conversion even of the illiterate masses.

As Aidan cautioned me at the end of his instruction, "Remember, Decius, the manuscript will not win over any souls unless the scribe works with a pious heart. To imbue the letters with spirit, one must approach the writing itself as a prayer. Only then will the Lord's magic work its way into the Word."

Magic? Now, this sounds like dangerous heresy to me too, brother. Maybe Druidic, maybe Pelagian, who knows. But if you sit in the scriptorium on a bright afternoon in the company of monk-scribes all copying the Lord's Word in this particular manner, you can see the truth in Aidan's statements.

Yet I say this only to you, and only in this letter.

To Gallienus, in my unsent messages, I say that I believe that the Abbey of Cill Dara contains many manuscripts of dubious church standing. I tell him that Aidan gives me access only to the standard texts, but that I've heeded the whispers of two other monks, Colum and Eadfrith. I listened to them describe Gospels of which I have never heard. I tell Gallienus that I need to see these manuscripts with my own eyes to judge their contents heretical or not. And to do so, I must enter the scriptorium under cover of night, when the other religious sleep soundly in their huts under God's own sky.

Of that endeavor, I will now tell you.

On my first foray, I waited until the moon waned—not until its complete disappearance, mind you. Indeed, I have come to know this abbey and its surrounding countryside well from my Sunday walks, but I needed the moon's guiding light to navigate across the grounds.

I steered through the huts and larger buildings easily enough. I saw no stirrings to deter me from my course, even though I had determined to stay steady regardless. Hesitancy only breeds suspicion.

The door to the scriptorium opened without force, as I expected. The abbey has no real security other than the guards posted at the *cashel*'s gates; it relies on Brigid's relationships with the local chieftains for protection and peace. Once inside, I knew the trick would be to locate and examine the more remote manuscripts—with little candlelight. Nothing would cause more alarm to a wakening monk-scribe than the sight of fire moving among the abbey's treasured possessions.

By touch, I worked my way to the staircase—in truth, just a ladder to the upper floor that can be lowered by a pulley. Without the need for additional light other than the moonlight, I lowered it with minimal noise and climbed up. This higher floor serves more as a wooden walkway than a proper second story, as its primary purpose is to access the manuscripts suspended in leather satchels for preservation and storage. Or so Aidan told me.

In one of these bags lay the concealed manuscript of which the monks had whispered. Of this I was certain, because I'd watched as Colum and Eadfrith returned the manuscript they were copying not to the cupboards but to the satchels. And I'd marked the precise one in my memory.

I squatted on the planks and reached across for the hanging bag. In the darkness, I misjudged the distance, and I teetered at the edge. But for the strap I grabbed, I would have crashed to the floor below. Instead, I fell back to safety, and the bag fell back with me.

I seized my candle and hastened to light it, for I knew not how long I had. My hands shaking, I untied the satchel and grasped the manuscript from it. Bringing the light as near as I dared, I thumbed through the brittle document.

Two curiosities struck me. Firstly, the pages were ancient, older than any I had seen before; and secondly, I could comprehend the text with ease. It was not written in Gaelic script, but in a more accessible Latin lettering.

Yet none of this compared with my reaction when I realized the precise nature of this manuscript. It purported to be the infamous Gospel of Truth.

Could this be one of the early Christian texts condemned by Bishop Irenaeus in the second century of our Lord, writings he banned as "blasphemy . . . an abyss of madness"? Brother, I know that three-hundred-year-old church history is hardly your expertise; thus I will tell you that Irenaeus is one of our great church fathers. He became so concerned about the dividedness of the early Christian movement, with its many so-called sacred texts, that he determined to unify the church by means of one biblical canon comprised of four Gospels only. In so doing, he wrote the Refutation and Overthrow of the Knowledge Falsely So-Called, which systematically dismantled the legitimacy of these rogue texts and revealed them to be "evil exegeses" beyond the church's elementary precepts. He then banned all Gospels other than the Gospels of Matthew, Mark, Luke, and John for true Christians, writing, "It is not possible that the Gospels can be either more or fewer than they are. For, since there are four zones of the world in which we live, and four principal winds, while the church is scattered throughout all the world, and the pillar and the ground of the church is the Gospel and the spirit of life, it is fitting that she should have four pillars, breathing out immortality on every side, and vivifying men afresh."

In 367, Irenaeus's proclamation was affirmed by Bishop Athanasius when he approved of the twenty-seven books of the New Testament— including the four Gospels—and rejected all the rest as "apocryphal books . . . filled with myths, empty and polluted." While I have heard rumors that manuscripts excluded by Irenaeus and Athanasius surface from time to time, I have never met any person, religious or otherwise, who has actually seen one.

I looked back down at the ancient text in my lap. It bore the same title as a particular text Irenaeus had specifically banished from the canon. Could this be that very work, the Gospel of Truth, not seen for centuries? Did one of the outcast religious here smuggle it to Cill Dara on his or her back, making the Cill Dara refugees not from the barbarians but the true church?

Brother, I scanned the Gospel of Truth as quickly as the dim light would allow. Beginning with the line "The gospel of truth is joy . . . ," on first glance, the text appears to be a sermon on the saving knowledge of God. According to it, the Word is our Savior, Jesus Christ. This is not objectionable in itself, yet it also hints that what we see in Jesus Christ depends on what we need to see and what we are capable of seeing. It does not describe His divine essence as a constant; thus, I can see the reason for Irenaeus's condemnation.

I began grabbing the other satchels and looking at their contents. I discovered a trove of other writings purporting to be gospels: the Secret Book of John, the Gospel of Thomas, and the Gospel of Philip, to name but a few. Some titles I recollect from Iranaeus's rantings, and some I have never heard mentioned. Surely, their age cannot be questioned; the very feel of the vellum tells me that they are indeed archaic.

I know I will return to read them every night the moon permits. I could lie to you and say I am drawn to them *only* so I can report back to Gallienus on the presence of heretical documents here at the abbey. So I can inform him that the abbey not only collects these profane works but actively copies them, presumably for dissemination. But I cannot lie to you or God, brother. I am fascinated by them for their own sake, for what oddities or truths they might contain. Let us hope and pray to our Lord that their attraction does not overtake my godly mission. More and more, I wonder if this is the "temptation" to which Lucius alluded.

Brother,

My hand trembles—nay, shivers—as I write these words. I pray that they will stop shaking, as I pray that God will give me a second chance. Yet my hands refuse my entreaties, and perhaps He does as well.

The Lord knows I have given Him cause enough to deny my request. I have not offered Him any reason to think me steadfast in my mission to rout out sacrilege in this hinterland. To the contrary, I have spent night after night in the darkness of the scriptorium, gobbling up the words of secret texts like a child with honey.

Oh, my brother, you should see what I found hanging from the ceiling of the scriptorium in this remote island abbey. I discovered sumptuous renderings of our Latin literature—Virgil, Plato, Horace—in which even you would delight. I unwrapped gilded copies of letters from church founders that would move even a stone to tears. Yet what continues to draw me are those banned Gospels.

Should I even dub them Gospels, though they call themselves such? None is in our canon. None of these have I ever seen before. Are they the writings of "madmen," as Irenaeus said, or are they truths? I know I should stop my speculations, for I came to excise this heresy.

Yet the Secret Book of John only feeds these conjectures. Purporting to offer a description of the events after Jesus ascended into heaven, the apostle John states that "the twelve disciples were all sitting together and recalling what the Savior had said to each one of them, either secretly or openly, and putting it into books, and I was writing what is in my book." If these words are indeed John's, can there be truth in these banned Gospels? Might they contain words from Jesus Christ's own mouth—recorded by His disciples—that we are prohibited from reading? As soon as these thoughts come into my mind, I try to cast them out, for I know them to be the fuel of Satan's heretical fire. Yet I find that I cannot purge them entirely; they have become like an opiate to me.

All the more so because the substance of these manuscripts so entices. This very eve, I found myself with moonlight enough to reach the scriptorium safely. I was eager to return to my reading of the Gospel of Thomas, with its inviting first line: "Whoever discovers the interpretation of these sayings will not taste death." Who could resist this invitation to immortality? Particularly when Thomas says that the kingdom of God is already here, and not a cataclysmic event or otherworldly place foretold for the future: "the kingdom of the Father is spread out upon the earth, and people do not see it." He dares to go further, proclaiming that we may find this kingdom by "knowing ourselves," by looking within to the "image of God" within us all.

Brother, with all this talk of images, you can see how these Gospels, true or not, heresy or not, transfixed me. I was sitting in a blackened corner of the second floor, the Gospel of Thomas in one hand and a candle in the other, when I heard the noise. It sounded like a rustle, and I strained to discern its origin. No swish, no crackle followed, so I attributed it to the wind in the trees.

Since my dark cocoon had begun to brighten with the onset of daylight, I clambered down the ladder. I slid it back to its designated place and settled at one of the tables, with lit candle still in hand. Pulling out a piece of parchment and a quill, I began to list the sacrilegious works I had uncovered, for these books contain certain heresy far beyond even that of Pelagius's creed or Arianism. I owed this much to Gallienus. Why I did not wait until I returned to my hut to create this report? I do not know—guilt over my interest in the texts, perhaps.

I heard the rustle again. I looked up and scanned the vast room. Seeing nothing out of the ordinary, I returned to my writing.

"Cannot wait until morning to labor for our Lord, Brother Decius?"

I turned; behind me stood a figure draped in white. I dropped to my knees and said, "Abbess, my apologies."

"Please rise. Why offer apologies if your work is for His greater glory?"

Recall, brother, I told you these Gaels speak in puzzles and multiple layers of meaning and innuendo. How could I answer her without stepping into one trap or another? My work was indeed for His greater glory, as defined by Gallienus and the Roman Church, though certainly not by Brigid if she knew my true motives. I said the only thing I could: "Abbess, I request forgiveness if my work disturbed your rest."

She walked around the scriptorium in a graceful perambulation— or the slow stalking of a predator; I could not be certain. "Oh, Brother Decius, I do not rest. Therefore, you could not have disturbed it."

I seized upon this statement. "Then, Abbess, you and I are alike in that regard. Restlessness brings me here to the scriptorium."

"Restlessness brings you out of your hut so late at night, does it?" Though her words challenged, her tone was even, bearing no trace of skepticism. I determined to take her words at their most benign.

"Yes, Abbess."

"Please call me Brigid. If Jesus Christ did not stand on ceremony, then how dare I?"

"Thank you, Abb—" I stopped myself. "Brigid."

"How are you finding the Abbey of Kild—" I saw a glint of her white teeth as she smiled to herself in the dark. "Cill Dara?"

This tease was Brigid's first reference to our initial meeting. I wondered if I should mention our encounter and offer further apologies for mistaking her for a common village girl on those plains. And for insulting the learnedness of the Gaels. But my situation was precarious, so I maintained the course of our conversation.

"I find Cill Dara and its people to be a wondrous gift."

" 'A wondrous gift' . . . ." The tenor of her voice shifted just a grade; how I should interpret it, I did not know. Did she mock me? "High praise indeed, Brother Decius. How is Cill Dara 'a wondrous gift'?"

"To be so welcomed when I was so outcast is a miracle unto itself. To have the further opportunity to work here in the scriptorium is a double blessing. Cill Dara is so much more than I expected or deserve."

Brigid grew quiet. In the growing light, I began to make out the details of her face: her strong jaw and cheekbones, her fiercely intelligent green eyes, and the unexpected, almost unwilling softness of her mouth. Brother, you would not find her beautiful in the Roman sense, but her looks arrest. Even more so when her strong character surfaces.

She placed her hands on her narrow hips and assessed me, much as she had on the plains. This time, however, I heard no cynicism or mockery in her voice when she asked, "Truly?"

I answered in an honest confirmation of my assessment of Cill Dara. "Truly."

The scriptorium door slammed at this very moment. We turned away from each other to watch as Niall, the keeper of the scriptorium, gaped at the sight of his abbess and a lowly monk alone in the hallowed building before dawn. With discomfort and haste, Brigid and I took our leave. I wonder what words might have passed between us next had Niall not interrupted.

Brother, I am left here in my hut to conjecture whether Brigid accepts my reason for being in the scriptorium. She gave no hint of disbelief, but I cannot suppose she accepted my reason wholesale; Brigid is too savvy for such blind trust. Even if she were a trusting sort, her presence could very well have been the rustle I heard long before I descended from the second floor—the home of the hidden manuscripts.

I shall wait until morning to hear her real ruling. For if she comprehends the true nature of my visit to the scriptorium, surely she will eject me from Cill Dara. Or worse. In the meantime, I will pray to our Lord for another chance to prove my worth, to Him and to Gallienus.

Brother,

Morning came, and I received no word from Brigid. Days passed, and still silence. Oh, I heard her voice at evening Mass and I saw her face at the refectory, but I received no judgment other than the tawdry murmurs of Colum and Eadfrith. Even here, smallness exists where largesse should triumph.

I resolved to abandon any further attempts to visit the scriptorium at night. I knew that if I persisted, Brigid would undoubtedly find me there again. In case God might deem me worthy of a second chance to do His bidding, I could not take such a risk.

Yet I longed to complete my readings of the hidden manuscripts, to answer their call. I yearned to accept the invitation of the Gospel of Thomas. But I knew that I must acknowledge the compulsion as the doing of Satan, and purge all thought of the Gospels from my mind. Still, I struggle.

I plunged into work. I prepared vellum, scraping and rubbing the young calfskin until it became like soft suede. I rendered insular script for a Gospel of Matthew and gilded a Chi-Rho cross on the Gospel's cover page while Aidan watched with guidance and approval. In all these acts, I tried to surrender to the Word.

Round and round through my mind, I uttered the Words I wrote: "One does not live by bread alone, but by every Word that comes forth from the mouth of God." In time, I could think of nothing else but the Words, Words that I could hear in my head as though God's own lips spoke them to me. And when I looked down at my quill, I watched the Words appear on the vellum as if scribed by God's hand, not my own.

The Words washed over me and through me, and I found myself entering a state of peaceful transcendence as I worked. Brother, I knew I had achieved the "Lord's magic" described by Aidan. And I knew I would never describe the experience—to Gallienus or anyone else—as anything other than sublime, wrought by our Lord.

This morn, I had just entered this rapturous state when the atmosphere of the scriptorium changed without warning. A quiver of excitement or agitation—which I could not tell—passed through the cavernous space. Similar ripples in the serenity of the scriptorium had occurred before and had yielded no cause for concern—once overturned ink had proved to be the source; another time, a misplaced text. Thus I continued with my work and my efforts to recapture calm.

The unease and sense of anticipation clung to me, though I could see or hear nothing extraordinary. I raised my head from the vellum laid out before me and turned toward the entry. There stood the source of the energy coursing through the room: Brigid.

I looked away. After days of praying for a moment with her, to make certain of her trust, I suddenly did not want to see her. In my time at Cill Dara, Brigid had not once visited the scriptorium while we scribes were working, and I suppose that her appearance seemed an ill portent to me.

My eyes refused to stay averted. I watched as she wandered around the various tables and gazed on the manuscripts in progress, offering gentle compliments as she advanced. I observed as she knelt next to an elderly monk, who had hands so gnarled I often wondered how he painted the gossamer figures of angels that the other monks requested of him. She took his hands in hers and they talked quietly for a time, after which he kissed her brow. The gesture shocked and embarrassed me; no such intimacy would ever pass between a Roman abbot and his monk.

She stepped out of view, but an instant later I felt her near me. Aidan and I rose in respect, but she placed a gentle hand on his shoulder. "Please sit. I come to watch Cill Dara's monks labor for the glory of our Lord, not to have His work interrupted."

Brother, I wondered whether her statement was a veiled reference to our conversation. Its similar phraseology seemed too close for coincidence. Yet her face belied no insinuation.

We settled back into our seats and resumed working, or at least assumed the pretense of work. "On what text do you labor, Aidan?" she asked.

"We are completing the cover page for a Gospel of Matthew, Brigid." He called Brigid by her given name, as she requested of all the religious folk—indeed, all peoples. The way Aidan spoke her name, however, instilled it with grandeur, almost as if "Brigid" were a title itself.

"May I draw closer, Aidan?"

"We would be honored, Brigid."

Aidan drew back so that Brigid could study the page on which my brush rested. As she leaned in to examine the sumptuous Chi-Rho cross, unique in its design, I could feel her white gown and loose hair on my cheek. It took all my effort to stop my brush from slipping at the distraction.

"Your work is exquisite," she said to Aidan rather than me, though I was the one painting.

"Many thanks, Brigid," Aidan answered.

"Are you pleased with the efforts of the young monk assigned to you? Decius is his name, I believe?" she asked as if she did not know.

"Yes, Brigid. He shows remarkable facility with our script, and he came to us already with an excellent ability with figures and decorative work."

The two discussed my skills as if I were not present. They reviewed my familiarity with various languages, the fluidity of my brushwork, and, most particularly, my piety. I was surprised to hear commendation from the reticent Aidan.

"Might you spare Decius for several weeks, Aidan?"

Aidan paused before answering. "If you wish, Brigid." Though he gave his accord, I heard wariness in his voice. As did Brigid.

She explained her request, though her position as abbess meant that she had no obligation. "I am in need of a scribe for a minor abbey matter, and I do not want to interrupt the labors of"—she gestured around the room—"our more accomplished scriveners. I believe Decius will suffice."

"I see," Aidan said in understanding. "I functioned well before Decius's arrival, and I will continue while he is in your charge."

"You have my gratitude, Aidan."

For the first time since she'd stood at my side, Brigid looked at me. "Finish the Chi-Rho cross, Decius. When you have completed it to Aidan's satisfaction, come to me."

Brother, you are a sophisticated creature, savvy in the machinations and intrigues of men in ways I am not. What make you of this assignment? Has Brigid accepted my explanation of restlessness and deemed my nocturnal work habits a sign of diligence, well suited for her abbey task? Or does she doubt me, and therefore want to secure better control over my activities? I cannot decipher her meaning, and need your insight.

Whatever the motive, I rejoice at the access to Brigid. Her alleged heresy is the reason Gallienus sent me to Gael. I can see no better way of assessing her adherence to the church and fulfilling Gallienus's objective—and surely God's as well—than to work on this "abbey matter."

I thank God for answering my prayers for another opportunity to serve Him in Gael.

Brother,

For nine days, I fashioned and refashioned the Gospel of Matthew's Chi-Rho cross. This magnificent Gaelic concoction, an ornately decorated composite of the Greek letters *chi* and *rho,* which abbreviate the word "Christ," swooped across the manuscript page in a swirling mass of knots, patterns, animals, and angels. I thought it beautiful, though Aidan sought more from my handiwork.

Nine days of gilding and regilding, nine days of reworking my brushstrokes, nine days in which Aidan grew increasingly more particular and more dissatisfied with my artistry. I surmised that he exacted upon me the irritation he felt with Brigid over her request.

No matter. I spent the nine days in the prayer Aidan insisted upon, though I entreated God not just for His assistance with the Word but also for His guidance with Brigid. Thus, when Aidan gave me leave to go and I stood at the door to the scriptorium, ready to walk the short distance to Brigid's own hut, I felt prepared to do His bidding and strong enough to resist any sibilant whispers of Satan to the contrary.

From the relative brightness of Gael's gray midday, I entered the cavelike darkness of Brigid's seemingly empty building. As my eyes adjusted to a space lit primarily by candles and a few small apertures, I noted that Brigid's structure could accommodate nearly four of my huts, as well it should, given its dual purpose of work and private space. Despite the larger size, her room bore the same minimal decoration as my own, but for a few critical differences.

A scribe's table and chair stood in the center. Brother, you can imagine my surprise. In the Roman world and even here in Cill Dara's scriptorium, women do not scribe; the sacred role of copying the Word is reserved for men. But then, in the Roman world, women do not preside over the Mass, either.

I tried to contain my reaction while I took full measure of the room, reassembling my composure for Brigid's arrival. Only then did I realize that she was present; she knelt before a small altar in a dim corner of the room. She faced away from me at an angle, and since I witnessed no alteration in her bearing, I assumed she was deep in prayer and unaware of my entrance.

My confidence, so bullish on the walk over, ebbed as I stared at her. Though I could see little, only her bright hair and profile, I watched as she mouthed the words of a silent prayer. Brigid seemed so serene in her worship, so tranquil in her supplications, I nearly regretted my motives. Nearly.

Her stillness gave me the opportunity to study the room further.

Aside from the altar and the scribe's table, the decoration was sparse. Only books and crosses sat on the few available surfaces, but for one oddity. A tiny sculpture, small enough to fit into the palm of a hand and familiar in subject, sat on a shelf. It depicted the Egyptian goddess Isis, positioned upon a large throne from which bison horns extended. Upon her lap rested her infant son, the god Horus. Brother, such statues are known to us Romans; they can be found on the ubiquitous pagan street altars of Rome, though banned by the church. To see such an object here, however, astonished me

"Decius, you have been a long time in coming," Brigid called out from her altar, startling me to attention.

The chiding took me aback, and I stammered out an answer: "Aidan had much need of me."

"I need to remind myself that the Lord's timing is not ours, and to stop demanding that people undertake His work on my time. In Acts, Jesus said, 'It is not for you to know the times or dates the Father has set by his own authority,' did he not?" She said this in Latin, without moving. Not for the first time, I marveled at her impeccable command of our tongue.

"He did indeed, Abbess." In my nervousness, brother, I slipped back into my hierarchical Roman habits.

She stood and stared at me. "Abbess? I thought we had settled on Brigid, *Brother* Decius. Just as we settled on Cill Dara, no?"

Brother, I knew not whether to take her words as quip or admonition. How these Gaels confuse. "My apologies, Brigid."

"You are forever apologizing to me, Decius. Without sin, there is no need for repentance. And I hardly think calling me 'Abbess' constitutes a sin," she said, with a melodious laugh that startled me with its girlishness. "Sit, sit." She gestured to the chairs on either side of her scribe's table, and I obliged.

"I see my Horus and Isis sculpture has caught your gaze," she noted, settling into the other chair.

"No, Brigid. I was merely admiring the tranquillity of your hut."

"Come, Decius. I am certain it must surprise you to see a pagan idol in an abbess's chambers. No?"

"It does a bit, Brigid."

"I know the statue is exotic, even unsuitable for a Christian nun. But it serves as a private remembrance of a beloved Egyptian friend of my youth, who settled here after long travels and much persecution. Not as an object of worship. In fact, that friend is now as Christian as myself."

"I see."

"Does the sculpture shock you as much as the scribe's instruments?" She gestured to the table between us.

"I am certain that you have many reasons—and uses—for such implements, Brigid."

"God called me to the life of an abbess, not a scribe. But if my life were mine to choose, I would choose illumination."

Brother, I sensed an opportunity for Gallienus and God to determine her purpose. I grew bold and asked, "Is that why the scriptorium figures so prominently in the abbey?"

She smiled. "One reason among many. Still, I wonder that you do not ask why I have all the necessary tools, since the scribe's work is obviously not my calling. Are you not curious, Decius?"

Her tone was light, so I answered as she wished. Plainly, she desired to tell me the reason. "Yes."

"I scribe the Word for myself, as a means of prayer. I do not flatter myself to think my skill would inspire conversion—and I am shamed to confess that my vanity demands I keep the results private—but the exercise puts me in a prayerful mind-set."

"I understand."

"I presumed that you would." At this pronouncement, Brigid rose and walked toward a cupboard near the altar. Though smaller than the cabinets in the scriptorium, it mirrored them in appearance. She pulled a text from a shelf and returned to her desk.

"I have been reading a most excellent manuscript, a small Gospel book much like the one I have been creating for my own use."

"The scriptorium has a most magnificent collection."

"Indeed. Though this particular work, so beautifully wrought, cannot be found in the scriptorium."

"Oh?"

She slid the manuscript across the table.

I recognized the item at once—the heavily tooled leather, the grooves on the bindings, the undulation of the pages from splashes of seawater. It was the manuscript I inadvertently handed to Ciaran upon my arrival at Cill Dara, the one formed by *my* hand.

"This Gospel book is your creation, no?"

I paused, though I know not why. No offense could be found in the production of a personal Gospel book.

She reached for the text, and opened it to the first page. "*De manu Decius.* By the hand of Decius. Am I wrong?"

"No, Brigid."

"I am relieved. Otherwise, I would have summoned you unnecessarily. And, I suspect, subjected you to Aidan's wrath needlessly," she said with a wide grin. She understood her monks well.

I smiled back.

"At last, we come to the 'abbey matter,' Decius. I have need of a scribe. A scribe who writes script understandable to a Roman reader, yet illuminates in our Gaelic manner. A scribe blessed with uncommon skill."

"It seems a tall order, Brigid."

"Not too tall, I hope. I believe *you* are that scribe."

"Me?" I blurted out. *Tact, brother, tact,* I can almost hear you sigh as you shake your head. You know I have an excess of reserve, but my natural caution disappears—rendering even my tenuous diplomacy and artifice impossible—when I am startled. Still, I try when I must, and this mission gives me ample opportunity to exercise the skills.

Brigid chuckled. "Yes, you. Aidan assured me of your skills in both, and your Gospel book confirmed it. You are gifted, Decius." She handed me my manuscript, and I was glad to have the comfort of my old friend in my hands again.

"Thank you, Brigid."

"I confess, though, this 'abbey matter' is not 'minor,' as I represented it to Aidan. I have prayed for forgiveness for this well-intentioned lie." She closed her eyes as if entreating God once again, and inhaled deeply. "Decius, I ask a monumental task of you."

"I will endeavor to meet your high expectations, Brigid." Brother, I can nearly hear you chuckle at my response and say, *Always the good soldier, Decius.*

"I wish to demonstrate to the Roman Holy See that this remote, backward island is capable of producing manuscripts of breathtaking artistry and undeniable piety. I want you to create the most magnificent Gospel book that Pope Simplicius has ever seen. We will inscribe this opus to him as a token of faith from the farthest ends of the earth—*extremis de finibus.*"

"Brigid, I am honored." Indeed I was, brother. And I was simultaneously sickened at the duplicity that lay in my heart, though I tried to comfort myself with the knowledge that the deception was necessary for His ends.

"There is more, Decius."

"Whatever you ask, Brigid."

"I wish this manuscript also to contain a history, much like the one we create for our martyrs. Although the subject is not a saint, and the subject is certainly not dead."

"Who is this subject?"

She swallowed hard. For the first time, I saw that this was difficult for her, that she bore a soft humanity behind her daily show of hard strength. "The subject is not a who, but a what: the Abbey of Cill Dara. We will write the history of the abbey. I wish Pope Simplicius to know us Gaels for true Christians and accord us a place in His house."

I must break off, brother, for I hear footsteps outside my hut. I will write again when I can. Pray for me, brother, as I need the supplications to our Lord more than ever. As I will pray for you.

Decius

GAEL

A.D. 467

BRIGID: A LIFE

The gold and silver chalice gleams in the candlelight as Brigid utters the secret words of transubstantiation. She admires its complex renderings as they spring to life in the light, and thoughts of Patrick fill her mind. For without his consecration and his instruction in the sacrosanct rituals known only to priests, deacons, and bishops, she could never have built her abbey or fulfilled the true role of abbess. She says a private prayer for his soul.

Though she has performed Mass in her church hundreds of times, nay thousands, the rite moves her still. She realizes the blessing of her position and the magnitude of her vocation. Ever grateful, she imparts the final prayer to her growing congregation with tears welling in her eyes. She is careful not to let them drop; goddesses do not cry.

As she returns the chalice and paten to its ornamental bowl, she watches the worshippers file out of the church, into the dying light of day. In the emergent shadows cast by the stone roof, barreled vault, and linteled doorway, she discerns Adnach. She is well pleased to see that the tough chieftain has attended her service, and with his brood, no less. For where the chief leads, his people will follow. She smiles with pleasure as she tallies the souls she has fished from the waters of the old Gaelic gods, but then stops herself. To calculate the number for purposes of impressing the Roman Church with Gael's growing orthodoxy is acceptable; to reckon that number for her own satisfaction serves only the devilish sin of pride.

Brigid hoists the ornamental bowl containing the chalice and paten midway to the ceiling, so it may serve as sublime decoration and constant reminder of His sacrifice. She looks up from the altar, expecting to see an empty church. Yet one parishioner remains. The worshipper sits at the very back of the room, almost entirely engulfed in shadow.

She squints into the darkness. The figure, seemingly aware of Brigid's gaze, rises and begins walking down the long nave toward the altar. As it nears, its shape grows familiar. The graceful carriage, the deliberate step, the elongated neck, and the resolute jaw can belong to no one but her mother.

Staring as Broicsech grows more distinct, she sees that her mother has aged. Her glossy black hair is shot through with dull gray streaks, and lines fan out from the outer corners of her eyes. Her jawline has softened, and her posture no longer bears the erectness of youth. Broicsech is still beautiful, but she is now old. Brigid wonders how time has treated her own face, as it has been years since she looked into a mirror.

"You conducted a beautiful service, Brigid," Broicsech says, her strong voice unchanged by time.

"You mean God conducted a beautiful service, Mother. For I am but His mouthpiece."

"Nicely spoken, Brigid. You have attained the veneer of piety and grace I sought to instill in you for many years."

"It is no veneer, Mother. Any piety and grace you observe in me is a gift from our Lord."

"I stand corrected and chastised, Abbess. Regardless, it is good to see you, daughter."

"It is a blessing to see you, Mother." Brigid steps down from the altar and reaches out to embrace Broicsech. Always the queen, she stiffens a bit at the human touch. Brigid continues to hold her close until Broicsech relents and surrenders into her arms.

Stepping back, Brigid examines her mother closely and whispers, "I have a confession, Mother."

"A devout soul such as yourself has a sin to confess?"

"Ah, it is not that sort of confession," Brigid retorts with a little laugh. "No, I confess that I have longed these many years to see you and Father. I dare not tread on his land uninvited, but I thought perhaps you and he might pay the Abbey of Cill Dara a visit during the royal progress."

"Do not think that because you have not seen us we do not yearn for a glimpse of you. We have had to satisfy ourselves with reports of your good deeds and conversions, and your magnificent abbey. You understand, of course, that Dubtach cannot both keep his honor and publicly acknowledge his daughter."

"I am saddened but not surprised, Mother. Still, I am content— nay, delighted—that you have decided to cast aside convention to meet with me."

"I wish I could claim such boldness, daughter. No, I came today— with Dubtach's secret sanction—because I must."

"What do you mean, Mother?" Brigid asks, but she cannot help noting that her fearsome mother did not defy Dubtach even once to see her over the ten long years of separation.

"Your father just returned from one of his slave raids on Britannia's coast. Unknowingly, he brought back with him a messenger from the bishop of Rome, who—"

"One of the pope's own representatives?"

"Yes," Broicsech answers, irritated at the interruption. "Just listen. This messenger carried on his person a letter to the bishops of Britannia from one of the pope's closest advisers. This letter bore the papal seal, which your father slit open with a flick of his knife, of course."

"Of course. What did it say?"

"Allow me to read it to you."

"If you wish, Mother."

Broicsech pulls the letter out from a pouch she has tucked into the front of her dress.

"Bishops of Britannia—

"You have among your midst a most unorthodox practitioner of our faith. This individual professes adherence to our Roman Church but baptizes in rivers and streams, like a Pelagian or a Druid, rather than in consecrated waters and churches, as mandated by our rule. This person does not separate women and men in church, as is seemly, but permits intermingling throughout. This alleged Christian celebrates Easter when it suits the whims of the congregation, instead of when Rome dictates. This individual openly defies Rome by encouraging religious monks and priests to adopt the Gaelic tonsure and rejecting the Roman tonsure of a shaved crown.

"These offensive infractions would hardly merit mention but for this practitioner's most abominable practice, a description of which I save for the last. This individual celebrates the divine sacrifice of the Mass sanctions with the assistance—or direction—of women called *conhospitae*. These women distribute the Eucharist, take the chalice, administer the blood of Christ—and even utter the sacred words of transubstantiation. This is unprecedented superstition.

"These practices should come as no surprise, however. For the person of which I speak is a Gael proclaiming the title of bishop, though but one set of hands lay upon this individual during the rite of consecration, instead of the mandated three. And this person is a woman. She is called Brigid of Cill Dara.

"His Holiness is concerned that her profane practices will spread from Gael to Britannia to the Continent like a Pelagian wildfire. Yet the uncertain times do not provide His Holiness with the independent military might to stamp it—or any other—out before it fully ignites. Thus, we charge you with seeking out opportunities to eradicate any evidence of these heretical practices that might seep into your own churches and congregants and to route out Brigid herself, should the opportunity arise.

Yours in Christ,
Gallineus"

Brigid is silent, but her mind screams. Has she undertaken all this work to court Rome on behalf of the Gaels only to be undone by her sex? She closes her eyes and inhales deeply, imploring the Lord for direction. A peace descends upon her. She reminds herself that she has labored not solely for Rome and the preservation of the Gaels alone, but for the Lord and the safeguarding of her people's souls.

When her mother speaks next, her voice is soft and caring. "Brigid, you have accomplished much here in Cill Dara. You have built an abbey worthy of Roman notice. You have converted thousands of Gaels to the church. You have accomplished all that your father and I asked of you when we released you to God. The Roman Church should be persuaded to Gael's cause."

"I appreciate your kind compliments, Mother, but Rome obviously does not agree. I set out to woo the Roman Church and my own people at once. And in so doing, in allowing the people to keep their own traditions as they revered their new God, I angered Rome. Particularly because I am a woman."

"True enough. Yet the leaders of Gael—your father and I among them—believe you have important work ahead of you still in proving Gael's Christian mettle to the Roman Church."

"Certainly more work is needed, but perhaps you should invest your confidence in another contender."

"There is no other we would consider for the role—assuming you soften some of your edges to satisfy the Romans, of course," Broicsech says with a smile. She then claps her hands and a parade of servants proceed down the nave of the church with chests in hand. "I have brought you inspiration for another way to entice the Roman Church into embracing the Gaels."

GAEL

A.D. 467–70

BRIGID: A LIFE

Brigid tempers her ways. She refuses to answer to the title "bishop," insisting that her congregants and religious call her "abbess" if they find "Brigid" too informal. The abbey celebrates Easter on the day Rome selects, and from the altar, she publicly encourages her religious men to adopt the Roman tonsure, though she does not punish those who adhere to the old style. She commissions a baptismal font out of an enormous stone slab and performs all baptisms within its blessed waters, as prescribed by Rome. Brigid even installs her newly converted foster brother, Oengus, as an abbot to oversee the religious men, though he ranks below her, and she segregates the male and female religious quarters. Although it bristles, she follows Broicsech's guidance almost in its entirety, believing she has led her well thus far.

Yet Brigid resists her mother's advice in one respect: Broicsech's insistence that she relinquish the Mass. She reminds her mother of the powerful female figure embodied in the Gospel of Mary the Mother and Broicsech's own charge that she preserve the Gaels' ways in the face of coming change—and that includes the traditions of Gaels' strong women. She withstands Broicsech's doggedness because she is called to follow Mary's commanding lead, even if it angers Rome. Otherwise, her sacrifices will be too great.

Rather than simmer over the grounds she has lost, she rejoices over her gains. For Broicsech has brought with her not only ill news and strictures; she has also transported a great gift: her library. Manuscript by manuscript, scroll by scroll, Brigid unpacks her old friends from her mother's trunks. She fills the scriptorium's empty cupboards and hanging shelves, thinking that they have been waiting long for their companions, but is careful to keep to the secluded second floor private texts Bishop Irenaeus banned long ago.

Her religious folk disseminate a message among the traveling merchants they encounter: the Abbey of Cill Dara contains an impressive library awaiting scholars and scribes. The message reaches desperate ears. Learned Christians persecuted by pagan barbarians tromping through Rome's former dominions begin to trickle into Cill Dara. Over time, they surge into a deluge.

The abbey becomes the center for religious study and reflection of which Brigid had only dreamed. She thrills to the sounds of different languages wafting through the abbey's air and the crackle of brittle manuscript pages turning. She delights in the heated debates among scholars about the meanings of certain words uncovered in her mother's ancient texts. The cupboards and shelves become so full of sacred books carried to Cill Dara on the backs on her refugees that she commissions more storage space for the crowded scriptorium.

Brigid trains the scholarly monks in the art of illumination. She instructs them not simply in the practical means of copying the sacred manuscripts—preparing the vellum, quills, and ink; forming the folios; and accurately replicating the Words—but also in how to bring His Words alive on the page.

She begins with the iconography of the text. Clarifying the symbols associated with His Words, she shows the monks how to depict aspects of Christ's life and message through interlaced drawing of spirals, swirls, braids, trumpets, and figures—be they beast, man, or spirit. With silversmiths and goldsmiths at her side, she provides the monks with metalwork and jewelry examples of this uniquely Gaelic style. Brigid explains that the scribes must enliven every corner of the sacrosanct page, because this honors His Word and sways the uniniti-ated and the illiterate who view the pages. Each stroke of the quill, each application of pigment, may bring a soul to God.

Brigid hopes, by these works, to build an unprecedented scripto-rium. She aspires to create a place where the Word is studied, where religious erudition is encouraged, and where new manuscripts capable of converting ever more souls are formed. She believes that the scrip-torium of the Abbey of Cill Dara will become that place. And she prays that the Roman Church believes it as well.

"Please come in, Cathan," Brigid says without looking up from her altar. She knows Cathan by her knock.

"My apologies. I hesitate to interrupt your prayers with abbey mat-ters."

"The work of an abbess is prayer unto itself, is it not?"

"If so, I suppose I am adding to your prayers. Am I not?"

"Indeed," Brigid says with a laugh and looks up at her loyal friend. With her interesting blend of pure piety and plain-speaking boldness, Cathan never fails to gratify. She makes Brigid feel human, not like some living emblem of the divine.

"I intrude only because a recently arrived monk from Gaul bears in-teresting news. When Ciaran interviewed him upon his arrival, this monk claimed that he fled Gaul not because the barbarians pursued him but because the Roman Christians did. Apparently, he preached a brand of Christianity that contained elements likened to Pelagianism." Cathan pauses.

"Yes?" Brigid encourages her to continue. The monk's story is nei-ther novel for Cill Dara nor disconcerting to Brigid. The abbey occa-sionally attracts religious folk with nonconformist leanings. After long reflection and consultation with her fellow religious, Brigid has deter-mined to grant them admittance as long as their faith is true and their deviation not extreme—particularly if they are gifted scholars.

"This monk says he came to believe that he would be welcome at Cill Dara because rumors abound that you yourself practice unortho-doxy. He heard this from his own bishop. Who heard it from Rome."

Brigid says nothing, for what can she add to Cathan's report other than her own distress? She has sacrificed much to appease Rome and has failed. Her sex is seemingly insurmountable. Feeling caged by her very walls, she begins pacing around her quarters. The urge to flee is strong. She grabs her cloak and pushes open her door to gulp in the fresh outdoor air.

"Brigid, are you all right?"

"Yes, yes." She waves away Cathan, who bows in respect and leaves her. Without looking back at the abbey, Brigid walks through the *rath*'s gate and onto the plains, alone.

GAEL

A.D. 470

BRIGID: A LIFE

She rambles across the plains, prayers and plans running through her mind and then drifting off, like the clouds floating across the horizon. For the first time since her visit from Broicsech, Brigid feels unmoored.

Unconsciously, she makes her way to a favorite niche near the base of a rolling hill. The heather covering provides a shelter of sorts, and Brigid settles in behind its welcome shield. She lies down in the inviting embrace of the soft, damp grass. Shedding the façade of the goddess, she allows herself to cry. It is her first succumbing to weakness in many years.

Her sobs subside as she feels footsteps approaching. Brigid presses her ear more closely to the soil and determines that the growing noise is man, not animal. She stills herself and waits to learn whether the source will divert its course or come even nearer. The footsteps do not quiet as if passing into the distance but, without warning, cease altogether. Fearing that her presence has been detected and an ambush planned, Brigid places her hand on the blade she always carries and rises from the heather.

A man kneels some distance off, his bow readied. At the very sight of her, he reels to standing and awkwardly drops it. His stark brown robes reveal him to be a religious man. Poor monk, she thinks; he believes he has stumbled across one of Gael's rumored warriors and is attempting a feeble defense.

From his proximity to Cill Dara, she assumes he journeys to the abbey, seeking sanctuary. Brigid draws back her hood and smiles, wanting to assure him that she bears no threat. Approaching him slowly, she is on the verge of introducing herself as the abbess of Cill Dara when he suddenly stammers in nigh incomprehensible Gaelic, "Do you know the way to the Abbey of Kildare?"

She understands him well enough to answer—in Gaelic, Latin, Greek, Hebrew, French, or whatever tongue is native to him, for that matter—but some aspect of his person causes her to stop and take stock. He seems different from the typical Cill Dara refugee, who hails from former Roman lands overtaken by barbarians, not from Rome itself, and he bears none of the downtrodden aspect of the persecuted. This monk gives her pause. Placing her hands on her hips, she stares the unusually tall monk up and down. His hair and eyes are black, his skin olive not from sun but from birth, and his nose aquiline—an unmistakable Roman from the Western capital itself.

She answers in her native tongue, "Cill Dara?" As if she corrects his pronunciation to better grasp his meaning.

He seizes upon the phrase: "Yes, Cill Dara."

Keeping to Gaelic, Brigid explains that she indeed knows the way and beckons him to follow. Panting as he tries to keep her pace, he asks a few inept questions about Cill Dara and its abbess, the absurdity of which nearly make her laugh. The monk clearly believes her to be a peasant woman and not an educated religious, and she enjoys playing the role.

They climb a precipitous mound near Cill Dara, and she points down at the breathtaking abbey. The monk's face reveals his astonishment. At first, Brigid feels pride at his stunned reaction, but then he ruins the compliment by saying, in Latin, "It looks near to a Roman village."

In an instant, the rejection of her mission by the Roman Church wells within her. Brigid can hold her tongue no longer; she will not allow herself and her people to be viewed as boorish simpletons incapable of self-rule. In Latin, she answers, "So they say."

The monk turns to her in shock. "You speak Latin?" His words incite her further.

"I do. Some of us Gaels are not as ignorant as rumored." As she speaks, Brigid watches his crestfallen expression. She realizes that, though his motives may be suspect, his heart is not entirely corrupt.

Still angry, Brigid rushes down the steep incline, knowing that the monk cannot match her stride. The guards race out to greet their abbess; Cathan must have alerted them to her absence. She passes under the gate's stone archway with the monk far behind and allows herself to be ministered to by her waiting, concerned nuns.

Before the nuns usher Brigid into her quarters, she looks back. She watches Ciaran shepherd the monk toward the refectory and the interrogation that all newcomers must face after receiving repast. The monk catches her eye, and she turns away. As Brigid leaves the tepid daylight for the candlelit darkness of her chambers, she allows herself a small smile. In her crushing despair, God has sent her a new chance, or so she thinks. She prays that it—he—will yield fresh hope rather than certain ruin.

XXV

DUBLIN, IRELAND

PRESENT DAY

Alex had divulged *nearly* all to Declan, an unlikely confessor for her sins. She'd told him about the Order of Saint Brigid commission, Sister Mary's oral history of the relics, her own assessment of the chalice and paten, and the manuscript's hiding place in the reliquary. But still, she'd said nothing about the other two books.

With each admission, Declan's face had grown more excited. She knew that her words confirmed his suspicions and more: Not only was her manuscript indeed the legendary Book of Kildare, but it predated the Book of Kells by hundreds of years. Alex wasn't so certain.

Darkness began to overtake the room as night fell over Saint Stephen's Green. Declan pushed back his chair from the worktable. "Come on, let's get out of here. We need to celebrate just a little."

"We're a long way from celebration, Dec." Alex's superstitious nature wouldn't allow her to tempt fate. "But call it a sanity break, and I'll happily grab a drink with you," she said as she wrapped the manuscript back in its protective sleeve and placed it carefully in her bag.

Declan practically skipped down the two flights of stairs to the landing. Linking his arm with hers, he dragged Alex down the block to his local pub, the Pearl. He settled her in a nook and dashed up to the bar to get two pints of Guinness.

"How can you be so sure it's the Book of Kildare?" she asked as soon as he returned to the table with their drinks.

"The similarity to Giraldus's description has been bothering me, and its likeness to the decorative scheme of the Book of Kells has been nagging at me as well. For example, both codices open with a full-page illustration of all four symbols of the evangelists and then introduce each specific Gospel with a separate page bearing the author's unique symbol. To be sure, the artistic style varies quite a bit. After all, it's done by the hand of a different scribe. But certain discretionary elements are almost identical—elements that aren't necessary to communicate the iconographical message of the Gospels."

"Like what?"

"Like the appearance of tiny mice figures holding communion wafers hidden within the elaborate borders."

"Couldn't the scribe of my manuscript have just copied the Book of Kells?"

"Sure, the practice was common enough back in the eighth and ninth centuries. That's why the date is so critical. Your sixth-century evidence—the dating of the Kildare communion vessels and reliquary and Sister Mary's history—helps establish that it is the Book of Kildare, and that it's earlier than Kells." He paused while he downed his drink. "I guess, in some ways, it doesn't matter whether your manuscript served as a model for the Book of Kells or not."

"Why?"

"It's a masterpiece regardless. To be sure, it'll enhance its value if Ireland's magnum opus modeled itself on your earlier manuscript. But if you want to leave behind crass topics like the exact euros your book will fetch and move into the scholarship, what really matters is proving that date of creation"—he smiled—"and your Virgin Mary, of course. That's where we'll really change history."

"What do you mean?"

"The Madonna and Child seen in the Book of Kells has long been thought to be one of the earliest known representations of the Virgin Mary in Western art. One of the great mysteries of the Book of Kells is why this image first appears in ninth-century Ireland and how it spreads to continental Europe, fueling the cult of the Virgin Mary. If, indeed, that's how it happened. After all, Christ's Mother was barely a biblical footnote for several centuries after the death of Christ. Imagine how shook up the crusty old academics will be if the first Virgin Mary dates from the sixth century rather than the ninth."

They debated Declan's theory over another pint and some dinner until two broad-shouldered men crashed into their nook. She'd instinctively grabbed her bag and started to run when she heard Declan laugh. "You bastards, get off me!"

"Just like you showed us mercy on the rugby pitch last week?" joked the man in the blue jersey who was continuing to pummel Declan.

"Gentlemen, play nice. You can see I am here with a work colleague."

The two men stopped their mock beating and looked over at Alex, as if just noticing her.

"Colleague? Is that what they're calling it these days?" the other man, also in a blue jersey, asked with a smile.

"So I'm told," Alex said with a laugh as Declan introduced her to his friends: Owen Daly and Dermott Rolley.

"It's nice to see Declan sharing a pint with a young lady rather than drinking and eating all by his sorry self at the bar like he does most nights," Owen said.

Although they all chuckled, Alex could swear that Declan reddened. She sat back and listened to the old Rathmines schoolmates torment one other over their rugby losses, but Owen's taunt kept running through her mind. Maybe the rogue was just a part Declan played.

After they finished their pints, Dermott said, "What do you say we sample the ales at Shanahan's?"

"Allowed out so late on a school night? I thought Helen and Sally kept you two on a tight leash," Declan teased.

"Ah, Dec, you know we always get a free pass from the wives on rugby match nights," Dermott said.

"Then by all means, we will join you," Declan said. As they rose, he moved toward Alex and slipped his hand behind her back to shepherd her toward the door.

"I think I'll just head back to my hotel. *I* have an early morning tomorrow," Alex reminded Declan, hoping it might prompt him to call it a night as well.

"I'll walk you to the Shelbourne. It's just on the way to Shanahan's."

Owen inserted himself between them. "We'll *all* walk you to your hotel, Alex. Dermott and I want to find out more about what 'colleagues' do these days."

XXVI

DUBLIN, IRELAND

PRESENT DAY

A bleary-eyed Declan greeted her at the door the next morning. Resisting the urge to tease him, Alex handed him one of the two coffees she'd picked up on the way to his place. Owen's remark had softened her toward him a tiny bit.

"I've been thinking about our proof problem, Alex."

"You have?" Alex said skeptically, putting down her paper cup to slip off the coat she wore over jeans and a blue cabled sweater. She found it hard to believe he'd thought about much other than rugby and Guinness during the eight hours since she'd left him at the Shelbourne's doors.

"I have indeed." He chugged his coffee and then left his cup with hers in the foyer before they entered his office. Neither one wanted a spill on the manuscript. Sitting at the worktable, he motioned for her to join him.

After they both put on sterile gloves, Alex pulled out the manuscript and opened it to the Virgin Mary folio page. She wanted another look at it under Declan's bright work lights. The image—and its ramifications—had haunted her all night. Could she really be staring at the first portrait of the Virgin Mary in history? If Declan's speculations were correct, why did her image appear in pre-ninth-century Ireland, of all places, where Christianity was just beginning to take hold among the isolated warrior people?

Alex knew, of course, that the early church bore a traditional hostility to women, and thus the Virgin Mary was barely mentioned—even in the Gospels. Luke referenced her a few times: in her election as Mother to the Messiah, in her giving birth to Jesus in Bethlehem, in her presentation of Jesus at the Temple, and in her discovery of Jesus discoursing with the Temple elders. John remarked on Mary's presence twice: once when she asked Jesus to assist the wine stewards at the Cana wedding, and once when she heard Jesus's last words at the foot of the cross. Matthew and Mark mentioned Mary only once each, referring to her visiting Jesus with his brothers. In each instance, the allusion was fleeting.

Not until the Council of Ephesus in A.D. 431 did the church sanction veneration of the Virgin as Theotokos, Mother of God. Even still, it was centuries before devotional images surfaced and worship of her took hold; this didn't reach a peak until the thirteenth century, when fervent "Mariolatry" helped raise women's status above that of sinful daughters of Eve. Alex had always figured that the Virgin Mary emerged despite the antagonism of the early church because the people needed a mother figure. But no one really knew how it occurred.

"Do you have a solution to our proof problem?" Alex asked, finally snapping out of her Marian musings.

"I do, but I fear you might not like it."

"Please don't tell me it involves taking a sample off one of the pages and submitting it to a lab."

"It does indeed."

"Dec, it's one thing for me to borrow the manuscript from Sister Mary for further research. It's quite another for me to damage it."

"So 'borrowing' is what we're calling 'stealing' these days?" Alex cringed, and Declan backtracked: "I don't mean to be harsh, Alex. But to my way of thinking, you might as well get what you came for."

"Is there no other way?"

"So far, my translation of the biblical text has revealed nothing definitive. Your book contains the standard four Gospels seen in all the other illuminated manuscripts. There is nothing quirky in the language or the writing style that permits authoritative dating. I don't see any other way to be certain about the date."

"But even with the sampling, the dating's not absolute, is it?"

"No, but it's as close as we can get." He motioned for her to draw closer to him. As she did, she smelled last night's beer seeping out of his pores, under the scent of soap from his morning shower. She found it oddly appealing. "I think I know a place from which we can take a sample and no one will be the wiser."

Spreading open the manuscript, he turned to the very last page. The scribe had affixed an unadorned piece of vellum to the back of the thick leather cover. Declan pointed to the bare folio page. "I think I can remove a tiny sliver of vellum here, and it will be undetectable. Plus, it won't affect the design or text in any way."

She wanted to scream. How had she come to this point? Unimaginably, she'd taken an ancient manuscript from the owner's possession and now she was considering allowing unauthorized invasive testing to be conducted upon it. It didn't matter that she planned on giving the book back once she'd verified her discovery. So why did her gut tell her that the amoral act was the right one? Was it that she knew she could solve the mystery better than anyone else? Or was it just her ambitious desire for glory urging her on?

Alex hated to admit it, but Declan was right. If he used his knife skillfully, he could excise a minuscule piece of the plain vellum, leaving the decoration unharmed. It seemed that there was no other way to get closure on the date. She closed her eyes and made the sort of decision she'd never thought she'd be capable of. "All right, Dec. But I can't watch."

"Why don't you just sit by the window and finish your coffee then? I'll tell you when it's all over." He sounded like a doctor reassuring a mother about her young child's impending surgery. And that was precisely how she felt.

"Okay."

Peeling off her gloves, she retrieved her coffee from the foyer and walked to the window. There was no way she'd be able to sit while he hovered over her manuscript with a blade. She stopped herself: "her" manuscript indeed.

Alex tried to keep her eyes fixed on the pedestrians strolling through Saint Stephen's Green, but her vision settled on a large clock tower looming over the park instead of on the people walking on its paths. She ticked off several minutes that seemed like hours. Impatient, she was about to turn around and find out what was happening when Declan called to her.

She ran to the worktable. "Is everything all right?"

"Yes, the piece came off easily."

"So now what?"

"I'll take it to a good friend—a discreet friend—who works at Trinity's labs. Then we wait."

"For how long?"

"Maybe a week. Maybe a bit more."

"A week? Dec, I don't have a week before I have to return this to Sister Mary."

"I don't know that we have any other alternative."

Alex knew they did. For her own reasons, she'd held off giving him the two books she'd found in the convent archives. But the time had come. She reached into her bag and handed them to Declan.

XXVII

DUBLIN, IRELAND

PRESENT DAY

"Oh my God," Declan whispered after he'd paged through the first of the two books.

"What is it?" Alex was almost afraid to ask.

"It's an ancient life of Saint Brigid."

"A saint's hagiography?"

"Yes."

As he turned his attention to the second book she had found in the convent archives, Alex began to believe that every rush of terror and dread she'd experienced since her decision was worthwhile. Before Declan even spoke, the reaction on his face told her that, whatever the risk, disclosing the two books might make the manuscript the stuff of dreams. He looked up at her and asked, "Alex, you found these books in Kildare as well?"

"Yes, in the convent archives. From the age of the vellum and the script, they seemed related to the manuscript." She couldn't wait any longer. "What's the second book?"

He smiled. "It's a bound packet of letters written in the same hand as the manuscript—and as the life of Saint Brigid, except for the final few pages of the life. It's early days yet, but I believe they might be letters written by the scribe."

"Really?"

"Really. I'm hoping these books might contain the evidence we need to prove the early date of the manuscript and the image of the Virgin Mary—proof that'll change everything."

After much deliberation, Alex and Declan decided to study the life first and the letters second. This time, however, Alex didn't sit in the upholstered chair reading research material while Declan translated. This time, she sat in the work chair next to Declan, literally looking over his shoulder. Alex didn't care if she distracted him. They had agreed that he would undertake a cursory translation first, to get a sense of the documents and see if any critical evidence jumped out. And she had no intention of missing a single word.

Declan began to skim the life, reading aloud key passages to Alex and entrancing her with the Brigid found there. He described a bold Celtic girl, a well-educated warrior of the fifth century. He told of an evolving young woman who defied her noble parents' wishes to follow Jesus Christ. And he revealed a woman brought to Christ through the love of His Mother, Mary, as Brigid read what she called "the Gospel of Mary the Mother."

For all her familiarity with gnostic and apocryphal Gospels alike, Alex had never heard of the Gospel of Mary the Mother. But as Declan began reading the lines from the Gospel excerpted in the life, the pieces of the puzzle began to fit together.

Alex asked, "You don't happen to have a copy of the gnostic or the apocryphal Gospels in your library, do you?"

"What self-respecting Irishman doesn't have the banned Gospels handy?" He smiled at her. Blushing, Alex was glad when he swiveled over to his bookshelves and plucked out three textbooks for her.

She stuck her nose deep into the textbooks while Declan continued with his translation of Brigid's mission to convert the Irish. Scanning the tables of contents, she found what she was looking for: the Protoevangelium of James and the Gospel of Pseudo-Matthew. The Protoevangelium was written around A.D. 150, and the Gospel of Pseudo-Matthew was a later version of it. Together, they described Mary's unique birth and childhood, including her training in the Tem-

ple of Jerusalem, her young adulthood and chaste relationship with
Joseph, and her close relationship with her son Jesus. It was a very different picture of Mary than that presented in the handful of mentions
of her in the accepted four Gospels of the Bible. It showed a well-
educated, bold woman who was the only human being her divine Son
would listen to.

In Christianity's early days, all sorts of Gospels floated around, and
the church had to sanction a few or risk splintering. To that end, in the
late second century, Bishop Irenaeus recognized four Gospels as the
pillars of the church, banning all others. Still, other Gospels continued
to circulate, versions of the Protoevangelium of James among them.
The church condemned the text multiple times: in 382, Pope Dama-
sus I did so; in 405, Pope Innocent I; and in 496, Pope Gelasius I. And,
in fact, the Gospel of Pseudo-Matthew was prefaced by an introduc-
tory letter—of dubious origin—that claimed to explain the church's
view on the Gospel's rejected status: "The birth of the Virgin Mary, and
the nativity and infancy of our Lord Jesus Christ, we find in apocryphal books. But considering that in them many things contrary to our
faith are written, we have believed that they ought all to be rejected,
lest perchance we should transfer the joy of Christ to Antichrist. . . .
You ask me to let you know what I think of a book held by some to be
about the nativity of Saint Mary. And so I wish you to know that there
is much in the book that is false."

Regardless of the repeated denunciation, parts of the stories found
within the Protoevangelium—and its later version, the Gospel of
Pseudo-Matthew—were seamlessly woven into the fabric of Catholic
practice by medieval times. Bits of the apocryphal Gospel's tales
formed the basis of the legends around the Virgin Mary and Christ
child birth and helped promote the worship of Mary within the church
through the Feast of the Nativity, the Conception, and the Presentation. Nowhere would ardent readers of the Bible find mention of these
events celebrated by the church; those accounts were described only
in the Protoevangelium and its related progeny. Having decided to ban
the Gospel as apocryphal, or legendary, the church—or its constituents—later determined that it had some need of the Mary found
within its pages after all. As Alex had suspected.

But she didn't need to tell Declan any of this. A scholar of early biblical manuscripts, among other things, he could tell her a thing or two about the rejected Gospels.

Alex interrupted Declan and asked him to reread the quotes from Brigid's Gospel of Mary the Mother. "She's referring to some version of the Protoevangelium of James," Alex said.

"Are you sure?"

"Listen to this," she told him, then read aloud the relevant sections from the Protoevangelium and the Gospel of Pseudo-Matthew. The text was almost identical.

Declan pushed his chair back from the table and let out a low whistle. "Brigid must have had access to the prototype for the Protoevangelium in her mother's library. Some scholars think that the Protoevangelium is a faulty copy of an earlier Gospel that has been lost—maybe this Gospel of Mary the Mother. This reference to the Protoevangelium in the life might have the additional effect of bolstering the credibility of that Gospel."

Alex asked, "There isn't a copy of the Gospel of Mary the Mother in the life or the letters, is there?"

Declan flipped through both quickly, then shook his head. "It doesn't look like it. Still lost, I guess. You're getting too big for your britches, Alex," he laughed. "Anyway, I'm happy to see the Protoevangelium surface. I love its mischievous picture of the young Jesus." He was referring to the descriptions of the youthful Christ child lashing out at other children with his powers when they acted against his childish will.

Alex smiled; of course the Protoevangelium was one of Declan's favorites. "Maybe that's why no fewer than three popes banned it?"

"Nah. I always thought the church was more put off by the world seeing his strong-willed mother."

They were interrupted by the rare ringing of Alex's cellphone. Hardly anyone ever called her on it unless it was an emergency. She reached for it, checking the number. It was the exchange code for Kildare. Her stomach lurched as she picked up.

"Alexandra Patterson, please."

"This is she."

"Alex, it's Sister Mary. I have some bad news."

Her heart beating even harder, she said, "What's happened?"

"The previous keeper, Sister Augustine, just passed away."

"I'm so sorry, Sister Mary," Alex said, although all she could feel was relief.

"We'd like to use the communion vessels and the reliquary one last time for her funeral Mass, and I'd like you to be here for that. To make sure that our usage doesn't interfere with your appraisal process—or the sale, of course. Can you make it down to Kildare for first thing Thursday morning?"

Thursday would give her only two more days with the manuscript, two more days to ascertain the date of the Book of Kildare. But what choice did she have? "Of course, Sister Mary. I'll be there first thing Thursday."

"Excellent. I hope you'll be bringing me good news, Miss Patterson?"

"God willing, Sister Mary."

GAEL

A.D. 470

Brother,

The history begins. I have never heard anyone speak the way Brigid speaks, with such frankness and intimacy. She bares her thoughts and feelings as she unfolds the details without a shred of self-consciousness. Brother, Brigid speaks only as I have read in Augustine's *Confessions* and only as I write to you.

The experience of capturing Brigid's words with my own is like painting a moving likeness with letters. I sit in a rigid wooden chair, with the scribe's table before me, and force my quill to race to catch her words. I disregard the splinters that lodge in my palm as my fingers fly across the rough table surface in search of ink. I steal glimpses of her face during her rare moments of pause. At day's end, if I have been quick and open, I find her vivacity, her soul, in my pages. In my darker moments, I wonder what will become of this history, as I do not have the same intentions for it as does she.

Each day, we start before the sun rises and the abbey along with it. Her duties, of course, demand that we break for meals and meetings and ministry and Mass, yet we use every spare moment between—as the noon sun brightens even a gray Gael, as the afternoon shadows takes hold, even as dusk settles like silt. I scribe furiously as she talks about the misty world from which she emerged.

While she performs her abbey responsibilities, I carry out my other charge: to create a wondrous Gospel book. Brother, I need not tell you how I delight in this task. I build on my early effort at illumination— my personal Gospel book—and meld its design with the uniquely Gaelic artistry. I hope you will not find me prideful if I share that even the recalcitrant Aidan finds time to watch as I paint and illuminate, that even he finds reason to praise me.

Yet the scriptorium and the hut do not confine us. Brigid desires the history to memorialize her current ministry; thus we tramp across the lush countryside as she tends her people with the dedication of a servant. No task, no person is below her care. No situation poses too great a danger for her, and dangers abound in this still-Druidic warrior world. She dismisses my cautions with a laugh and a wave, saying, "You know that I am the daughter of two warriors."

In my days with Aidan, I often heard the other monks tell tales of her wondrous selflessness, but I thought the vignettes tall. I was wrong. If you ever perchance read the history, brother, you will see an account of her good deeds, and I endeavor to animate them well. I must admit, however, to witnessing her works firsthand moves in a manner words cannot share. In fact, she is so kindly and maternal in her ministrations, I once asked her whether she did not regret forgoing motherhood.

Her answer to my somewhat impertinent inquiry vastly informed my understanding of her. She said, "How can I be mother to all, if I am mother to one?"

Her statement casts an interesting shadow over all our dealings, for she is indeed mother to her people. I recall one afternoon when Brigid dragged us on horseback through near-blinding rain over hills that slid like ice. She seemed to have a particular destination in mind that day, though she did not always, and we arrived at a small cluster of structures in a knoll.

The inhabitants, rough Christian men and women indistinguishable in their dun-colored cloaks, emerged at the rare sighting of their abbess. They threw themselves prostrate at her feet, and Brigid knelt down in the puddles to draw them up to her level. She spoke to each person in a low voice, such that I could not overhear, and their faces softened at the conversation.

When the group rose, Brigid addressed the whole: "I understand that one of your daughters wishes to enter the abbey life as a nun. May I meet this young woman?"

A man scrambled into one of the structures and came forth dragging a writhing girl under his arm. "Here she is, Abbess." The local community insists on calling Brigid by her title, regardless of her efforts to the contrary. "My daughter Maeb wants to take the veil," he said, shoving the reluctant girl forward.

The unkempt, towheaded girl, who could not have been more than twelve, stumbled at the force of her father's push. Brigid bent down to help her up and took her hand in hers. She looked into the girl's face and asked, "Is it your intention to enter the Abbey of Cill Dara as a religious?"

The girl did not answer.

Still holding the girl's hand, Brigid turned to the little crowd and said, "It seems she would prefer not to join us in Cill Dara. And that is fine." Brigid offered the girl the kiss of peace.

The father stepped forward and said, "Maeb wants to go, all right, but she cannot talk. She's a mute and has been since the day of her birth."

Brigid's hand tightened around that of young Maeb, until her own knuckles shone white. "It saddens me to see our strong Gaelic culture absorb the Roman beliefs that women are chattel. I will force no woman to act against her wishes, regardless of her father's command. I will not relinquish Maeb's hand until she tells me her desires—in whatever way she can."

Brigid turned away from the parents of this poor girl—no doubt pushing her into abbey life because no man wanted to marry a mute—and asked the girl again, "Is it your intention to enter the Abbey of Cill Dara as a religious?"

I could feel the crowd tense, and I worried that they might turn against Brigid, abbess or no. The girl, whose face altered inexpressibly at the loving attention given her by Brigid, emitted a croak.

The mother gasped at the sound, but Brigid merely smiled at the girl, who tried again. With a rasp, she said, "I wish to do nothing but what you wish."

While the crowd watched in amazement as the girl made these first utterances, Brigid continued their conversation as if it were quite normal. "I wish for you to speak your own desires."

"I wish to join you," the girl whispered.

Brigid hugged the girl tight. "Then join us you shall. Maeb, welcome."

We said our farewells, and left the knoll with Maeb. I have recounted this story in the life, and I have no doubt that many will call it miraculous. And perhaps it is. Or perhaps it is the result of Brigid's goodly kindness. Only He knows.

Oh, I can hear your knowing laugh, brother. Yes, I confess that Brigid fascinates. Worry not. Daily I remind myself that Satan can take many forms, even that of a well-intentioned, pious-seeming woman. So may I share with you my efforts to ensure that no fresh temptations of Satan worm in? I dedicate the evenings, when the light fails and illumination grows impossible, to shoring up my defenses. After evening Mass, I rush to my hut. Once I secure the door behind me, I throw myself facedown on the dirt floor and assume the penitential position of the cross. Silently, for I cannot risk another religious overhearing my supplications, I cry to God for His help to strengthen my heart against any of Brigid's sacrilege or allure.

Hours pass in this manner, so many I cannot account for all of them. I rise from the floor only when my body aches and my forehead bleeds. Then, filled with fervor, I pry loose the stone in the hut's floor where I store my secret writings, these letters to you among them. Exhausted and near collapsing, I force myself to report to Gallienus.

I recount in excruciating detail Cill Dara's heretical practices of which I've been told and which I've observed—the tonsures, the suggestion of the Druid in certain rituals, the renegade celebration of Easter, Brigid's performance of the Mass, and the unorthodoxies of her life. I list all the banned Gospels I saw in the scriptorium's satchels, knowing that this profanation is so deep Gallienus need not call it

Arian or Pelagian. Even an Arian or Pelagian would take offense at the copying and dissemination of the prohibited texts.

As I lie down to rest on the rock that served as pillow, I pray to arise renewed to God's task. And so you find me, in the prayerful moments before sleep.

Brother,

I heard from Brigid's own mouth that she was warrior-born. And through the tales of the abbey's history, she told me that she was warrior-trained. Yet I have a confession. I thought that all her talk of martial instruction and practice was common Gaelic boasting or, cast in a more flattering light for Brigid, a show of might to the warrior society lurking outside her walls. I did not believe her.

Brother, I am no innocent, clinging to visions of His peaceable kingdom. I understood that the Abbey of Cill Dara's peace stood on vulnerable ground in an unstable culture. Too often, my time with Brigid was interrupted by urgent requests for her skills in mediation. Though she never described the disputes she arbitrated, I learned from others that she adjudicated upsets among chieftains and bloody disputes between neighbors. Yet somehow, these clashes and the ensuing carnage seemed far from the calm world of Brigid's hut and the scriptorium. I do not know why. Perhaps my obsession with the Gospel book and the history distracted me. Or perhaps Brigid shielded me.

But even I heard grumblings about the Liffey decree from the other monks. The river Liffey cuts through the plains of Cill Dara, passing through or touching upon by means of swampland three adjoining territories. Each of these provinces was governed by a different chief, and the most pugnacious of the three—Caichan—had proclaimed by writ that they must join together to build a wide road through the three regions, the design of which would sit upon the Liffey riverbed and swampland at certain points. At the outset, the three chiefs agreed that the region needed the road, and set their people to labor creating a solid foundation with tree branches and stones, utilizing Caichan's plan. Within weeks, however, it became clear that Caichan had allocated the most arduous work on the soggy riverbeds and marshes to the people of the two other chiefs, Miliucc and Dichu.

Although she never mentioned the nature of her work, I watched firsthand as Brigid trudged out to settle countless disputes about this decree. I knew that she recognized the benefits of the road and desired its furtherance for the abbey purposes. Yet as the road building grew ever more challenging, the tensions escalated.

One afternoon, Lochru and Daig, two of Brigid's Gaelic monks whose abbey roles were nebulous but who appeared whenever peace-keeping measures were called for, interrupted our work. Instead of receiving them inside, as she did other visitors, Brigid talked with them outside the door for nearly a quarter hour. She finally stepped back into the hut, announcing that she'd have to stop our labors for the day.

"The chiefs are drawing battle lines over the Liffey decree, are they not?" I asked.

She looked at me with surprise. "Yes. How did you know?"

"It is no secret within the abbey. I assume that you will try to stop them. May I join you?"

"I do not think so, Decius. It isn't safe."

"I need to witness the full history of the abbey to record it, do I not?"

Brigid smiled. "I suppose you are right. If you insist, come." Her robes swirled around her as she exited the hut. She did not wait for my answer.

We set out on horseback to the west, on a route unfamiliar to me. I had grown accustomed to roaming the countryside with Brigid at my side, but instead, Lochru and Daig flanked her. The threesome rode so quickly that I pushed my horse to keep their pace.

By nightfall, we reached a grove. I spotted a large bonfire at its center, and we veered toward it. Tall oaks wove a canopy over our heads, but the moonlight was so strong and the fire so bright, I could easily make out the men gathered there. At the core of a large circle of soldiers stood three exceptionally tall men, two with long hair and the other with short hair, spiked with a chalky substance. All three wore outer cloaks of a heathery fabric over short, brightly colored tunics and sword belts hooked with blades so long they touched the ground. They were screaming.

To my astonishment, I recognized these men. They often attended Sunday Mass with their vast families in tow and their sword belts empty, yet I had no idea they were the chiefs so often criticized in conversation. I could not believe that Brigid had managed to convert these hardened warrior souls.

Though we dismounted and drew close, the chiefs' exchange was so heated they did not take notice of our presence. Until Brigid drew herself to her full height, cleared her throat, and called out, "Chiefs."

"Abbess, my apologies," Caichan said. In unison, the chiefs and their men knelt before Brigid.

"Shall we leave the weapons outside the grove?" she asked, though it sounded more like a command.

The chiefs nodded in agreement, and their men began to gather the shields, chain mail, helmets, and swords that rested behind each as a declaration of impending battle. The men took leave of their chiefs, and we religious and warriors stood facing one another.

"I understand that the accord we reached has been undone," Brigid said.

The chiefs began shouting at once, each pronouncing the inequity of the decree and the impracticality of the accord. Brigid stayed absolutely still while they aired their grievances and then said, in a voice quieter yet mightier than any of their own, "You will not behave in this offensive manner in this sacred place, under God's blessed sky. You will abide by the accord I painstakingly wrought with His guidance. Did Patrick teach you nothing about the destruction and sinfulness in warring against your brothers?"

The chiefs stopped their bellowing and stared at her. As did I. As did Lochru and Daig. The power in her voice was inescapably God-sent.

Caichan's scrape-metal voice interrupted the still night air: "My apologies, Abbess. For bringing you from the warm safety of your abbey on a cold eve. For dragging you into this quarrel once again. And for disobeying your request for adherence to the accord. The battle will proceed at dawn, as we discussed."

As the chiefs took their leave, Brigid acted. She walked slowly to Caichan's side. Then I saw a flash of silver as she reached into the

sleeve of her cloak and pulled out a knife. She pressed it against
Caichan's throat and disarmed him of a blade hidden in his own
sleeve. Lochru and Daig did the same to the other chiefs.

"You think us harmless because Christ teaches us to turn the other
cheek, do you? Because Patrick schooled us to abandon our swords?
Never forget that, unlike Patrick, I am also the daughter of Dubtach
and Broicsech, thus a warrior just like you. When you battle, you
wound God's Abbey of Cill Dara and His people. Through my hand,
He will punish you if you persist."

Brother, I know not what more I should add to this account. I could
tell you of the humble apologies and fealty offered to Brigid after her
show of force, or I could tell you the manner in which the three chiefs
proceeded with the river Liffey project. Yet what I must divulge is that
Brigid proved me wrong, and I pray forgiveness from Him for my
doubts. She is indeed a warrior.

Pray for me.

Brother,

I am in need of confession, yet cannot secure it here. The Gaels have
a curious practice for confession. They do not stand in church and
proclaim their sins publicly, as we do. For they do not view sin as a
public matter, a crime against the church. Instead the Gaels see sin as
the penitent's private business with God and, as such, deserving of a
private confession between the sinner and his or her confessor, whom
they call *anmchara,* or soul friend.

Curious, is it not? I do not think it quite rises to heresy of the sort
Gallienus seeks, but it is an oddity nonetheless. Inexplicably, I have
grown quite fond of this *anmchara* confessional concept, and since I
cannot make a soul friend of anyone here, may I make you my *anmchara* for a particular sin?

A new monk, called Valens, arrived in Cill Dara several days ago.
Though from a central region we would deem provincial, he is indeed
Roman. He is learned in scribing, illumination, sacred texts, and lan-
guages. He and I share many similarities, and one would think we

might incline toward a natural friendship, however artificial and guarded, given my situation.

Outcast monks, priests, and nuns arrive in Cill Dara with regularity, so this particular addition would not typically merit mention. Why then, brother, you ask, do I write of this Valens to you? And why, pray tell, do I convey this information to you in the context of an *anmchara* confession?

Because I revile him. My stomach churns as I watch him walk from the refectory into the scriptorium. My fingers clutch as I observe him settling into his seat at the scriptorium and dipping his quill into the ink for that first brushstroke of the morn. My eyes narrow as I witness his careful application of pigment to the vellum. I loathe the very sight of this black-haired, charcoal-eyed Valens.

I can imagine you readying your arms to defend me for whatever offense this Valens has inflicted upon me. For surely, I can hear you proclaim, any man who has so incited your pious brother deserves to be punished for his transgressions. As you have so punished wrongdoers before, real and perceived, though we need not speak of these past matters.

Here lies my sin, brother: Valens has done me no wrong. He goes about his business as a monk-scribe with regularity and piety. He appears kindly and soft-spoken. He seems to pay me no heed out of the ordinary.

I hate him because Brigid favors Valens.

No, brother, I do not mean that she bestows her *favors* upon him, as you would insinuate. I mean that, Brigid assigns small illustrations to him that I am guessing are designated for her Gospel book, though he could not possibly know this, and, as she does, she nears Valens, and I watch in agony as her white gown and loose hair brush against him as they once did to me.

Brother, in watching this display and gauging my reactions, I realize how deep my attraction to her has grown. I must purge my feelings and this jealousy from my soul or surely it will corrupt me from the inside out, and taint me not only for Gallienus's mission but for my own eternity. And all the measures I have taken to bolster my heart and soul against her glamour and her heresy will be for naught.

This venomous resentment of Valens spreads through me and begins to poison my dealings with Brigid. At midday, we set out for a trek across the plains. We stopped at a nearby farm that supplies the abbey with milk and butter, run by what I thought was a Christian family. As is the Gaelic way, they welcomed us into their home and offered us their best foodstuffs—hearty bread and ripe cheese. I stared as Brigid interacted with the family. I noted the kind compliments she paid the wife for her tidy home, as well as the linking of Brigid's hand with the farmer's as we prayed before eating.

I watched the slow stroke of Brigid's hand on the sleeping baby's pink cheek. She said, "We will need to baptize this babe soon."

The mother said, "Ah, surely there is no rush. A sweet babe such as this is born pure; she has not chosen to sin as yet."

Brigid did not pause in her caresses, just simply answered, "Let us make the arrangements."

Instead of admiring her gentle, caring way, I grew angry. Inwardly, I raged at Brigid's indiscriminate squandering of her affections. As we left the family's warm hearth and faced the blowing winds of our return walk, I lashed out at Brigid by seizing upon the mother's remark.

"Did you hear the mother's pronouncement about the baby's purity?"

"I did indeed."

"Does this comment not trouble you? It sounds as though the mother believes that there is no such thing as original sin. "

Brother, this query drew dangerously close to accusing Brigid of harboring Pelagianism in her midst. I did not need to speak the name of the heretical faith aloud for her to understand my meaning, for the essence of that doctrine is the absence of original sin and the presence of free will. Yet I could not stop myself.

Brigid did not take offense, though she had cause. She did not unsheathe her deadly warrior's tongue, as I have seen her do when she is challenged. Instead, she placed her hand on my shoulder and asked, "What ails you today, Decius? I have never known you to harshly judge your fellow Christians."

Her kindness acted like kindling for my fury. "Christian—you call them Christian? A true Christian would baptize her child at the first opportunity, to wash clean the sin with which the child was born."

"Decius, I know these Gaelic beliefs and practices seem archaic, even profane, to your Roman sensibilities, but remember, my people are new Christians. They surrender their old ways slowly, and I take care to heed their pace to ensure their steadfastness to my flock."

"So they may baptize their babes whenever they wish and reject the notion of original sin if it does not suit their fancy?"

Her eyes flashed at me in anger, but she tempered her tongue. "Decius, you speak as though you stand on the floor of the Roman Senate, deliberating politics and theological nuances. I care not for such a debate. It does not render souls unto Christ, as He commands me to do and as I have so done. But I understand it."

"How so?"

"Forget not that I am the daughter of warriors. Even men who are not soldiers need their wars."

With this, she silenced me. For, brother, if I close my eyes to the theological unorthodoxy of the Gaels and their lingering Druidic customs, Brigid's logic holds and her people's practices seem close to the earthly goodness Christ espoused. But I have not the luxury of such beliefs. My duty to Gallienus and my vows to our Lord require that I care for this mission. My feelings endanger both.

Anmchara, brother, let my confession serve as the means by which my covetousness of Brigid and hatred of Valens are purged from my soul, and pray God forgive me for it. Pray for me, brother, as I pray for you. I am much in need.

Decius

GAEL

A.D. 470

BRIGID: A LIFE

Brigid collects information on this new arrival. Sidelong glances at Mass tell her of the monk's piety. Surreptitious observations in the refectory divulge his quiet way with his peers. Reports from her senior scribes on the progress of their illuminated works reveal his unusual skills with the brush and the Word. Yet a single encounter uncovers the purpose and true nature of this monk, this Decius.

Brigid awakens from her sleep in the darkest hour of a cold night. She rises and kneels before her private altar, seeking the solace only the Lord provides her. Though her head lowers as she silently mouths her prayers, a tiny light dancing in the corner of her vision distracts her. She walks to her window and sees that the light comes from the scriptorium. On the verge of calling for the guards, she realizes that a single candle emits the light and that a lone figure bears it.

Brigid watches as the light passes from one aperture to the next— on the scriptorium's upper level. The figure moves through the higher floor with purpose. Without hesitation and without assistance, she dons her cloak and steps into the night.

Creeping across the abbey grounds, Brigid pushes open the scriptorium door soundlessly. She scans the room, a space she knows so intimately she has no need of a light herself. Spying the candle on the second floor, and a deeply shadowed figure seated alongside it, she settles into a chair in a far corner of the main room and waits.

Listening to the brittle pages of an ancient manuscript turn, Brigid wonders which text entrances the reader. Only the rarest or most controversial tomes are stored upstairs, so perhaps a racy work of Greek mythology has captured the wandering imagination of a wayward nun. Or maybe one of her more unconventional priests seeks out a Gospel variant of challenged origins. Either way, the errant religious must be set upon the righteous path.

Daylight begins to replace the scriptorium's shadows, and still the figure remains fixed in place. Brigid does not want Niall to stumble upon the scene. So she rustles her cloak a bit, hoping to rouse the individual, who, as if alerted, scuttles across the floor and down the ladder—but, instead of leaving, inexplicably sits at one of the scribe's tables and begins to write.

The anonymity of the religious garb and the clinging shadows necessitate that she draw closer to identify the trespasser. She rises and treads quietly up behind the person, who is still engaged in writing. She recognizes the profile. It is Decius.

"Cannot wait until morning to labor for our Lord, Brother Decius?" Brigid says, breaking the silence.

Decius jumps up from his seat. He offers apologies, and from the sincere expression on his face, she understands that he is abjectly sorry. She knows that this occasion provides her the finest opportunity to assess the man.

She is never overt in her questions, and he is never plain in his answers. When she nears the topic of the reason for his nocturnal visit, his repentant, guilty expression resurfaces. And when she inquires as to his thoughts on Cill Dara, he replies in earnest, "I find Cill Dara and its people to be a wondrous gift. To be so welcomed when I was so outcast is a miracle unto itself. To have the further opportunity to work here in the scriptorium is a double blessing. Cill Dara is so much more than I expected or deserve."

By the time Niall bursts into the scriptorium, Brigid is convinced that Rome has indeed sent Decius to Gael to scrutinize the rogue abbess Brigid—but it unwittingly sent a conflicted spy. One of which she will make good use.

Brigid spends the next weeks praying for His guidance on how best to use His gift. A rough strategy emerges from the swirling mass of her dreams, but she is not certain of its power. She makes a rare, clandestine visit to her mother and explains this idea of creating a portable Gospel book for the pope's own hands—one of such breathtaking beauty that His Holiness will surely be swayed by the talent and loyalty of the Gaels. Broicsech deems the tactic worthy of her and Dubtach's prayers.

Though she settles on a plan, Brigid leaves Decius alone to stew for several days. She is certain that the long wait will make him anxious as he wonders what she suspects. She predicts that his apprehension will encourage him to overcompensate and become a willing conscript for her designs.

Finally, Brigid calls for Decius. She watches from the corner of her eye as he enters her hut warily. As she presents him with the mission to create a magnificent Gospel book for His Holiness Pope Simplicius and a history of the abbey, one she has no intention of sharing with anyone but him and, even then, only to sway him to her and the Gaelic people, she studies Decius's eyes. She sees a flash of excitement in them as she explains that the book will demonstrate Gael's breathtaking artistry and undeniable piety, and then notes the shadow of guilt that passes across them. Decius's conflicted response proves her suspicions correct. He embraces her plan and will undoubtedly work diligently upon it, but he is also a spy for Rome. Albeit an inconstant one.

GAEL

A.D. 470–71

BRIGID: A LIFE

Brigid delights in the collaboration. Decius is indeed the scribe and illuminator of her wishes. With ease, he captures the unusual Gaelic style and imbues it with his own artistic Roman vision, fashioning a Gospel book of unprecedented beauty, meaning, and structure. He encapsulates the abbey's history so skillfully and persuasively, she often forgets it is her own as he reads bits of it aloud to her. She comes to believe that the Roman Church will be convinced of Gael's deserved worth when Pope Simplicius is presented with a Gospel book so powerful.

To that end, Brigid undertakes every measure possible to ensure that Decius receives a most favorable image of Cill Dara and Gael. She invites him to accompany her as she works among the people, in the secret hope that it will further convince him of Gael's Christian fortitude and sincerity. With the Roman at her side, she ministers to the sick and the religiously unsure, encourages her people to engage in the sacred Christian rites, and gives them the unconditional love of Christ. She shows him the beauty of the Gaels and their lands and the mounting power of Christianity in her people.

Yet she grows exhausted from the constant vigilance she must maintain to shield Decius from the dark underbelly of Cill Dara life. The abbey's success breeds envy among neighboring tribes, and she must hide from Decius the raids on the abbey's lush farmlands and the physical threats to her monks and nuns. She conceals the fact that, among the religious, she has trained a band of warriors to protect the abbey and its inhabitants from attack. She secretes the nature of the potential attackers: the abbey is beset not only by covetous neighbors but also by remaining Roman-trained religious who had served Bishop Patrick but, after his death, do not embrace his love of the Gaelic people—or their female bishop. Brigid must be certain that Decius carries back to Rome an idyllic picture of a unified Christian Gael. She believes that she is successful in keeping her secrets, except for one occasion when she has no choice but to grant Decius leave to accompany her on a mission to halt a battle among local chieftains over the Liffey decree.

And Brigid faces another challenge to her plan: her emotions. During the months that she and Decius traverse the countryside, sharing thoughts neither has imparted to another soul, Brigid finds herself growing dangerously attached to the Roman monk. Unlike the rough warriors of her youth and the soft religious of her adulthood, Decius is both strong and gentle. Never shying from a confrontation, though admittedly of a more intellectual nature, he is also quick to offer empathy and consolation when needed. He is the most learned person of her acquaintance, Broicsech notwithstanding, and the most unwaveringly pious. She never forgets the real reason for his presence in Gael, but she knows that it rankles him like a painful, untended wound, and this knowledge makes her care for him all the more. For she bears a festering secret of her own.

In another life, without the yoke of her particular vow of chastity, Brigid might have selected Decius for her husband, even for a shared religious life. She prays nightly for the strength to keep her feelings hidden from him—though she knows she cannot keep them from God. And for that offense, she constantly asks Him for forgiveness.

DUBLIN, IRELAND

PRESENT DAY

"I thought we'd have a bit more time," Alex said.

"We may have enough time—if the letters have what we need."

Declan stopped his translation of the life, and they turned to the letters. There was their date, on the second page. Decius described himself as a scribe in the service of Pope Simplicius. Alex jumped up from her chair and ran over to Declan's bookshelves. Simplicius reigned from A.D. 468 to 483.

"That's it, Dec. We have the name of the scribe's pope, and we know the years of Simplicius's papacy. The Book of Kildare was written sometime in the late fifth century."

Declan remained seated, with a curiously reserved expression on his face. "We're nearly there, Alex. Nearly."

"Oh my God, what more do you want?"

"I want what all the other scholars and museums and collectors will want: a secondary source verifying this Decius. Otherwise, the whole thing could be labeled a hoax, a forgery."

"Even with testing done on vellum and ink samples?"

"Even with testing done on vellum and ink samples."

She knew he was right; their profession was rampant with forgeries, and all the players were raising the bar on proof. But she didn't want to hear it. "You're looking for a miracle, Dec, and these are not biblical times."

"What if you visited the Vatican's secret archives?"

"You actually think I'm going to be able to find mention of a lowly fifth-century scribe in service to Pope Simplicius in that football field of records?"

"Those archives contain all the manuscripts concerning the exercise of papal power since the apostles' times, acts that Decius might have recorded. And the archives aren't secret anymore. As long as you have scholarly credentials, you can access them. Most of them, anyway."

"I know. I've been there."

"Then you know we might find some mention of Decius in whatever's left of Simplicius's pontifical records."

Alex was torn. She knew it was possible—though highly, highly unlikely—that she'd find a reference to Decius, but she believed that the full translation of the texts was important too.

"What about finishing the translations? We need to get that done."

"I can stay behind working on that while you go to Rome."

"I don't know, Dec. I guess I was hoping to completely assuage my guilt by returning the manuscripts to Sister Mary tied up in a nice bow—translated, dated, and appraised."

"If that's your goal, then the Vatican archives are the only way."

Alex crossed the room to the windows looking out over Saint Stephen's Green. Declan's suggestion was sound, but did she trust him with the texts? And why didn't he stress the importance of the additional proof before? Still, he'd proven himself to be an invaluable resource thus far, and he'd shaken off some of his roguishness. But leaving him with the texts required an enormous leap of faith, and she's been secular in all respects for a long, long time.

"Come on, it's getting late," Declan said. "Let's have a bite to eat before you decide what to do."

They left the office area of his flat and entered his living space for the first time. Like his office, it surprised her. He had decorated the living room with edgy, modern furniture and paintings, and the kitchen was outfitted with stainless-steel chef's-quality equipment. She was stunned; she'd expected some Irish version of a fraternity house, with dirty clothes heaped in the corners and half-empty bottles of beer scattered about.

He poured her a glass of red wine and sat her down at the kitchen table. Pulling out pots and pans, he began boiling fresh pasta and sautéing garlic and Roma tomatoes in olive oil. The kitchen smelled wonderful, and after two glasses of wine, she felt wonderful too. They opened another bottle and sampled the simple, delicious pasta while they talked about themselves. They talked about everything—careers, families, lives—except her decision. But she had made it.

"I think I will go to Rome, Dec. And I'll leave you behind to translate."

"Really?"

"Yes," she said, but she couldn't keep the last vestiges of hesitation from her voice.

"You can trust me, Alex."

"Can I?"

He got up from his chair and knelt next to her. Placing one hand on her cheek and one on her knee, he said, "Yes, you can."

Declan leaned in toward her, but she drew back. The manuscript, the trip to Rome, their intimate conversation—it was all happening fast. It had been a long time since she'd been with someone. Her last relationship had been over two years ago, with an Australian artist who, she learned too late, needed to explore his creativity through other women's bodies. She hadn't trusted anyone since then. Even for a night.

She had already taken the biggest leap of faith—by entrusting Declan with the manuscript. And she really wanted to take another; she didn't want to be that lonely looking woman at the Silken Thomas Inn. But she couldn't allow herself to trust him further.

"I'm sorry, Dec," Alex said. And she slipped out into the night to her hotel.

DUBLIN, IRELAND, AND ROME, ITALY

PRESENT DAY

Alex woke up to the ringing phone. Assuming it was her wake-up call, she sleepily reached for it. But it was Declan. "I'm coming with you," he said.

"You needn't, Declan. I know my way around the Vatican well enough."

"Oh, Alex, there you go again, underestimating your charms. Maybe I can't keep away from you," he added, in his typical half-mocking tone.

She couldn't help but laugh in relief to hear his familiar personality resurface. She'd feared they'd be awkward with each other, when they still had so much work to do. "What a compliment," she bantered back.

"Ah, but that isn't the *only* reason I'm coming with you."

"No?"

"It occurred to me that, while you have access to the archives, you won't necessarily be able to translate what you find."

"The Vatican has translation services available for scholars. I've used them before."

"Sure, if you don't mind waiting three or four weeks to get your one page converted into English."

She sat up. He was right. "But what about the main translation of the life?"

"We'll bring everything with us, and I'll work on it while we travel."

"All right, Dec. You seemed to have thought of everything."

"If only."

Alex and Declan settled into a comfortable silence on the plane. True to his word, Declan buried himself in his translation; he'd gotten through only two-thirds of the life and the first few pages of the letters, those that had helped them with dating. Meanwhile, Alex read up on the papacy of Simplicius.

During Simplicius's rule, from A.D. 468 to 483, the great Roman Empire teetered on the edge of a perilous precipice, challenged on all sides by barbarian tribes: Burgundians, Vandals, Ostrogoths, Lombards, Franks, Angles, Saxons, Jutes, and, most of all, the Visigoths. The empire existed primarily in name, divided as it was between an eastern emperor and his western counterpart. Turbulence and chaos ruled the day, and Rome clung to its past glory by its fingernails, manned by Roman functionaries yet challenged by Germanic kings. During this unsteady political time, Roman society, no longer able to rely on the Roman government, reorganized itself around a new entity, Christendom, a mystical commonwealth that unified believers across the shifting boundaries of the barbarian kingdoms. These believers helped rule behind the scenes, and critical to their power base was the eradication of all heresies, including any springing up in increasingly Christian Ireland. It made sense that the Roman Church officials would send a spy to assess the Irish situation, especially since they didn't have troops at their command to deal with sacrilege among their churches.

Though Alex was immersed in Roman history, she was constantly aware of Declan's presence. And she was glad of it. After working alone for so long, she found his company surprisingly welcome, despite the events of the previous night.

Disembarking from the plane, they eased through customs and security, looking like a couple on a romantic holiday. Having landed during that quiet window between rush hour and lunchtime, they grabbed

a cab without difficulty and made good time through the notoriously
congested streets of Rome, to the Vatican. Declan directed the driver
to leave them off at Saint Anne's Gate. From there they'd head to the
Vatican Library, where they'd arranged for passes.

They stepped out into the golden sunshine of the Roman spring.
After more than a week of Irish rain and gray clouds, Alex thrilled to
the warmth. She stripped off her leather jacket and put on her neglected sunglasses. Declan looked her over and slipped an arm around
her back. "Now I'm *really* glad I came with you," he said.

Alex allowed them to walk arm in arm until they reached the
somber Swiss Guards. They registered with the admissions secretary
before the morning deadline, and waited as he reviewed the scholarly
credentials they'd arranged to be faxed over early that morning to a
contact of Declan's. Even though they'd both consulted the archives in
the past, there was no guarantee they'd be granted admission today. A
gap in their qualifications, a red flag for their specialties, an unknown
security risk, or even the sheer number of visitors could block their
entry on any given day. But fortune smiled upon them, and after consulting the database, the secretary returned with their entry cards.

A guard checked their coats and bags. To Alex's dismay, he refused
to allow her to keep her black bag containing the manuscripts even
though she insisted it was her purse. The guard escorted them to the
door to the first of three rooms containing the Vatican Secret Archives.
The name was a bit of a misnomer for the records of the Holy See, as
the collection wasn't secret but had been opened to scholarly use in
1881, by Pope Leo XIII. At least ostensibly. Most academics believed
that the Vatican kept private the most interesting, controversial documents.

Scholars of all varieties visited the collection in droves, containing
as it did the history of the Catholic church and the details of the
Roman pontiffs' rule. The documents had survived religious up-
heavals, political turmoil, and constant moving until the Vatican created a permanent home for them in the sixteenth century. Pope Paul V
chose three rooms next to the Sistine Hall—named the "Paoline"—to
house many of the archives. The three Paoline rooms were decorated

with exquisite frescoes honoring the donations made by various European rulers to the popes and lined with poplar cabinets furnished with the coats of arms of the Borghese, Pamphili, Chigi, and Pignatelli families.

Over time, the archives grew. At first, attics, unused crypts, and tower rooms were appropriated, but they proved inadequate. So in the twentieth century, vast subterranean halls—inaccessible to all but the inner circle—were built to accommodate the ever-expanding annals.

Immediately within the door of the first Paoline room sat a young priest, undoubtedly one of the esteemed Vatican librarians who screened all the research activities. They submitted their request for late fifth- and early sixth-century archives of papal activities, and without even looking at his computer screen, the priest shook his head.

"We do not have what you seek. Our manuscripts tracked the papacy only from the eleventh century onward," he said authoritatively in perfect, but accented English.

"What about the *Liber diurnus romanorum pontificum* and Codices A, B, and C?"

Alex was startled. How had Declan known precisely what document to request?

"Those codices do date from the eighth century. But you are seeking fifth- and sixth-century documentation of the papacy."

"The *Liber diurnus romanorum pontificum* and the related codices contain *copies* of papal documents from the late fifth century."

The priest smiled, as if they'd passed a test. "They do indeed." The smiled faded. "But the *Liber diurnus* is one of our most important records of the church and our history. I would need to understand your reason for consulting it."

"We have found a manuscript that the *Liber diurnus* may help us in dating to the fifth or sixth century."

The priest looked startled. And impressed. "Excuse me a moment." He pushed back his chair and hastened to a back office, his black robes trailing behind him.

"Why the hell did you tell him about the manuscript?" Alex whispered. Already angry over having to leave her bag with the guard, she was now furious. Declan's impulsive, brash behavior was precisely why she'd hesitated to trust him—with the manuscript and herself. But it was too late.

"He'd never let us look at the *Liber diurnus* without that information. And, anyway, he doesn't have any idea how important the manuscript is. It could be a list of liturgical vestments, for all he knows."

"Dec, he knows that the manuscript is important enough to have some tie to the *Liber diurnus.* I just can't believe you." She shook her head. "Why would you think Decius might be mentioned in it anyway?"

"It holds copies of the official papal documents from the late fifth century through the ninth, things like popes' elections, papal dealings with the other countries, the building and consecration of churches, appointments of church officials, and other important administrative matters. Decius was a key papal scribe recording those sorts of affairs. If we're going to find a reference to Decius, it'll be in there."

The priest returned. "You will have to wait here for Father Casaceli to take you to the *Liber diurnus* and the codices."

ROME, ITALY

PRESENT DAY

Alex and Declan waited for hours for Father Casaceli. When the Vatican guards began locking the doors and shutting the gates in the early afternoon, the young librarian priest informed them that they would have to return the next morning if they wanted to see the *Liber diurnus*. Without a single apology.

Alex retrieved her black bag from the coat check. Strapping it across her shoulder, she stormed out of the Vatican and across the wide yard fronting the complex. Declan chased after her; he didn't need an explanation as to why she was still mad. "Alex, I'm really sorry. But we need to see the *Liber diurnus,* and explaining why was the only way."

"You could have at least asked me first. I might have decided to abandon this whole dating verification. Since this visit has proven to be *so* productive anyway."

Declan pleaded with her: "Please, I know it's hard for you and we don't have a long track record working together, but please trust me. I really have your best interests at heart."

"Don't forget about your own interests. If the manuscript really turns out to be the Book of Kildare, and we really do have the first image of the Virgin Mary, it'll benefit you too."

He refused to back down. "Of course it will. There's no shame in that. Our goals are completely aligned. So why do you think I'd do anything to hurt our success? Or you?"

Once again, Declan was making complete sense. But she still could not surrender to his logic. Was it her own inability to trust or was it a sound internal warning? She didn't know, but she determined to keep her feelings—and decision making—in check.

He then dramatically changed the subject. "We have a free evening in Rome. What would you say to peeking at the Catacomb of Priscilla?"

"Why the Catacomb of Priscilla?" Alex couldn't understand why he'd want to head to one of Rome's oldest catacombs—on the outskirts of the city—when they had so much to accomplish and so little time.

"I think we should take a look at one of the only other contenders for the first Virgin Mary image."

Alex knew that the Roman catacombs were often thought to contain some of the earliest Christian imagery, although there was some evidence of early churches dedicated to Mary. But Alex wasn't up for a tour. "Don't you think the time would be better used in translating?"

"If I promise to get you what you need before Thursday, would you agree to go to the catacombs with me? It's not just a field trip, Alex; it's research."

Before she could say yes—or no—he hailed a cab and they were tearing down the city streets. For a hefty tip, the cab dropped them as close to the catacombs as possible. For another tip to the curator, Declan and Alex cut to the front of the line of tourists waiting to get into the catacombs and descended alone down the staircase into darkness. Alex's nose had to adjust as well as her eyes; the smell of mold and standing water was overwhelming.

Alex must have seemed disoriented because Declan grabbed her hand and expertly led her through crypt after crypt of narrow passageways and low ceilings. She'd been in the ancient catacombs twice before—once as a young tourist and once to study the frescoes deemed to be the earliest Christian art—but she didn't remember the closeness of the crypts or the stagnancy of the air.

Not a moment too soon, they stopped in front of a wall painting of the Virgin Mary holding the Christ child, alleged to be from the third century. The mother and son were not alone. The three Magis bowed to the pair, while one of the kings pointed to a star above Mary, presumably the star of Bethlehem.

"Here she is," Declan said.

Alex had noticed the other figures before, but she hadn't focused on the full nature of the scene. Her new knowledge changed her perception of the painting, as if she were looking at it through a prism. "It's not really a Virgin Mary icon. It's an Adoration of the Magi scene."

"That gets left out of the literature, doesn't it? It's always proclaimed as the first image of the Virgin Mary."

"But I don't think that was the intention of the artist—or its patron. I think the artist was commissioned to paint a biblical scene, one that also included Mary and Jesus. And even if I'm wrong, this Mary was obviously meant to be not a widely disseminated devotional figure but a private picture for the deceased's grieving family."

Declan started pulling Alex through the catacombs toward another image, a mosaic. As they drew closer, Alex saw that it was another mother and child, one declared to be from the fourth or fifth century, depending on the source, and often heralded as another very early Virgin and infant Jesus. Squinting in the dim light, Alex stared at it: the picture indeed more closely resembled a Byzantine Madonna image, but it bore none of the iconographic hallmarks of either the Virgin Mary or the Christ child.

A guard motioned for their departure, and Declan and Alex wove through the catacomb without talking. Once they got outside, Declan hailed another cab. He turned to Alex with a wide grin. "So, do you think we've got the first icon of the Virgin Mary?"

For all her anger earlier that day, she couldn't help but smile back. "I think we just might."

ROME, ITALY

PRESENT DAY

The next morning, Alex and Declan made it to the research desk in the first Paoline room the very moment it opened. But Father Casaceli was already waiting. The older, dour priest had no time for their conversation; he led them toward the *Liber diurnus.*

Father Casaceli guided them into the third Paoline room, though both Alex and Declan doubted that the rare manuscript was stored there. Most delicate documents resided in specially designed, acclimatized rooms. Still, the priest made a show of unlocking one of the poplar cabinets and withdrawing the famous book and its related codices with great delicacy.

Without a word, he indicated that they should sit in one of the study cubicles and put on their sterile gloves. They followed his instructions to the letter, and he finally agreed to place the surprisingly small *Liber diurnus* before them. Father Casaceli pulled up a chair alongside them, and the security guard who had escorted them from room to room remained nearby.

Alex sat back and let Declan take charge. He skimmed the pages with relative ease, commenting from time to time when he came across an interesting tidbit of history. But within an hour and a half, he'd reached the last page. Alex was incredibly disappointed, even though she knew she shouldn't have expected anything. He hadn't found their Decius reference.

"May I see Codex A, Father Casaceli?" Declan asked.

"Not finding anything of interest in the *Liber diurnus*?" Father Casaceli answered.

"It's extremely interesting, Father. I'd love to dig into the sacred rites for electing popes, but I haven't the time, you see? Maybe Codex A will point me in the right direction."

Father Casaceli withdrew the *Liber diurnus* and replaced it in the poplar cabinet. As he laid Codex A before them, he said, with an ill-suited casualness, "Father Lipari tells me you are trying to verify a fifth- or sixth-century manuscript. Perhaps if you tell me a bit about it, I might be able to guide you."

Alex's stomach lurched, but Declan just smiled and turned to Codex A, saying, "I appreciate the offer, but I think I'll just muddle through on my own." As he flipped through the pages, he asked the priest, "So Father Casaceli, do you get many requests for the Gelasian Decree these days? You know, after *The Da Vinci Code*?"

Declan had switched the subject to one near to their hearts—banned Gospels—but also one undoubtedly reviled by Father Casaceli. It was a gamble, but it worked. The priest winced at Declan's deft topic change and abandoned his own line of questioning. "Fortunately, we are a scholarly institution and not a tourist destination. That seems to weed out much of the riffraff seeking imagined church conspiracies and banned Gospels."

"Glad to hear it." They listened to the priest rant on about the conspiracy seekers while Declan turned the pages for another hour. Finally, he paused at a particular page in Codex A, and said, "You'll be glad to hear that we're nearly done taking up your time. I think I've found what we need. Would we be able to get a copy of this page?"

The priest quickly stood up and looked over Declan's shoulder. "You are certain that this is the page you require?"

"Absolutely."

"I should be able to get you a facsimile of that single page within an hour." He picked up Codex A and walked off to speak with one of the librarians on duty.

"What was on that page?" Alex whispered to Declan.

"A late-fifth-century papal formulary of an apostolic exemption for a monastery."

"Fascinating," Alex said sarcastically. "What does it have to do with Decius?"

"It seems our scribe returned to Rome after his time in Ireland and took up his old role as papal scribe. The codex formulary is signed—'so scribed by Decius.' We have our proof."

GAEL

A.D. 471

Brother,

Imbolc came to Cill Dara. The word "Imbolc" means nothing to you, brother, for how could you know of this festival celebrated by a backward people who teeter on the very edge of the world? And how could you, or anyone else, ever imagine that this common fair hailing spring, no doubt grafted onto a Druidic ritual, would so change me? Yet I am transformed.

The winter-darkened Cill Dara enlivened in the days approaching this holiday. The religious and common folk of the abbey grew more animated than I had witnessed over the holy days of the birth of our Lord. Brigid invited me to participate in the ceremonies and revelry along with the rest of the community, and I tried to view it as a fresh chance to assess the unorthodox customs of the Gaels rather than another prospect to be with her. I found it nigh impossible to maintain this perspective.

You see, brother, *anmchara,* my desire for Brigid has not lessened over the days. If anything, watching her power in the grove only enhanced my feelings. Nor has my loathing of Valens abated. Though I

redoubled my efforts at resistance nightly, my feelings returned by daylight.

As to Imbolc, I knew not what to expect. Thus when the day's work
of ended and we entered the refectory, which was aglitter with candles
and resplendent with Cill Dara's finest food and ale, I was astonished
at the splendor. After this repast, the merriment swept me up and out
into the church, where Brigid conducted a particularly beautiful service before the sun set. Brother, I love to watch her preside over the
Mass, staring at her to my heart's content, though I know I should not.

The celebrants began to file out of the church, and I presumed the
festivities had concluded. I'd started to walk in the direction of my hut
when I heard a call.

"Decius, where are you going?"

I turned to see the leviathan Aidan lumbering toward me. "Come
with us to the hilltop, Decius, or you will miss the finest part of the festival," he said. "You must watch the sunrise ceremony with us."

I joined his little assemblage of monk-scribes, and we headed toward
the flat hill that presided over the plains of Cill Dara. As we rounded the
near side of the hill and drew closer to the even crest of the mound, the
sky grew bright. To my amazement, dozens of bonfires raged, and hundreds of people were already sitting in an enormous circle.

Brigid sat in the circle. She gestured for me to join her. While
Aidan and the others found openings elsewhere, I lowered myself to
the narrow space she'd indicated, to her left. Turning to the right, I saw
Valens in the other space flanking Brigid. I thanked God for the darkness of night, for my face would have betrayed me.

Just then, Brigid rose, and the crowd rose along with her. She
walked to the center of the circle as everyone joined hands. She raised
her arms as if performing the rite of transubstantiation on the altar. In
the setting, I expected sacrifices and rituals worthy of the pagan ceremonies of lore. Instead, Brigid invoked the Lord's Prayer and then
asked the participants to pray along with her.

"Glory to you, word. Glory to you, grace," she began.

The assembly responded, "Amen."

"Glory to you, spirit. Glory to you, holy one. Glory to your glory."

"Amen."

"We praise you, Father. We thank you, light, in whom no darkness lives."

"Amen."

The supplications and praise continued on. The words grew more and more familiar, though I could not place them until Brigid said, "I am a lamp to you who see me."

"Amen."

"I am a mirror to you who recognize me."

"Amen."

"I am a door to you who knock on me."

"Amen."

"I am a way to you, passerby."

"Amen."

I identified the phrases then. Brigid was incanting the words from one of the Gospels I'd found hidden in the scriptorium, one that purported to be a song Jesus taught His disciples just before He was crucified—the Round Dance of the Cross. Irenaeus, of course, had banned it centuries ago, but the verses were alive and well in Gael.

As we entered the blackest hours of the night, Brigid stopped speaking and settled next to me. Deep drums reverberated through the frigid air, and melancholy stringed instruments joined them in a song yearning for renewal. While Brigid swayed, her eyes closed in private prayer, I noticed that other celebrants had begun trailing off in pairs toward dark nooks in the plains where the light of the bonfires could not reach. I did not need to guess at their pursuits.

I closed my own eyes and surrendered to the drums' low, sonorous rhythm. I began to experience that sense of submersion I'd felt on my arrival on Gael's shores. This time, however, my vision wavered as if I rushed headlong into the conflagrations, and I felt born of fire, not water. I entered into a pure, elemental state so near God that I comprehended Brigid's blend of the Gaels' ancient rites and the church's new teachings; together, they carried the power to transcend.

Suddenly, I felt a tap on my shoulder. Startled out of my meditative mind-set, I needed a moment to regain my sense of time and place. Finally, I opened my eyes to see Brigid looking into them.

She gestured for me to follow her, and I wondered where—and to what—she would lead. No words passed between us as I tracked her from the fires and the circle. She descended down the far side of the hill, onto the plains, with seeming purpose in her stride.

She arrived at a tiny crescent tucked into the hill. The niche was covered with low bushes, emptied of their leaves by winter's chill. Even so, the recess felt snug and protected against the night. I recognized the place.

Brigid turned to me. "This site holds special meaning for me, Decius."

Brother, I knew not what to say. The spot bore significance for me as well—I often visited it on solitary walks and relived those first few moments with Brigid—but I feared the admission. I feared that it held different importance for her than for me. "It does?"

"Yes. I first spied you from this place."

"I remember well."

"You do?"

"Yes. I saw small movements in the heather, and I thought you were a hare. And then you appeared before me."

She laughed. "So that is why you grew pale when I stood before you. You had expected a rabbit, not a woman. Well, I certainly had not expected a tall Roman to materialize from our Gaelic mist."

I laughed with her, and then grew silent, thinking about the conversation that had followed. "I offended you that day."

She seemed surprised. "You could never offend me, Decius."

"I must apologize, Brigid, for my insolence on that afternoon. I mistook you for a villager, I offended the learnedness of the Gaels with my surprise at your excellent Latin, and I—"

She interrupted me: "Decius, I am the one to offer apologies on this of all days. On Imbolc, we Gaels ask for forgiveness and new beginnings."

I sensed that she wanted to continue, but I needed to speak. "Brigid, if you only knew of my sins. . . . You have done nothing meriting an apology."

"Oh, but I have."

I stared into her face, just able to visualize her aqueous green eyes in the growing light. "Brigid, I am guilty as well."

"In truth?" Her voice was earnest, raw.

"In truth." Without intention, my tone matched hers.

Her eyes searched my face. "Oh, your black eyes are so hard to make out in this dim light. I need to see into them to make certain you can forgive what I confess. This work I ask of you, the Gospel book and the history for Pope Simplicius, I—"

Before she could continue, I interjected: "Brigid, I too have a confession about this work—"

The chant "Brigid" sounded out from the hilltop. The recitation grew louder as a single beam of sunlight shot out over the peak. It illuminated Brigid's face like gilt on vellum.

"We must return to Imbolc, Decius. I am needed for the final prayer of dawn. But please let us continue later, when Imbolc has ended."

In thoughtful silence, we climbed up the hill. Before we reached the summit, with its throngs of celebrants, I asked her one last question: "What of Valens?"

"Valens." She looked at me, her brow knitted in confusion. "What put Valens in your mind?"

By her response, I knew he meant nothing to Brigid, that his place next to her in the Imbolc circle had occurred by happenstance. This was all the reassurance I needed. "It is of no consequence."

We reached the hilltop, and I released Brigid to her people. Brother, my future—nay, my very soul—awaits my conversation continued with Brigid. Pray for me. Please pray for me.

Brother,

Somehow, brother, I returned to the scriptorium and the last of my great Gospels, that of the apostle John, after I finished the words of my last entry to you. Somehow, I pushed to the recesses of my mind the long wait for Brigid. And somehow, our Lord deemed me worthy of letting the words of John overtake me.

Brother, I have spared you the finer details of my illuminations thus far, but I must share the sublime experience of crafting this Gospel book. Gaelic tradition calls for each Gospel to be introduced by a portrait of the evangelist, which faces the opening text of the Gospel with elaborate decoration of the type I have described before. To this convention, I added my own design: I prefaced each evangelist portrait with a full-page painting containing all four evangelist symbols, the lion, the ox, the eagle, and man. By this device, I intended to unify the emblems of the Gospel book and to emphasize their cohesive message. If nothing else I undertake in my life brings Him joy, I pray that this celebration of His Word—displayed in my own melding of Roman craft and Gaelic artistry—pleases Him. I hope my delight is not sinful vanity alone.

When the light waned, I gazed up from the page for the first time in hours. As I scanned the empty room, I appreciated that the other monks had left the scriptorium for the evening meal. In my creative fervor, their departure had gone unnoticed.

I finished the final brushstroke of the multilayered lattice border around the evangelist symbols. As I began returning to safe storage the metalwork samples I used for inspiration, I touched the golden torc Brigid had loaned me as a guide for the delicate scrollwork I planned for John's portrait page. I thought about the curve of her neck in which the torc rested. My mind brimmed with thoughts of Brigid, and I wondered what kept her from me that very moment. I began to imagine the unusual life we might fashion together, pairing our devotion to each other with our devotion to sharing our Lord's message.

I felt a tap on my shoulder, and I jumped. I turned around with a smile, thinking that Brigid had snuck into the scriptorium before the meal began. Yet Brigid's countenance did not greet me—Valens's did.

His grin wiped the smile from my own face. Though I no longer seethed at the sight of him, I did not relish a conversation with him either. "Valens, you startled me. I did not realize anyone remained in the scriptorium."

His smile stayed in place. "You seemed rather lost in your work."

"When the Word moves through you, the world recedes. But surely you understand."

"Yes, of course. May I see the page that so fixated you?"

Brother, I wondered at his motive, as he had never before shown

the least interest in my work. Nevertheless, in my newfound munifi-
cence, I wanted to oblige. At least until Brigid summoned me.

I turned toward my worktable. As I peeled back the protective
parchment from my page celebrating the four evangelists, I heard him
whisper, "Gallienus sends his regards."

I froze. I wanted Valens's words to vanish into the air, desired his
own disappearance.

He said the reviled words louder: "Gallienus send his regards."

I had no choice but to face Valens. "Gallienus?"

The smile was gone. "Yes, Decius. Gallienus sent me to Gael to collect your evidence." So this was the means of conveying the fruits of
my mission to Rome.

"The evidence for Gallienus?" Brother, I stumbled over every word
as if I were an infant learning to speak. He must have thought me ob-
tuse, but I knew not what to say.

"Yes, Decius, the evidence that the Abbey of Kildare practices a
heretical form of Christianity," he said with impatience and irritation.

I collected myself. "So that the church might replace Gael's religious leaders and unite the land under the true faith in tribute to the
emperor?"

"Or offer Gael to the barbarians if the emperor falls and the church
needs to present an inducement to maintain its standing. . . . I am certain Gallienus will use Gael in whatever manner he deems most polit-
ically profitable," Valens said with a shrug.

I could not believe my ears. "Hand Gael over to the barbarians?"

Brother, you have seen from my letters that doubts about the god-
liness of my mission have plagued me for some time. I had attributed
my qualms to my allegiance to the Gaels, and to Brigid, of course. At
that moment, I identified another source of my unease, and I realized
I could never do Gallienus's bidding.

"Do you have the evidence?" Valens insisted.

"I, I—"

Brother, God blessed me in that moment. For with a bang, the door
to the scriptorium slammed open, and in Niall lumbered. I have never
wanted to embrace the prickly keeper of the scriptorium before, but I
gladly would have done so then.

"What are you two doing in here?" he bellowed.

"Finishing up," Valens answered for us both.

"Hurry then. Brigid has been asking for you, Decius."

I thanked Niall and hurried to take my leave. Valens did the same, and whispered as we walked: "I will come to your hut tonight to collect the evidence and you. A ship awaits us on the nearest coast."

Niall grabbed Valens's arm. "I am not done with you, Valens. I noticed that your worktable was untidy when you retired to the refectory last evening, and I want to make sure that—"

Brother, I seized the chance the Lord provided, and I ran into the night. To Brigid.

Brother,

Brigid awaited me. The moment I closed the door of her hut behind me, we were silent, though we each had much to say. Our earlier approach toward boldness had made us shy.

Yet I knew we must begin. So I closed my eyes, let my reserve and caution slip away, and started. Brother, I told her *nearly* everything: the reason for my journey to Gael, the truth behind my nighttime visits to the scriptorium, the real destination and use for her Gospel book and abbey history, the details found in my report to Gallienus, the location of the stone under which I secreted my evidence against her and Gael. I even told her of Valens, and of Gael's role in the impending power struggle between Rome and the barbarians. Holding back only my deepest feelings toward her, I laid bare my soul, and waited.

She was quiet throughout my confession. This quiet state, so unnatural for one so forthright, unnerved me. I had expected a warrior's rage and an angry withdrawal of her affections. Or worse, if I could conceive of worse. Instead, she smiled with such tenderness I thought perhaps she'd neither heard nor comprehended my words.

I started to repeat my admission, but she interrupted me with a finger to her lips. "Decius, there is no need. I know who you are. I have always known."

"You know?"

"Yes. From the moment I saw you stride across the plains of Cill Dara with determination in your Roman eyes rather than the exhaustion of subjugation, I knew. I'd thought Rome would send you sooner. I'd waited long for you."

"You do not hate me then?"

She looked shocked at the question. "Hate you for doing the hard duty your church asked of you? Hate you for performing a dangerous task you believed would serve God? I do not hate you for the truth, Decius; I admire you for it."

"Admire me?"

She smiled. "Yes, Decius, I admire you. I admire your veneer of reserve and the way it shatters when your righteousness bursts forth like a spring too long underground. I admire your keen, curious mind and your talent with the brush. And I—" She stopped abruptly, but looked deeply into my eyes with a mixture of longing and regret. I saw that she loved me as I did her.

Yet if I'd ever thought that Brigid and I might profess feelings for each other despite our vows, I knew then that I was wrong. I felt the possibility of a life with her drain away from me, and I realized that our feelings must be made stronger and more constant by our shared silence—and our dedication to God.

She paused and looked away, her eyes growing unfocused and distant. "I hope you can say the same of me once you have learned *my* truth."

Brother, I could not imagine that her deeds could be worse than mine. I looked into her face. "No words that you utter can change my admiration for you."

"Your admiration for me . . ." She sighed and said, "Decius, I chose you to create the Gospel book and the history of the Abbey of Cill Dara because I knew the truth of your presence here among us. Though I may have intended your Gospel book to leave Gael as an honorarium for Pope Simplicius, I never intended the history to leave Gael at all. The history was for you alone."

"For me?"

"Yes. I only hoped that hearing our story—the story of my people and our God—would sway you to return to Rome and persuade your church leaders."

"Persuade them of what?"

"Persuade them that, though different, our brand of Christianity is true. Persuade them that we Gaels should continue on our own path, be it religion or rule. With Valens's arrival and his words, I see now that they will never be so persuaded."

"You do not know that for certain, Brigid."

"One need not be a prophetess to see that change is coming." Her head dropped down. "I am sorry for my duplicity."

This time I was silent. She had deceived me. Yet I could not be angry with her, not when I looked into her eyes and saw that she had lied to me out of love for God and her people. I could not rage at her for her dishonesty when I knew her to be just in her motives.

"You have no reason to be sorry."

"You do not hate me then?" she asked me, as I had asked her.

I responded in kind. "Hate you for performing a dangerous task you believed would serve God? I do not hate you for the truth, Brigid; I admire you for it."

We smiled at each other in relief. As our smiles subsided, however, so went our mirth; the immediacy of our circumstances forced our happy reprieve to be short-lived.

Brother, I needed to speak the unspoken. "I will not go with Valens," I told Brigid. "I will not give him that which Gallienus seeks."

She searched my eyes. "Are you certain, Decius? I would not want you to act against your conscience because of your feelings for me alone. Forget not that life is short but our Lord's eternity is long."

"Brigid, I believe the religion of your people to be nearer His purpose than Rome's creed. Pardon my bluntness, but I act for my conscience, not for you."

"Truly?"

"Truly."

"I am well pleased, Decius. Nothing brings me greater joy than your shared conviction, not even my lost hopes that Rome would grant us Gaels leave to continue as we go."

"Lose not your hopes, Brigid. Perhaps we can fashion a way to re-claim some shred of them."

"You would jeopardize all to help me? To help us?"

"Yes, I believe it is why He sent me here. And furthermore, I need to hear the end of the history, do I not?" I said with a grin. We had come close to completing the abbey history in recent days.

She smiled back. "You do indeed."

"Before we return to our roles as abbess and scribe, I must address Valens."

"Yes, you must. What will you do?"

"I think it best if you leave that to us two Romans." With the great-est of difficulty, brother, I left her and reentered the night.

Brother, I cannot imagine your reaction to the seeming rashness—perhaps the apparent foolhardiness—of your normally cautious younger brother. Please know this, for whatever small comfort it might offer: I feel in my soul that this is His course. Pray for me, brother, please.

Brother,

I waited in my hut for Valens. I assumed the penitential position of prayer, hoping that it would bring me much-needed strength for my dealings with Gallienus's messenger. For His strength I would need in abundance.

Deluging myself with our Lord's prayer, I let the words of Jesus Christ still my racing heart and mind. Silently chanting the sustaining "Give us this day our daily bread," I entered a state of tranquillity so deep that I barely heard the creak of my door or the footsteps of Valens. I became aware of his presence only when he spoke.

"Bolstering yourself for the vagaries and hardships of the long jour-ney, I see." Valens's voice revealed a disdain toward my prayers that I did not like.

I struggled up from the floor with difficulty. Maintaining the rigid position of the cross had seared my limbs, a small reminder of all Christ had suffered for us and the least I could endure for all I asked of Him. "I could see no better way to prepare for our meeting."

"Indeed. Let us make haste. Ready yourself."

"I am ready."

Valens scanned the small space. "I do not see your bags."

"No."

"No matter. I can understand why you desire to bring little of this godforsaken place back to Rome."

"I imagine you would think that." Brother, I could not resist the small gibe, though Valens was too arrogant to recognize it.

"Come, we have not the time for leisurely conversation. Secure Gallienus's report and let us go. The ship will wait only for this night."

"I do not have the evidence assembled."

"What do you mean? You have had nearly a year here."

"Gallienus did not give me to understand that my time would be so short. I have only begun my search for heresy."

"What have you done with these long months?"

"As I was instructed. I integrated myself into the Cill Dara community and secured their trust, so that all sacrileges may be revealed to me. Did you think that this would occur immediately upon my landing?"

He was incredulous. "So you have nothing for me, nothing for Gallienus."

"Only what you have witnessed with your own eyes."

"That Brigid presides over the Mass?"

"Yes."

"Her unorthodox transubstantiation is not enough to topple this miserable land. What am I to say to Gallienus? He will be beyond displeased with you, and you know how he manifests even his simple displeasures."

"Tell him the additional time will bear the necessary fruit. Haste will only deliver unto him a fraction of what he seeks."

"The church may not have the time you seek. I doubt the barbarians will linger patiently at Rome's gates until you disembark from the next ship from Gael." He seethed.

"If the church wants Gael, it must wait."

Valens shook his head. I could see that only the constraining situation and his need to rush tempered his anger. "I hope she is worth the risk of delay."

"What do you mean?"

"Brigid."

Brother, I froze. I knew not how to respond. Did he know what had passed between us, or was he baiting me?

Valens saw my discomfort and continued, delighting in this torment. "I see how your eyes follow her across the room and stare at her on the altar. She is fetching. It almost makes me wish Gallienus had assigned me your mission rather than my own."

"You do not know of what you speak."

"Not to worry, Decius. I will deliver your stated message to Gallienus, not my own suspicions. I will do this not because I like you or believe you, but because I care too much for my own neck to be the bearer of such bad news. But you best board the next ship we send for you, or I will make certain we deliver another monk to do your work. Perhaps a monk like me."

Brother, the moment I was certain of Valens's departure, I hastened back to Brigid to begin our true work. Though the Lord delivered to me the strength for which I prayed, He did not deliver much time.

Pray for me, brother, and for Brigid, if you will. I will pray for you, as always.

Decius

GAEL

A.D. 471

BRIGID: A LIFE

Imbolc arrives in Cill Dara. Though Brigid has strived hard to elimi-
nate or soften the traditional pagan rituals of her people, particularly
since the arrival of Decius, she knows she cannot ask them to part
with Imbolc. Forsaking the springtime festival that honors the Dagda
and his daughter the goddess Brigid, above all, would alienate those on
the fringes of her flock—and lessen her perceived power.

With the Mass and the feast over, at midnight the people retire to
the flat hill looming over the plains of Cill Dara. Brigid takes her place
at the center of a large circle, noting with mixed emotions that Decius
joins the crowd. She extends her arms as if performing the familiar rite
of transubstantiation at the altar and invokes a number of traditional
Christian prayers. Then she utters the banned words of the Round
Dance of the Cross, words that have become familiar to her people
from years of Imbolc celebrations but are inaccessible to most Christians. The mysterious words speak to her—and her followers—much
as the poems of the beloved Gaelic bards do.

Her work finished, Brigid settles into a place in the circle next to

Decius. At first, his presence distracts her, but in time, she loses herself to the throaty beat of the drums and the otherworldly strum of the harps. She enters a state of prayer so deep she does not call it prayer. It feels like direct communion with God.

Without warning, Brigid awakens from her transcendence. An epiphany has descended upon her during her deep contemplative state. Tapping Decius's shoulder, she draws him away from the circle. She knows where she must go and what she must do.

Talk seems sacrilegious to Brigid. They walk in silence until they reach a secluded niche tucked into a hill behind an expanse of heather: the place where she first saw Decius. Standing before him, she readies herself to admit all. She knows not why He directs her to undertake the very act that would seem to destroy her plans—yet she knows she must confess or lose everything.

Emboldened, Brigid says, "This site holds special meaning for me, Decius."

His eyes widen in surprise and flicker with hope. In that moment, Brigid realizes that Decius shares her feelings. "It does?" he answers, sounding hesitant and fearful.

They are scared to rush along the clear pathway to the truth. So they delay, laughing over that first moment. Yet deep within Brigid, an inexplicable urgency propels her onward.

"I have not been honest," she says.

"I am guilty as well."

"In truth?"

"In truth."

Yet she knows that He asks more of her—and less. "Decius, this work I ask of you, the Gospel book and the history for Pope Simplicius—"

He interrupts: "Brigid, I too have a confession about this work—"

Brigid knows full well the nature of his confession, for her own lies encapsulate it like a seed. She squares her shoulders, ready to cut through the dishonesties and obfuscations like a plow through thick soil. For she senses that He awaits them both on the other side.

Satan lurks in their brief delay. The chant "Brigid" calls out from the hilltop. The people are summoning their abbess and the goddess. Brigid and Decius heed the call, putting off the moment when they will be free to heed each other, which she prays will be soon.

Her prayer goes unanswered, as duties prevail for hours after the close of Imbolc. When she is finally able to summon Decius, the wait for his arrival seems unbearable. Brigid paces the floor of her quarters. Her steps are so anxious and heavy, it seems to her that her route leaves a trench in the dirt floor. She knows not what He will call her to do when Decius arrives, but she wants to follow where He leads. And she prays that He will permit Decius to join her on her course.

A knock sounds. Brigid hesitates before opening it. Smoothing her hair and straightening her robes, she stares into the reflective surface of the silver pitcher on her table, an act of sinful vanity unpracticed for many long years. She is surprised at the peaceful countenance that stares back at her, an expression that hides the turmoil of her heart, mind, and soul. Only then does she rush to pull the door ajar.

Decius awaits her, his face bright and eager against the pitch black of the night. She wants to fall into his arms, to surrender after so long at playing the imperturbable goddess. And she sees that he wishes the same. But she knows that her vows prevent her—prevent them.

So they make their confessions. He reveals his true purpose, and she divulges hers. And though they keep their feelings unspoken, they are patent. Still, they share private relief that they are of like mind—and heart.

Decius dispatches with Valens and buys them time. Though Brigid understands that the time allotted to them by the Lord and by the Roman Church may be short, she finds it hard to speed through the minutes with Decius. She wants to savor every glance, every heartfelt exchange, every shared effort on the Gospel book, every walk through the fields, and every touch. Only prayer gives her strength to keep her vows, though Brigid often wonders whether He truly begrudges their union.

Yet it seems that He does.

DUBLIN, IRELAND

PRESENT DAY

Alex had doubted Declan's motives and the wisdom of his suggestions, but he turned out to be right. Again and again.

They returned to Dublin Wednesday evening triumphant and pleased. But Alex's early-morning meeting with Sister Mary required that they throw themselves into work. Declan tackled the last half of his rough translation of the life, and Alex devoted herself to a preliminary appraisal of the manuscript.

The more she wrote about it, the more convinced she became that she had indeed discovered the lost Book of Kildare and more. She now believed that the masterful late-fifth-century Book of Kildare had served not only as the model for the famous Book of Kells but also contained the first known image of the Virgin Mary.

Alex looked at the clock. It was after three A.M. Her train to Kildare left in less than three hours, and she still had her room at the Shelbourne to pack. And Declan still wasn't done translating.

"I've got to get back to my hotel. How far have you gotten?" she asked Declan.

"I still have about a quarter of the life left to translate. And I haven't even touched the letters yet, except for those first few pages."

"What am I going to do? My appraisal seems questionable—at best—without the full translations of the life and the letters attached."

Declan stood up and placed his hands squarely on her shoulders. For a moment, Alex didn't know if he was going to kiss her or shake her. "Alex, I don't think there's anything in the last few pages of the life or in the letters that could change your conclusions. You *have* found the Book of Kildare and the first icon of the Virgin Mary." He handed her the life and the letters, and a printout of his rough partial translation. "Anyway, I'll finish up once you've run all this by Sister Mary, right?"

"Right. Assuming she forgives me."

Alex packed the three texts and their work carefully in her bag, and started walking toward the door. Before she reached the foyer, Declan pulled on his coat to escort her back to the hotel. He asked, "Have you thought about the possibility that Sister Mary may not want to sell the book?"

"Yes, and I wouldn't be surprised. Even though she'd probably get a small fortune for it at auction, she might want to build a shrine to it herself, right in Kildare. Just like she wants to do with Saint Brigid."

"No, I mean have you considered that she might not want to go public with it?"

"No." For Alex, whose personal religion revolved around uncovering and freeing past secrets, the very notion of keeping such knowledge hidden was inconceivable.

"Alex, Sister Mary might not like the description of the strong-willed, nearly defiant Brigid; Brigid comes across as only paying lip service to Rome but really following her own agenda. Not to mention, Sister Mary might object to her beloved Brigid's reference to the Gospel of Mary the Mother."

"I cannot fathom Sister Mary making that decision. You don't know her."

"But what if she does?"

"What are you suggesting, Declan?"

"I'm suggesting that you consider alternatives."

With a sudden, resounding clarity, Alex comprehended Declan's endgame. The betrayal she'd feared—suspected—from the beginning stood before her. She guessed that he'd planned it from the start, so-lidifying it with their trip to Rome and his attempts at intimacy. Her internal radar had been right all along. But she wanted him to say it out loud. "Like what?"

"Like not returning the book."

"And doing what with it instead?"

"We could unveil it as our own discovery sometime down the road. Sister Mary doesn't even know it exists, after all."

She baited him a bit more, to make absolutely certain of his proposal. "I see. And you'd know how to go about doing that?"

"I know some people."

She couldn't pretend a moment longer. "I told you from the beginning that I planned on returning the book to Sister Mary once I'd studied it. I would never consider keeping it."

"Never? Don't tell me you've never thought about it?"

Alex shook her head. In truth, she hadn't. She'd been more worried about preserving her relationship with Sister Mary upon the book's return, so the nun would give Alex the chance to reveal the Book of Kildare to the world as her discovery.

She slipped her old stoicism over her wound. "Thank you very much for your services, Declan. I'll make sure you get credit for your translation and your research assistance. And, of course, you'll be paid. Just send me a bill for your time." She slammed the door behind her.

KILDARE, IRELAND

PRESENT DAY

Alex watched as the undertaker shoveled dirt into the open grave. The other nuns wept quietly for Sister Augustine, but she wondered if they had really known her. Maybe they cried for the woman Sister Augustine wanted them to think she was, a quiet religious, bookish, and an obedient passive vessel, like the Virgin or the Brigid they imagined.

Alex's hair stuck to her cheeks as she peered out from under her umbrella and looked deep into the grave site. The undertaker's shovel had left a deep scar in the wet earth. Inexplicably, tears joined the rain on her face. Alex wondered for whom she was crying. Sister Augustine? Herself? Brigid? All the other women who had to refashion themselves to fit society's mold? Or the women whom society refashioned, like the Virgin Mary?

She jumped when a finger tapped her shoulder. It was Sister Mary, her face bereft of tears. "The loss of Sister Augustine seems to have upset you, Miss Patterson."

"Death is a sad business, isn't it?"

"Not for believers, Miss Patterson. I rejoice that Sister Augustine has entered the presence of the Lord."

"I suppose the thought must console."

"You don't believe, Miss Patterson?"

"I'm not sure what I believe anymore, Sister Mary."

Sister Mary looked Alex up and down, but did not offer any gesture of comfort. "Why don't we go to my office, Miss Patterson. I can get you a cup of tea, and you can tell me what you've discovered about my relics."

They walked in silence from the graveyard to the community center. The rain continued its merciless lashing, but Sister Mary seemed impervious. Alex supposed that years of Irish rain, as well as decades of painful convent realities, had made her resistant to many hardships. Neither spoke until Alex had a steaming teacup in her hand and they faced each other across Sister Mary's desk.

"I have a confession to make, Sister Mary."

"I'm not a priest, Miss Patterson."

"It's you to whom I must confess, not a priest."

For once, Sister Mary didn't know what to say. She started and then halted, finally saying, "Well then, I won't stop you."

"I did a thorough examination of your chalice, paten, and reliquary and some intensive research in Dublin, and I was able to confirm that all three hail from the late fifth century."

Sister Mary's eyes gleamed. "That is welcome news, indeed. Even better than my sixth-century attribution, I'm guessing. Though I'm confused about why you're calling it a confession, Miss Patterson."

"Because of the way I was able to make my conclusive determination."

"I don't understand."

"Your reliquary contains a false bottom. Within that space, I found an ancient illuminated manuscript. I took it to Dublin for analysis without telling you."

Rather than explain further, Alex handed Sister Mary everything: the Book of Kildare, the life and the letters, Declan's partial translation of the life, and her appraisal. Then she waited.

She averted her eyes as Sister Mary slowly turned the vellum folio pages of the Book of Kildare, the life, and the letters. When the nun put them aside and took up the appraisal and the translation, Alex stood up and stared out the window. Anything not to witness the religious woman beholding the evidence of her duplicity.

"Miss Patterson?"

Alex spun around to see Sister Mary's smiling face. Confused and astonished at the nun's contented reaction, she said nothing.

"Thank you for finding our Book of Kildare, our Brigid, and our Virgin Mary."

Not trusting herself to remain standing, Alex sat back down in her chair. "You're not furious?"

"Well, you might've asked permission before you took our fifth-century manuscript off the grounds. But you brought it back, didn't you? And I bet you always planned to—am I right?" Sister Mary gave Alex a knowing look, with one eyebrow cocked.

"You're right."

"All's well that ends well, Miss Patterson. And we've ended very well indeed."

"How would you like to proceed? Would you like me to get a colleague to finish the appraisal? I can find an expert to complete the translation, if you like."

"Why on earth would I want anyone but you? Don't be ridiculous. I want you to finalize your appraisal, oversee the translation, and I want you to find a proper buyer."

"So you still want to sell?"

"Can you imagine the good our order can do with the proceeds of this sale?"

The nun was exultant. Alex didn't want to deflate her hopes, but she needed to make certain that Sister Mary really understood the ramifications of the Book of Kildare.

"You want to sell even though the life depicts a very different Brigid from the one you know? A Brigid who didn't always follow the Roman Church's rule?"

"The life's Brigid may not be my Brigid, but maybe she's the real Brigid. Perhaps she's a better Brigid." Sister Mary smirked. "And you know I don't always agree with Rome."

Alex was so relieved she started sobbing uncontrollably.

Sister Mary walked over to Alex's chair and placed a reassuring hand on her shoulder. "It seems you needed to make a confession after all, Miss Patterson. Even though it's unnecessary, if you feel that you are in need of absolution, I'll grant it to you. Particularly since I have a confession of my own."

Alex peered out at the kneeling nun through her interlaced fingers. "You do?"

"I knew about the reliquary's false bottom. I knew that the Book of Kildare lay inside."

Alex stared at the nun. Instead of remorse, she began to feel the rumblings of anger. "Why didn't you tell me?"

"I am the keeper of the Book of Kildare. I took a vow of silence about its existence."

"You must have known that my research would uncover it. Why did you let me discover it?"

"It is time for the Book of Kildare to be revealed to the world. It is time for the world to see what our Brigid was capable of—what the early Irish Christians were capable of. But my vow prohibited me from telling you about it directly. So I prayed and prayed that you would find it on your own." She crossed herself. "And He answered my prayers."

"So you obeyed the letter—if not the spirit—of your vow?" Alex was now furious at having been used by the nun.

Sister Mary flashed Alex a hostile look. "That breach is between me and God." Her look softened. "We each have practiced our own deceptions, Miss Patterson. Maybe we can agree to forgive each other as we work together on the Book of Kildare."

Alex gave Sister Mary a hard once-over. How could she stay angry at the nun for her lies of omission when she herself had practiced dishonesty? And didn't she want desperately to finish what she'd started with the Book of Kildare? "Maybe we can."

"Good. I hope you will be well pleased with your decision, especially when you finish the translation of the life and the letters."

"What do you mean?" Alex wasn't thrilled with the specter of another surprise.

"I have never read the life or the letters myself, though I'd heard about them from Sister Augustine. They have been hidden away by an earlier keeper, as you saw. Maybe she wanted to conceal the heretical texts but couldn't bear to destroy something so very close to our Brigid. I don't know. In any event, they were lost in plain sight, in a manner of

speaking. But I am so thankful that you discovered them, as they seem
to confirm what the keepers' oral tradition has long told us. And I know
the world would never believe mere words passed down from one nun
to another for over a thousand years. As we saw when we tried to pass
down some of the history to Giraldus Cambrensis more than nine hundred years ago."

Alex was astonished by Sister Mary's mention of Giraldus, the very
same twelfth-century historian whose description of what must have
been the Book of Kildare Declan had read to her only days ago. The
pieces began to fit together. But she hoped that Sister Mary wasn't
going to wait until the completion of the translation to tell her the
story. "What does the keepers' tradition say?"

"Our history tells us that the Book of Kildare reflects the making of
a saint and an icon—the Virgin Mary. It demonstrates the dedication
of two early Christian figures—Brigid and a Roman scribe—to fashion
a female image worthy of worship, against the opposition of the
Roman Church."

Alex whispered, "The life and letters indeed support your oral tradition."

Sister Mary smiled a smile Alex would've described as mischievous
if she didn't know better. "But our tradition never told us that Brigid's
image of the Virgin Mary was based on the text that converted her to
Christianity—the Gospel of Mary the Mother."

GAEL

A.D. 471

Brother,

So it began, my dear brother. So began the moment that changed all subsequent moments. So began the months that altered me for all eternity, as God alone knows. So began my genuine time with Brigid.

On that first evening, we did not begin our real work, our true calling, as we have both come to think of it. No, on that first evening, Brigid finished the abbey history, a vital prelude to our work.

What is this "real work"? I can hear you ask impatiently. To what labor could He possibly call you that would compel you to abandon your fidelity to the Roman Church, even if the church would trade Gael to the hated barbarians? Knowing your proclivities, I imagine that you could almost condone my disloyalty if it had involved revelation and consummation of my feelings for Brigid. I am sorry to disappoint you on both fronts.

Brother, I am loath to describe our work with my words rather than His, for I fear I cannot do it justice. Or for fear that committing our mission to parchment will somehow endanger it. Yet, for you, I shall try.

How the final chapters of her history moved me. I will tell you of a young Gaelic woman, noble and warrior-born, educated by tutors and exposed to Druidism and Christianity. I will tell you of a young woman entranced by this Jesus but mystified by the absence of women in His world, when women were so prevalent and powerful in hers. I will tell you of a young woman given a rare, perhaps singular manuscript by her mother, the Gospel of Mary the Mother. I will tell you how the Mary of this Gospel—bold, brave, learned, and convinced of her special role—led this young woman to Him and secured her place alongside Him. I will tell you of a young woman asked to become a savior of her people—to preserve the Gaels if she could, or protect womankind if she could not. And I will tell you of a young woman who said yes.

That young woman became my Brigid, and her charge became my own.

Brigid came to understand, brother, that she could not shield her people and their ways from Rome and the barbarians. I fought her conviction at first, but in my heart, I knew she was right. It pained me, as it pained her, that she could not deliver the gift of shelter to the Gaels. Yet her people had entrusted her with another care: womankind. I became determined to assist her—in preserving some glimmer of her fading Gaelic culture, rough, proud, and imperfect as it is, and in thwarting Gallienus's total victory over this land, whether he seeks it through Roman rule or barbarian domination. And if I could help her achieve this by helping her preserve and exalt women, so be it.

Yet we danced round and round the means to meet this exigent charge. Until our Lord showed us the way.

"I know I will not be remembered as I am, Decius. Strong, generous, bold, some would even say capable of rule and compassion in equal measures," Brigid told me with a falsely modest smile and a wink. Then a dark shadow crossed her face, as if the hut's light had changed. "This does not sadden me. What saddens me is that, as with all women, I will not be remembered at all in the rising tide of the Roman Church—much as Irenaeus's Gospels pass over my Mary in silence, relegating her to a scant few phrases and ignoring her intellect and power as witnessed by the full Gospels."

"Not so, Brigid. You will be recollected," I hastened to reassure her, though I knew not how.

She laughed. "Decius, if the church deems Jesus Christ's own mother worthy of only a few lines of canonical text, we can be certain I will garner less recognition and even less commemoration."

Brigid rose from her chair and began walking around her hut with restless agitation. She had been born—and groomed—to act, and act she could not. I said nothing. Brother, what could I offer other than empty consolation?

"What of Mary . . ." Her voice trailed off, and her eyes grew distracted. She continued her amble around the hut, though with diminished agitation and with increasing intensity of gaze.

"What do you mean?"

"I know better than to strive for dissemination of her Gospel; Irenaeus made certain of its suppression. But what of preserving Mary's essence? What of securing some reverence of women through her?"

"By what manner?"

"To start, we must abandon all hope that we will propagate Mary's real self or her actual Gospel. We must suppress all desire to share her natural intelligence, her supreme conviction in her own anointedness, her education among the holy of holies in the Jerusalem Temple, where no woman had been schooled before, and her intimate relationship with Jesus Christ as His Mother, the one human being permitted to correct and instruct Him—the one human being whose counsel He sought."

"How will we share this modified Mary with other believers?"

She turned to me with a smile. "We must create an image, Decius."

I watched as Brigid paced around the room once again, muttering to herself and gesticulating in the air. "What form will this image take?" I asked.

Her eyes met mine, and I saw within them such fervent light. Brother, it took my breath away. "We shall emblazon upon all Roman Christians a Mary they will comprehend and embrace. Since purity is so prized by the Roman Church, we will emphasize her virginity and cleanse our new Mary well, washing her of all boldness and forming her into a beloved passive vessel. Decius, we must create an image that all people, illiterate and erudite alike, will worship."

"What will we create?"

"Let us call her the Virgin Mary."

Yet Brother, this epiphany was only the beginning. Pray for me, brother.

Brother,

The precise form of our Virgin Mary eluded us for ten days. Ten days in which we settled on one image only to supplant it with another. Ten days in which Brigid grew increasingly disheartened about our ever capturing some quintessence of her Mary, however infinitesimal compared to her total glory, in a likeness that would appeal to Rome and its people.

On the morn of that fateful tenth day, Brigid paced across her hut in the fitful tread that had become routine since we'd embarked on this work. She clasped in her hand the delicate yet worn copy of the Gospel of Mary the Mother passed down to her from her own mother, and she read aloud passages from it in the hopes of inspiring in us His vision of Mary.

Yet we were sheep caught between two rams, to use a phrase of Brigid's; we wanted desperately to share the Mary who had drawn Brigid to Christ, but we knew that the church's condemnation of the very Gospel depicting the empowered Mary and her Son with loving intimacy constrained that effort.

Brigid's face drooped from exhaustion. I knew she toiled through the night to accomplish the abbey work she could not tend to while daylight reigned and our work could proceed. Stopping her constant pacing, she lowered herself to her knees in front of her small altar. I heard her begin to chant in prayer. I could not abide watching her offer supplications alone, so I put aside my scribe's instruments and knelt next to her. She reached out for my hand, and our voices joined and rose to our Lord.

As our prayers lifted into the air, I felt the unusual compulsion to open my eyes, an act I typically shun during worship. My eyes fluttered open, and my gaze settled on the wall shelf near Brigid's altar. My vision fixed on the statue of Horus and Isis resting toward the back, the one I had noted on my first visit to Brigid's hut but had paid little attention to since.

Brother, as I stared at that pagan figurine, the Spirit inexplicably passed through me, and I knew precisely how to proceed. I immediately rose from the altar and sat at my scribe's chair. I threw aside the rejected scraps of parchment littered about the desk and grabbed my brush. It moved furiously across the rough page without any strain or thought on my part.

Before my eyes, a serene and confident Mary, seated on a richly decorated, high-backed throne, appeared on the blank parchment. Draped across her lap, a youthful yet knowing infant Christ materialized, facing left. He reached out toward His mother with his left hand and, with his right, clasped her own.

My hand continued on as if of its own accord, framing the mother and child's throne with the wings of four ethereal angels. My brush enclosed the figures with a very Gaelic border of swirling forms and shapes. I believe that my brush might have persisted in its creations, but its inspired handiwork halted when Brigid appeared at my side.

I dared not look at her. Though I sensed that this image was different, special perhaps, I feared further disappointing her. Instead, I stepped back and stared at the painting, a rendering which I intended to fill with brilliant color. Brother, I saw it anew, as though I had not been its creator. I felt almost as though I had tapped into the divine "image" described by the banned Gospel of Thomas, as the way to discover the divine within us and the kingdom of God here on earth.

"It is perfect, Decius," Brigid whispered.

"Truly?" I turned toward her, surprised that I had so contented her. Her green eyes brimmed with tears.

"Truly. You can feel her human spirit and her divinity at once, as though they were one and the same. I see all the tenderness and trust and respect between the Mother and Child described in the Gospel of Mary the Mother, yet none could call it profane. It does not diminish His divinity to show her maternal feelings and His childlike love for and dependence on her. It is beautiful, and none could object to it."

I said, "I hope my work does justice to your vision and goal."

"Oh, my Decius, your Virgin Mary and Christ child achieves much more than my paltry aspirations. You have even hinted at her power by enthroning her. More than that, even. She is literally the throne upon which He sits, the source of His power just as He is the source of hers." She smiled at me. "Though none might intuit that message but us. And those who are seeking it."

I looked down at my creation, and appreciated that God's own hand must have guided that aspect of the depiction. For I had not knowingly aimed to that end.

"Does it not bother you that it harkens to the Horus and Isis image?" I asked, nodding toward the small statue on her shelf.

"No. The divine endeavors to course through all peoples and religions, Decius. It is only in Christianity that it has best found its home."

"As long as the Roman Church does not spy the likeness and reject it on that basis alone."

"I am not troubled. The Roman Church leaders will undoubtedly see your Mary's throne not as the empowerment it truly represents— for the Egyptian gods' and pharaohs' claim to royalty flowed through their mothers' veins—but as her virginal claim to the throne through her Son. In any event, we will endeavor to make our Mary and Child different enough to avoid seeing the similarity, will we not?"

I smiled. Here was the Brigid I knew, charming and demanding at once. "We will indeed, Brigid."

"Decius, you have brought me such a gift. You have delivered unto me sweet relief that Mary might be remembered, perhaps even revered. Maybe one day, when the world is ready, she will be fully recalled and resurrected, if you will. And womankind along with her."

Brother, what you must think of me? I break with my beloved Rome, though secretly. I stray from the dictates of my church, in private. I even endeavor to deceive Rome and her church to meet the objectives of a *woman* living on the outer edge of the known world, in the utmost concealment. What have I become? you must ask.

Of this alone, I am certain: Through my brush, I have become His instrument. Pray, pray for me brother.

Decius

GAEL

A.D. 471

BRIGID: A LIFE

With Decius at her side, Brigid settles into the most blessed chapter of her life, and the most despairing. While they are free to revel in each other's company without a wall of secrets separating them, a new barrier looms—Decius's departure. And while they collaborate on the Gospel book with renewed vigor, their creative energies prove barren—for they realize that Decius cannot return to Rome as a willing ambassador to Gael's greatness with the masterwork gospel book in hand. Gallienus will never embrace Gael, and so neither will the Roman Church. Together with God, they must find an uncommon pathway to achieve their now-shared goal to preserve at least one core aspect of her Gaelic culture, a society that may fade as Romans or barbarians descend and destroy in the coming days. Yet they cannot.

In her anguish, Brigid rides to her father's *cashel*. Strolling along the merchant stalls set up along the fortified walls, she lingers until she sees Broicsech stepping out for her daily walk around the grounds. She knows that her mother likes to bathe alone, without the attendance of her maid Muireen, so she waits until Broicsech approaches the riverbank.

Though Muireen stands guard, her position is distant, and she is distracted. Brigid slips behind the privacy tent erected near the river-bank. When she enters, Broicsech's back is to her. Brigid tarries until her mother turns around; she does not want to unduly alarm her.

Their gazes meet, and Broicsech does not seem surprised at Brigid's presence.

"I was wondering when you'd come."

"Why would you expect me?"

"I assume that you near completion of the Gospel book. You must be considering the best way to present your masterwork to Pope Simplicius."

"I wish that was the nature of my appeal. A papal councillor, Gallienus, sent an envoy to collect Decius and his damning evidence. From their discussion, it seems clear that the Roman Church will never stomach a positive message about Gael; Rome is determined to cast us as disobedient heathens."

"Undoubtedly for their own motives—"

"Yes, it seems the Roman Church would like to use Gael to hedge its bets, and portraying us as heretics is necessary for both tactics. Should Rome prevail against the barbarians, the church will replace Gael's 'unorthodox' religious leaders and present the country in tribute to the Roman emperor. If the Roman government topples, then the church will offer the cleansed Gael as a bribe to the barbarians in order to maintain its standing as the state religion."

"I see."

"Decius has appeased the envoy for now, but another will be dispatched in due course. Decius is willing to return to Rome and help us in whatever way we conceive, but I cannot foresee a successful path."

Broicsech begins pacing the length of the tent, and Brigid cannot suppress a smile. She sees the source of her own nervous habit. Broicsech says, "We may have to leave Gael's independence to your father and his efforts at unification."

"I feared as much." Brigid sinks to the ground, bone-weary from her constant efforts and her relentless worry.

Broicsech sits down beside her, dirtying her exquisite plum gown in

the mud of the riverbank. "You may still protect something of your people, Brigid."

"Enlighten me, Mother."

"What of our formidable women?"

"How might I protect our women when I have failed at using the
might of our Lord to protect our borders from Romans or barbarians?"

"Remember Mary, the Mother of Jesus Christ. Perhaps you can
fashion an image that will make all Christians revere her as did her
Son. Much as you refashioned yourself to make the Gaelic people revere you."

ROME, ITALY

PRESENT DAY

They would have to deal with Rome.

"You're certain about this?" Alex asked Sister Mary as they crossed Saint Peter's Square on their way to the Vatican.

"You've seen how hard I fight to keep the real Brigid from receding into the mists of history. Why would I allow the real Mary to disappear when I have the means to do otherwise?" Sister Mary looked at Alex with a quizzical expression. "Anyway, what's wrong with a strong Virgin Mary or a bold Brigid?"

The translation had confirmed every aspect of the keepers' tradition, and although Sister Mary's order had concurred that their title to the relics—and thus the manuscript—was beyond reproach, the order insisted that Sister Mary consult Rome before the sale. The order believed that the manuscript raised monumental theological implications, of which church hierarchy had to be informed. Put another way, the members weren't sure how to feel about this Brigid or this Virgin Mary, and they wanted Rome to tell them.

Sister Mary was not of like mind. "Some days I lament my vow of obedience to my order. Must we all look to Rome like lemmings? Can't we trust ourselves to deal with the manuscript in a manner befitting a saint and the Mother of God? After all, we treated the relics properly for over a thousand years, sometimes in *spite* of Rome and its betrayals—like selling Ireland off to the English in the late twelfth century," she said to Alex as they walked through the main gate into the Vatican, in a rare moment of personal disclosure. "Ah, ignore my babbling. I took the vow, and now I must abide by it."

Entering the Vatican, Alex experienced a surge of déjà vu. Although the warm welcome Alex received at the side of a respected nun bore no resemblance to the anonymity of her visit with Declan, she was constantly reminded of him. And there was a tiny, rebellious part of her that questioned whether she'd been harsh in her judgment. She tried to shut her feelings off by replaying his last words, but they squeezed through nonetheless.

Numerous priests and nuns emerged from their desks and offices to greet Sister Mary as they walked through the Vatican hallways on the way to their appointment. Alex shot the nun a puzzled look at the breadth of their reception, but Sister Mary only smiled and whispered, "I've spent a lot of time here lobbying for my Brigid and for recognition of the early Irish Church. Some take to my message and others abhor it." She smirked and said, "The latter are hiding in their cubicles. Or maybe they're all cowering in the office of Father Benedetti."

A young priest escorted them directly into the office of the secretary-general of the Secret Archives. From the sumptuousness of his office and the obsequious treatment by his underlings, Alex deduced that the older priest clearly held a senior role, though he wore no visible evidence of his rank. Father Benedetti stood when they entered, and he and Sister Mary shook hands with seeming respect, but they immediately squared off like old enemies.

"You requested a meeting to discuss a matter of some urgency?"

"Father Benedetti, I'll leave it to my expert, Alexandra Patterson, to explain just what we've got at Kildare."

Alex made the presentation she'd rehearsed repeatedly with Sister Mary back in Kildare. She stressed the historical and artistic importance of the Book of Kildare, the Life of Brigid, and the Scribe Letters, as they'd come to call them. But she was ever cognizant of her audi-

ence, and tried never to overstate the religious implications of the finding or even mention the Gospel of Mary the Mother. She allowed the
texts to speak for themselves.

Father Benedetti stayed silent for a time, staring at Alex and Sister
Mary as if waiting for some information more befitting his station.
Then he begrudgingly turned his attention to the appraisal. He re-
viewed it with excruciating slowness, designed, no doubt, to unsettle.
Alex started to get uncomfortable, but Sister Mary remained as still as
a statue.

"How can I help you with this book of yours? Books, I should say,"
he added in a belittling tone.

"We're not here asking for help," Sister Mary explained. "We are
here out of courtesy. My order insisted that we notify you that we are
planning to sell the texts." Her tone made clear that she did not agree
with the necessity for such an announcement. "And Miss Patterson
here tells me that, at auction, the texts will garner considerable publicity—and bidding. We just wanted you to be apprised."

Alex knew that the nuns of the order wanted Sister Mary to do
more than just forewarn Rome of the sale; they wanted theological
guidance and approval. But Sister Mary would never deign to ask for
it. For all her adherence to the Catholic Church and her faith, she
bore the old Irish distrust of Rome. The Irish should be left to the
Irish, she believed.

"I do appreciate your courtesy visit. But you understand, of course,
that the church can never sanction the sale of these items."

"We are not asking for sanction. We are merely providing you with
information and notification."

"Then I am sorry to inform you that we will have to ban the sale,"
he said, although he looked anything but sorry. He looked delighted.

"On what grounds?"

"That the theology on which the manuscript and its imagery are
based is heretical."

"Interesting. Well, you have no legal basis on which to ban the
sale."

"What do you mean?"

Sister Mary handed him a legal opinion prepared by a solicitor of

Alex's recommendation. It set forth the Order of Saint Brigid's unbroken chain of title to relics—and thereby the manuscripts—for over a thousand years. The church's awareness of the relics and its failure to assert any claims of ownership to them barred it from making such claims now.

Father Benedetti no longer appeared delighted. "If we cannot operate by law, then we will operate by God. We will declare you in breach of your vows."

"My particular vow is not to Rome but to God and my order. I will try to abide by Rome's views, but I will sell these pieces."

"Even if you are deemed disobedient?"

"To my way of seeing, that's not a label you'd like to slap on an old nun like me. Wouldn't it just draw unwanted public attention to the manuscript? Everyone would scurry off to steal a peek at a book so scandalous that the church censured an old nun for selling it. You might be getting lots of requests for information about why the church banned the Gospel of Mary the Mother in the first place, and why it continues to do so. In this climate, you might not fare so well."

His eyes narrowed in anger, but he said nothing. He understood that this was her opening move.

Sister Mary knew that it was time to crack open the door just a bit. "You'd be better off going along with my sale. I'm not unreasonable, you know."

"Do you have a proposal?"

"I may be a gambler, but I'm not a fool. I don't think I'll start off by bidding against myself."

"I see. You'll leave it to me to bid against myself."

"Exactly."

Father Benedetti shot Sister Mary a look of such unbridled loathing it astonished Alex. "Please excuse me." He rose and left his office through a back door disguised to blend in with his extensive bookshelves.

Alex turned to Sister Mary to ask a question, but the nun placed a finger on her lips to silence her. She nodded toward the shelves as if to say, The books have ears.

Within a half an hour, Father Benedetti returned with a red folder.

He made a show of pulling out a report and reviewing it before speaking. "It has been drawn to my attention that the Holy See will be publishing a paper in our newspaper, *L'osservatore romano,* suggesting that the church's position on the Virgin Mary might not be inconsistent with the Protoevangelium of James, the successor text to the alleged Gospel of Mary the Mother. In that paper, His Holiness explains that the Virgin Mary has *always* been specially venerated by the church and points to the Infancy Gospels—including the specifically named Protoevangelium of James, as well as the Gospel of Pseudo-Matthew—as evidence of her special place in the hearts and devotion of all faithful. His Holiness even notes that one of the earliest depictions of the Madonna and Child—the painting in the Catacomb of Priscilla—offers confirmation of the early church's adoration of the Virgin Mary. In this way, permitting the circulation of an image such as yours—one founded on the Protoevangelium or its predecessor, or even its successor, for that matter—is consistent with the papal view."

Alex was flabbergasted. Could it just be sheer coincidence that the church had at the ready a position paper that addressed the controversial issues raised by the Book of Kildare? If not, how had the church known what she and Sister Mary would say in their meeting? Then it dawned on her. The Vatican had had access to her black bag, containing the manuscripts, for nearly a day and a half while she and Declan had waited for Father Casaceli and had reviewed the *Liber diurnus*—and it had had the impetus to search it after Declan had told the librarian priest about their fifth-century finding. The church must have undertaken a cursory interpretation of the books before Alex and Declan returned to get them. Father Benedetti had come to their meeting well prepared.

Although Alex believed that Sister Mary understood this as well, she gave no sign of it. "That is welcome news indeed."

"Might you be amenable to a sale that would place certain conditions on the buyer?" Father Benedetti asked. "Conditions that might position the object in the context of His Holiness's recently expressed—though long held—opinions?"

"Depending on what those conditions are, I might."

"What if the church were given the chance to explain its historical and emerging view on the person of the Virgin Mary as part of a larger exhibit displaying the Book of Kildare, the Life of Brigid, and the Scribe Letters?"

"Would you deny that the Gospel of Mary the Mother ever existed?"

"No, the church would not."

"Even though we do not have a copy?"

"Even though you do not have a copy."

"Would you in any way undermine its depiction of a strong, forceful Mary?"

"No. His Holiness has decided that the time might be right to embrace a more generous image of the Virgin Mary—one that might prove more appealing to our younger female constituents. And, as I am sure you can see from His Holiness's recent opinion paper, the church has always welcomed the view found within the Protoevangelium of James and its progeny, the purported successor texts to the alleged Gospel of Mary the Mother."

"Even though it once banned the Gospel?"

"The condemnation of the Protoevangelium and the Pseudo-Matthew was the decision of an earlier Holy See, a product of a different time. We will make that distinction abundantly clear."

"Then Miss Patterson and I will ensure that whoever purchases these manuscripts will provide the church with an opportunity to explain itself."

GAEL

A.D. 471

Brother,

I labored over the image's completion, brother. I confess this small deception to you only. I knew that my long days with Brigid would cease when she became satisfied with our Mary, even though my actual departure from Gael might be months away, when Gallienus's next ship came for me.

But I could not bear parting from Brigid yet. Not yet. Just one more layer of lattice border, I told myself. Just another palm frond in an angel's hand, I said in silence. Just a spare copy of the painting so Brigid may have one for her own collection, I whispered to the walls. I prayed that my slow brushstrokes could deliver just one more week, one more day, even one more hour with her. Though, in truth, the two images, identical in every aspect, drew as close to perfection as I believe I am capable.

And I do not regret my dishonesty, though I was frank with Brigid in almost all other respects. For we had so many happy hours in each other's company in those last three months. We were free to roam the countryside under the pretext of abbey business and our project—though none knew of its nature. Measure by measure, Brigid revealed to me the hidden treasures in the mild rolling hills near Cill Dara's plains, and I described to her the searing beauty of our family's lands in the summertime, born of a heat unfathomable to her.

Though we could not join our words or our bodies in an expression of our emotions, we could join our minds and secret hearts. And so we did. Those twelve weeks were the happiest of my life. Yet no matter my efforts at delay, the end came sooner than I could have ever supposed.

After evening Mass on a particularly stormy evening, I returned to my hut. I'd lowered myself to the floor, ready to assume my prayerful position to help cast out the temptations of the day, when I heard a rapping noise. One of Cill Dara's few rules, albeit unwritten, forbids the interruption of the religious once they retire to their hut, thus I attributed the tapping to a wayward branch blown against my hut's outer walls by the fierce wind. Yet I heard the noise again, more purposeful this time, and I knew it was someone knocking.

I rose and opened the door. A man dressed in monk's garb, thoroughly drenched from the downpour, stood outside. Though he was unfamiliar to me and his appearance at my door most unusual, I motioned for him to enter; such hospitality is the Cill Dara way. I handed him a cloth with which to dry his face, and asked in Gaelic, "May I help you, Brother?"

He pulled back his cloak and wiped his face clean of rain. He then answered in Latin: "You may indeed, Brother Decius."

He spoke with such familiar address that I grew confused. Had I met this monk before? Given my distracted state and the constant influx of religious to the abbey, it was possible I had forgotten the introduction. "How may I assist you, Brother? I am at your disposal."

"Please join me in a short journey to the coast, Brother Decius. Gallienus diverted a ship destined for Britannia to Gael—to secure your homecoming to Rome."

Brother, I was shocked. Only three months had passed since Valens's departure, and I'd never anticipated that a return voyage could be secured so readily. I'd believed I had at least three months left in Gael, three joyous months left with Brigid. But my joy was of no matter. Our Lord called me to His mission—different from the one upon which I'd embarked—and I must follow when He calls.

The monk grew impatient with my silence. "Are you ready?"

I wanted to say no, to cry out that I needed more time with my Brigid. But I knew that our work demanded that I give my accord. "Yes, Brother. I am ready."

"Good. Gather your belongings, and let us go. The ship awaits us, and the seas are rough."

"I will need but an hour."

"An hour? We have little time."

"For safety, I have not kept all the necessary documents here in my hut. I must collect the remainder." I spoke in generalities, as I knew not what information Gallienus—or Valens, for that matter—had made him privy to. He seemed to understand, and nodded his acquiescence.

"One hour. Let us meet near the large oak in the curve of the hill to the east of the abbey walls. Do you know the one?"

I did indeed. It was a tree much beloved by Brigid. "Yes. I will be there in one hour."

The monk, if he was in fact a monk, let the wind slam the door to the hut behind him as he entered the night. I waited until enough time had elapsed to be certain of his departure, then assembled my few possessions, including my carefully crafted "evidence" for Gallienus, and ran from my hut. To Brigid.

One thought coursed through my mind over and over again as I hastened to her. How can I leave her? She has become more than just my world; she has become my true *anmchara*. Yet I knew I must. I knew I must marshal my limited skills at artifice, infiltrate the world of Gallienus, and make him believe. Believe that, though mildly heretical, the Abbey of Cill Dara posed no threat to Rome's Catholicism. Believe that Gael did not make a useful tool in the church's machinations to secure power, whatever the forthcoming political landscape. And believe that the church must embrace Brigid's and my own image of the Virgin Mary.

I knew all this. And I knew I would never commit the sin of choosing myself and Brigid over God. Yet those desires restrained me at Brigid's door, as if an actual physical presence. Only against my will did I manage to overcome the resistance and knock.

The door opened and revealed a disheveled Brigid lit by a single candle. To me, she looked more beautiful than ever for her tousled state. She ushered me in and whispered, "Whatever is wrong, Decius?"

"The time is at hand, Brigid." I did not need to say more. She knew what had befallen me.

"No, Decius. Not so soon."

"Yes."

"I thought we had longer."

"As did I. Oh, Brigid, I pray I can make this heartless Gallienus embrace our Mary."

"Convince Gallienus thus. Convince him that, in time, his people will clamor for a woman to worship, and that our image of the Virgin Mary alone will satisfy his Roman believers. Convince him that it would be better to control the object of their devotion, lest they venerate an unpredictable living woman such as myself rather than worship a virtuous dead one."

"Indeed I shall." I nodded, then whispered, "I have come for the painting."

"Of course. Let me gather your things." She hurried to her cabinet.

"Might I have a minute with your scribe's instruments?"

She gazed at me, with that lovely hint of a smile curling on her lips. "You need not ask, Decius. All that I have is yours."

Brother, I took the last few minutes before my departure to make this record of my last days in Gael and finish Brigid's life as best I can, the life I cobbled together from her abbey history. For I realize now that I can never bring these letters back to Rome with me. It would endanger not only my safety but yours. I pray that a day will come when I may recount my story to you in person, rendering these letters obsolete. But, until then, I have left them in Brigid's care for her perusal and safekeeping. As I have left my masterwork of the bound four Gospels and the image of our Mary—my Book of Cill Dara—as well as Brigid's life. I take only Gallienus's evidence and my original painting of the Virgin Mary. For I will serve as its disseminator and its keeper.

Let us pray.

Decius

GAEL

A.D. 472

BRIGID: A LIFE

The spring rain whips the outer walls of Brigid's quarters. Brigid stands at the open door to her beehive, letting the downpour lash her. She welcomes its sting. It penetrates the numbness that has enveloped her since Decius's departure.

She returns to the grueling work of the abbess of Cill Dara, pretending that Decius's disappearance does not merit mention. Other religious folk, ill-suited to the monastic life, have drifted away from the abbey before, and she behaves as if he were one of their ilk. She tends to her work ministering to the sick and needy, securing the protection of her people's bodies and souls, and glorifying His name—as if her heart had not broken.

All the while, she thinks of little else but Decius and their Virgin Mary. She tries to keep her focus on the image. Reflecting on the morning when Decius created their Mary, she consoles herself with the knowledge that together they have become His instrument. Their spiritual union has been His design from the very beginning, perhaps from the moment Gallienus selected Decius for this mission and the time Brigid resolved to take the veil. For only together did they stand a chance at creating a woman—the Virgin Mary—the Roman Church might adopt as its own and foster through the ages.

Yet her mind always returns to Decius himself. She replays their last moment together in her quarters before Gallienus's latest envoy whisked him away to Rome. Imagining his journey by sea to Britannia or Gaul and through the dangerous barbarian lands, she prays for his safety. Closing her eyes to kindle the images, she envisions his hero's welcome in Rome and Gallienus's disappointment at the paucity of evidence against her and Gael. She guesses at the ways in which Decius will ingratiate himself with Gallienus once again and begin his subtle campaign of introducing the Virgin Mary.

She constantly wonders where he is—where they are—and longs for him. Prayers for consolation as to Decius's well-being and relief from her hunger for him go unanswered. She supposes that she deserves His punishment for even considering the abandonment of her vows, and determines to forgo all entreaties except those protecting Decius and their Mary.

In her prayers' stead, Decius's Gospel book provides her with solace. Most days, she needs only to delight in the artistry of his Gospels and caress his fine brushwork and imaginative figures to feel the touch of his hand. But on the dark days, she requires more. She turns to the life of Brigid that Decius fashioned from her abbey history—and she finished in her own hand—and then unrolls the packet of letters that Decius has left in her care and rereads the private words that tell her over and over of his love for her. And for Him.

Brigid smiles. Perhaps there is a way she can honor Decius as he honored her. She will summon her artisans to fashion a sumptuous reliquary to house his masterpiece, and she will be its keeper.

DUBLIN, IRELAND

PRESENT DAY

Adam's auction house positively buzzed in the minutes before the Book of Kildare went on the stand. Sister Mary had selected the premier Irish art auctioneer to oversee the bidding, even though she'd had interest from Christie's, which had garnered a record sale of over $30 million for Leonardo da Vinci's Codex Leicester and over $13 million for a rare sixteenth-century illuminated manuscript. Sister Mary had chosen Adam's because it was Irish and, after all, the Book of Kildare was *the* quintessential Irish masterwork.

Because of its relative inexperience with ancient illuminated manuscripts, Adam's needed Alex to help prepare for the auction. With her boss's blessing, she contacted potential buyers, an unusual mix of private collectors and institutions; finalized the catalog; dealt with the media flurry; and, in particular, worked on the estimates. The latter was a tricky business because no true comparables for the Book of Kildare and the first Virgin Mary image existed, and she had to factor in variables such as the future income stream from reproductions.

But when the lights dimmed and the Book of Kildare took the stage, Alex was pleased with her efforts and her decision to proceed. Sister Mary reached over and squeezed her hand as the auctioneer began announcing the book. Until the bidding commenced.

The first bid matched the $10 million reserve. The second doubled it. And the third bid took it from there. Paddles flashed and numbers were called out in the most frenzied auction Alex had ever attended. In disbelief, Alex watched as the gavel finally slammed at $52 million, the highest amount paid at auction for any book or manuscript, including da Vinci's famous Codex Leicester.

The crowd erupted when the auctioneer announced the buyer as Trinity College Dublin, the keeper of the Book of Kells and the perfect owner for the Book of Kildare, the Life of Brigid, and the Scribe Letters. Reporters converged on Sister Mary. The media was just beginning to understand that the Book of Kildare reflected the moment of creation of one of the world's most beloved and revered devotional images, that of the Virgin Mary. And journalists hungered for more details on how the Life of Brigid and the Scribe Letters proved that the iconography of the first Virgin Mary had secretly derived from an apocryphal Gospel banned by the early Catholic Church.

Alex stepped aside to let the star take center stage. She and Sister Mary had worked through the night to prepare sound bites for this precise moment. As Alex expected, Sister Mary delivered them perfectly—with her signature mix of humble religiosity and feisty Irish common sense.

One of Adam's principals called over to Alex, offering congratulations. She headed across the auditorium to thank him for all his hard work and bumped right into Declan.

"What are you doing here?" She couldn't believe his audacity.

"You forget, Sister Mary invited me."

"She did it out of thanks for your initial translation and research work—and only because I didn't tell her about your real intentions for the books. I never thought you'd dare come."

"You never gave me a chance to explain." Declan had phoned Alex repeatedly since she'd slammed his apartment door nearly three months ago. She had not returned one call.

"What's there to explain? That you didn't really mean that I should keep the Book of Kildare from Sister Mary? I don't think your 'suggestion' was open to any other interpretation. And I don't think your overtures toward me were open to any other interpretation either."

"Alex, I'm not going to lie about what I proposed. But did you ever consider that my motivations might have been other than financial gain? That maybe I didn't want the Book of Kildare to go underground forever in some morass of Catholic theology and bureaucracy? I would never have guessed that the church would permit the auction of the book with such publicity. And did you ever think I might have had—still have—real feelings for you?"

Alex's head spun. Was Declan speaking the truth? "I can't talk about this today."

"Does that mean you'll talk about it another day?" He grabbed her hand. "Please, Alex?"

She thought about Brigid and Decius, and the second chances they'd freely granted each other despite all the deceptions. Although she felt like she couldn't breathe, she whispered, "Yes."

Freeing her hand from Declan's grip, she pushed past him to gulp the fresh air of early summer outside Adam's walls. Just before she reached the door, another hand grasped for her. She turned around, ready to shake Declan off again, but it was Father Giuseppe, the representative from the Vatican. Father Benedetti wouldn't lower himself to attend the auction.

"We wish to thank you for your assistance with the sale of the Book of Kildare," he began.

Alex just wanted to move past him and get outside as quickly as possible. "It was my pleasure, really. Now, if you'll excuse me."

The priest reached for her again. "You've done the church a great favor. We will be happy to repay that favor one day." He passed her his business card.

"What do you mean?"

"For some time, we've struggled with the reality that our Virgin Mary—the unassuming mother of God and protector of mankind that we have fostered in the minds of Catholics—has become insignificant to and far removed from our modern faithful. And yet we had no female figure with which to replace her in their minds and hearts. Your discovery and your hand in selling the Book of Kildare with the special condition requested by Father Benedetti allows us to resurrect the Virgin Mary, if you will, and bring more believers to God."

Alex couldn't listen to any more. Stumbling out of Adam's and into Saint Stephen's Green, she threw herself onto the first empty park bench she could find. Given her ambivalence about organized religion, she felt unsettled by the thought that all her efforts had gone to reinvigorating the Virgin Mary for the church's private aim—even if that reinvigoration was based on the Mary formed by Brigid and Decius rather than the church's created Mary. Perhaps she should have quieted her ears to the tale the Book of Kildare Virgin Mary had to tell and let her recede into respectful obscurity.

But then a curious peace descended upon Alex. Maybe He—whoever He was, if He even existed—meant for the image of the Virgin Mary to be a helix, bending and twisting and morphing to fit the needs of the times. Perhaps He intended Alex to use her gift of listening to the secrets of sacred images to save the Virgin Mary, not for the benefit of the church but for the people. Just like Brigid, its first keeper.

KILDARE, IRELAND

A.D. 1185

They led Giraldus blindfolded through the dark forest. He did not know why or how they had taken him from the guarded campground he shared with Prince John, the new vice regent of Ireland. Stumbling over the dense undergrowth, Giraldus nearly fell, and would have but for the saving hands of his captors.

Those same hands directed him to a clearing and then removed his blindfold. Before him waited a young woman dressed in the white garb of a nun. They stood several feet apart in a grove of oak trees.

"You are Giraldus Cambrensis, Welsh clergyman and adviser to Prince John, heir to Henry, king of England?" she asked in perfect Latin.

"I am."

"You have fought for the independence of the Welsh Church from the control of the English Church?"

"I have, though never from English political rule."

"It is enough that you sought freedom for your church. We have something to show you."

She raised her hand almost imperceptibly. From the oak trees emerged a man wearing the brown robes of a monk, with a sword strapped to his belt. He carried a large rectangular box that gleamed gold and silver in the moonlight. She motioned for the monk to bring it to her.

Before she opened it, she said, "You see before you the greatest treasure of Ireland. It was crafted by the early Irish Church, long before it became shackled to England and Rome."

She reached deep within the box and withdrew a large manuscript. "This Gospel book was written at the time of Saint Brigid. We are told that an angel furnished the designs, while Saint Brigid prayed and the scribe copied. You may approach."

Giraldus walked toward her. The monk held a newly lit torch while the woman opened the book for Giraldus. A Virgin Mary of breathtaking beauty stared up at him from the very first page. As the woman turned the pages, divine images, delicately and exquisitely crafted in brilliant colors, gazed out amid the Words of the Lord. He had never seen anything like it. It seemed a miracle, the work of angels, not man.

"We understand that you will accompany England's Prince John on his tour through his new lands." She paused, as if awaiting his confirmation.

"I will."

"We also understand that you will be at his side as he fashions his policies toward the Irish Church."

"I hope to assist him in that regard."

"Then we ask this of you. Remember this book and let it remind you of what the men and women of the Irish Church are capable when free from outside rule. And ask yourself what your Welsh Church might have accomplished—might still accomplish—without the yoke of England."

A second monk appeared, holding the blindfold in his hand. Before he drew too near, Giraldus asked the woman, "May I know your name?"

"It is the book that is important. I am only the keeper."

AUTHOR'S NOTE

While I was writing my first two books, *The Chrysalis* and *The Map Thief*, I came to realize that what truly intrigued me was the notion that an object—be it a piece of artwork or an artifact, real or imagined—can tell a story, and that the story can resolve a monumental historical mystery as well as divulge something secret about the creator of the object. I became fascinated by the idea that I could answer those historical mysteries through fiction.

So when I began researching my third book, I undertook a voyage through time's riddles and characters. I've always been partial to Irish history, and in my readings, I learned about the lost Book of Kildare. The last recorded sighting of this mysterious, very early medieval Irish illuminated manuscript was by twelfth-century Welsh historian and clergyman Giraldus Cambrensis, during his tour of Saint Brigid's Abbey of Kildare in Ireland. Giraldus became so entranced by this manuscript—"the work of angelic, and not human skill"—and its legendary creation at the guidance of Saint Brigid herself that he wrote:

Among all the miracles in Kildare, none appears to me more wonderful than that marvelous book which they say was written in the time of the Virgin Saint Brigid at the dictation of an angel. . . .

> Aided by divine grace . . . the book was composed, an angel fur-
> nishing the designs, Saint Brigid praying, and the scribe copying.

As I read Giraldus' description of the book, I became captivated by the
idea of the possible rediscovery of this lost masterpiece and the historical questions it might answer. For the Book of Kildare might have possibly contained some of the very first images of the Virgin Mary. The
question of how these initial pictures of Mary originated in, and pro-
liferated from, remote Ireland when Mary played a relatively small role
in the accepted Biblical canon is a source of debate, particularly in
the context of the famous Book of Kells, which seems to bear a striking similiarity to the Book of Kildare.

Placing this legendary book into its historical context, I became
even more intrigued by the Book of Kildare and its possible ability to
address this question. If one credits Giraldus' narrative, the book was
written and illustrated during the late fifth or early sixth century when
the Roman Empire teetered on the edge of destruction at the hands of
barbarian tribes. Some of Rome's outcasts began fleeing the crumbling
kingdom to the recently built abbeys, monasteries, and scriptoriums in
the newly Christian Ireland. These exiles brought with them many
classical and religious texts, and in scriptoriums such as the one found
in Brigid's Abbey of Kildare, the religious folk set to reading, preserving, and copying them. What if the Book of Kildare—and the first
Marian portraits—were influenced by the texts flowing in to Ireland's
scriptoriums at this time? Brigid and the scribes of Kildare would have
had access to a wide range of ancient manuscripts and in fact might
have had familiarity with certain gospels banned by the early Christian
church, such as the Protoevangelium of James, which paints the Virgin Mary in a strong, powerful light and offers much detail about her
life.

Viewing the Book of Kildare through this historical prism, it seemed
that the rediscovery of this lost masterwork might reveal much about
why one of the first portraits of the Virgin Mary appears in remote, early
medieval Ireland. It also appeared that the manuscript might illuminate
just how Mary's image and persona—indeed the true influential roles of
many women of the early church, both Brigid and beyond—were al-

tered and suppressed by society over the centuries. So I delved into the histories and legends of the formidable Mary and Brigid.

Indeed, unearthing the Book of Kildare might answer a more personal question, one raised by the wonderful woman who sparked my interest in this period and place—my late aunt, Sister Therese Coyne: "Why must Mary be so passive?" Perhaps the historical Mary wasn't passive at all. Perhaps the times and people that followed shaped her so. As they did with Brigid.

Thus, *Brigid of Kildare* was born.

ACKNOWLEDGMENTS

Brigid of Kildare would be as lost as The Book of Kildare if not for the encouragement of so many people. I want to begin by thanking my indefatigable agent and champion, Laura Dail, who unfailingly provides indispensable advice, tireless brainstorming, and humor. Starting with my talented editor, Paul Taunton, I would like to express my appreciation to the amazing Ballantine team for their constant efforts, support, and enthusiasm: Libby McGuire, Kim Hovey, Christine Cabello, Brian McLendon, Lisa Barnes, Rachel Kind, Jane von Mehren, Scott Shannon, the art department, the promotion and sales departments, and the managing editorial and production departments. And I am so thankful for the Pittsburgh book community, especially Mary Alice Gorman, Richard Goldman, and the many book clubs, libraries, and organizations where I have been invited to speak.

Family and friends offered unremitting optimism, including but by no means limited to: my parents, Coleman and Jeanne Benedict; my siblings, Coley, Liz, Lauren, Sean, Courtney, Christopher, and Meredith, and their wonderful families; my in-laws, particularly Catherine, Alison, and Marilyn; Illana Raia; Ponny Conomos Jahn; the Sewickley Book Club Ladies; the Six; Michael Volpatt; and Patti Vescio. And I reserve a special debt of gratitude to my late Aunt Terry, who is responsible for *Brigid of Kildare* in more ways than I can begin to express.

Yet, *Brigid of Kildare* truly *belongs* to my husband, Jim, and our sons, Jack and Ben. They provided me with such boundless love, unwavering faith, and steadfast support during the writing process that *they* made *Brigid of Kildare* possible. Thank you, thank you.

HEATHER TERRELL is the author of *The Chrysalis* and *The Map Thief*. A lawyer with more than ten years' experience as a litigator at two of the country's premier law firms and for Fortune 500 companies, Terrell is a graduate of Boston College and the Boston University School of Law. She lives in Pittsburgh with her family.